Acts Chapter 16

Heart Cry of a Dreamer

Acts Chapter 16

Heart Cry of a Dreamer

Myrtle Wilgis McDaniel

Pleasant Word
A Division of WINEPRESS PUBLISHING

ISBN 1-4141-0425-1
Library of Congress Catalog Card Number: 2005901942

Table of Contents

CHAPTER 1

Thyatira

Loukas arrived earlier than usual to place his offering of fresh figs, pomegranates, and an amphora of wine on the temple steps leading to the seated statue of Cybele, mother of earth and procreation. The marble figure was undercut so deeply it seemed a separate work from the throne pedestal upon which it rested. From the top of her tiara, studded with four enormous gems representing the four seasons, to the sandals protruding from under the folds of her simple gown, the statue exuded a sense of control and power. A loaf of bread held in her left hand offset a scroll in her right hand, believed to contain the names of future generations of those who would be granted her favor.

A white-robed priest stood immobile before the deity, an olive branch in his hand. Two priests and two priestesses clad in diaphanous white robes stood on each side of the stone figure. They were available to offer their services as temple prostitutes for those who cared to worship in this manner.

Only one or two other worshipers appeared at this early morning hour to kneel before the gilded altar rail and offer prayers and seek blessings from Cybele.

Loukas left the temple area and wound his way down the hillside, back toward town, contemplating why he bothered to come every morning to bring an offering. Like every Greek man, he served as priest to his household and led his family in paying homage to their household god. But he did not believe the gods made any real difference in his life. They did not care whether he was happy. He did not worship to gain peace, but simply to placate the gods in the hope of avoiding their displeasure. So he came daily to this temple.

He believed there were gods who exercised power over the lives of men, but their behavior was like that of other humans, the only difference being their immortality. Even Zeus, the great god himself, lusted after women the same as mortals, knew what it was to be angry, to be jealous, to have desire and revenge.

Furthermore, the gods needed nothing to add to their happiness. Their actions in the mortal sphere were neither productive nor practical, but based simply upon their whims. It was to avoid this interference that Loukas brought offerings and, at special times, made sacrifices.

Actually, he did not spend a lot of time thinking about the gods. More urgent matters called for his attention. The marketplace usually served to stimulate and occupy his mind, though even that did not hold his attention for long. He had turned more and more to his business since the day his wife died giving birth to their only son. The baby died two weeks later, leaving Loukas to care for a three-year-old daughter.

Other men, left alone with a young child, especially a girl, would have simply turned her over to slaves. But Loukas had not done that. He insisted on having Lydia with him as much as possible, perhaps as a way of keeping the spirit of his beloved wife alive. Over the years his daughter became as much a part of his business as she was a part of his home life.

Loukas sighed as he thought about those early days when he inherited the weaving and dying business started by his grandfather and handed down to his father and finally to him. He worked long hours training his workmen to become the best weavers and dyers to be found. This resulted in delicate colors and rich blends of such quality that dressmakers for the rich and influential were willing to pay handsomely for cloth from his looms. In time the business grew, and Loukas the weaver began exporting rich linen, cottons, silks, and sheer gossamer cloth to merchants throughout the Roman Empire as far north as Britain.

Strange how things seem to travel in cycles, Loukas mused to himself as he strode along, impervious to the beauty of the sunrise turning the sky from the gray of early dawn to pink and then lavender, rimming the clouds with golden trim as the first rays of the sun appeared on the horizon. He thought of how his grandfather arrived here as a colonist from Philippi and quickly realized the potential of Thyatira as more than a garrison town. Other merchants soon recognized the value of a city located at the end of caravan routes from Galatia to the east, Ephesus to the south, and Pergamon and Troas to the north.

Loukas continued to reminisce about his heritage from his wise grandfather, who had formed trade guilds for craftsmen as they moved into the colony. This enabled them to enjoy the peace and protection of Rome and the freedom to conduct their business as long as they behaved and paid their taxes.

Now the affairs of the trade guilds were also Loukas's responsibility. They took up almost as much time as his weaving.

Loukas jealously guarded the rights of the crafts-men under his supervision, which included weavers and dyers, carders and spinners of wool, and needle workers directly connected with his own interest as well as metal smiths, carpenters, and tanners. He had a large voice in setting prices and shipping fees, and a certain percentage of the drachmas paid to the guild found its way into his copious pockets.

The wheel has turned full circle, Loukas thought. Lydia, to whom he'd always expected to leave his holdings and at least some of his responsibilities, would be married in a few days and returning to Philippi, land of their ancestors. *Do the gods know about all this? Do they care?* He sighed, then resolutely put the morbid thoughts behind him.

The sun was beginning to make its presence felt. The heat was already bringing beads of perspiration to his forehead. It would be good to get back to the coolness of his marble house on the colonnade. The pain in his leg was beginning its familiar nag. By evening it would be screaming through his body, claiming his total attention.

Loukas spoke briefly to the porter as he stepped across the threshold of his villa. The household slaves had been busy in his absence. The mosaic tile pavement was polished like a mirror. Flower girls arrived with their daily assortment of fresh blossoms and greenery, placing vases of flowers on pedestals adorning the oblong colonnade surrounding the small garden.

A shaft of sunlight entered through an opening in the ceiling of the main hall, giving a mellow glow to the room, dominated by a long dining table. Backless couches, with one arm raised for the comfort of reclining diners, were draped with coarsely woven cotton cloth.

The muted sounds of cooking pots being moved about came though a doorway at the end of the columned room leading to the kitchen. Loukas glanced up the small stairway ascending to the second floor. He looked past the picture room containing paintings and busts of his ancestors to the doorway opening into Lydia's apartments. Apparently she was not ready to accompany him to the marketplace. It was just as well. He had business to take care of at home this morning.

An indication of the wealth enjoyed by Loukas was the presence of a bath. Most of the population of Thyatira used the public baths. A desire to socialize added to the mania for cleanliness. The baths were a gathering place for the town to hear the news of the country, consummate business deals, and exchange local gossip.

Few private homes had baths and their own sewage system. This was a privilege Loukas thoroughly enjoyed. He was especially glad to keep Lydia away from the women's baths and the tongues of those who gathered there. She had been saved from all manner of gossip and ideas that might change her sweet, trusting nature.

Loukas stepped out of his tunic and stood naked before a polished steel mirror. He saw the reflection of a man of medium height, grown a bit pudgy in the middle. His face still retained a youthful look with lines etched near his eyes from squinting against the sun. The past months had revealed a small bald spot in the middle of his thick black hair. Muscles in well-developed arms and legs rippled under curly black hair that also grew on the backs of his hands and the knuckles of his stubby fingers. He did not look old. In fact, he looked younger than most of his colleagues. Only the gray tinge to his skin tightening over his cheekbones betrayed the pain that raced through his body with ever-increasing force.

He summoned Elias, his body servant, a small man, a Jew from the area of Rome. Elias had fled that city under the reign of Tiberius, whose treatment of the Jews was becoming more and more harsh. He managed to secure passage on a ship to Ephesus and then joined a caravan coming north to Thyatira.

Loukas first noticed Elias fingering the lengths of material on display in his textile shop in the agora. He watched the slightly stooped figure move around the shop. His long, thin fingers touched the cloth as if he were familiar with texture and weave; his lips moved in appraisal as he talked with himself concerning the quality of this or that piece.

Inquiry revealed Elias was a tailor without a client. He could not open a stall in the agora or even sell his services to one of the merchants or rich men in the city because he did not belong to a guild. As a worshiper of the Hebrew God, Yah-weh, he refused to participate in the rituals of sacrifice common at the social gatherings of guild members. Strict laws of diet and behavior left him completely alienated from the entire Greek community.

Elias was down to the very last of his resources when Loukas noticed him in the agora. Something in his bearing struck a chord in Loukas's mind and heart. The destitute tailor did not bow to try to impress the Greek merchants who operated the shops. Nor did he attempt to be familiar with the working class. Loukas could not see any difference in the way he greeted the slave passing on an errand for his master or the master himself. Perhaps it was the man's quiet air of being his own person that held the attention of the weaver.

Unable to work at his trade, Elias was open to a proposition put to him by Loukas and readily agreed to enter the service of the weaver as his personal servant—not as slave, but in exchange for food and shelter for one year. At Elias's insistence Loukas followed him to the stall of a public scribe, and a contract was signed.

Though obedient and courteous as a servant, Elias was never servile. Loukas had the good sense to accept him as a man. He often used Elias as a sounding board for his ideas and his frustrations. The man never gave his opinion unless it was asked for, but when his thoughts were offered, Loukas found them to be more realistic and reasonable than those suggested by some of his most learned friends.

Today the written contract expired. Loukas pulled the scroll of their agreement from a niche where he kept some of his other papers. and handed it to Elias without a word.

Elias accepted the contract. The two men looked into each other's eyes as they shook hands.

"I've been thinking," Loukas said. "I will need some time to train a new body servant. None of the slaves presently in the house seem to meet my requirements. I was wondering if we could make some arrangement for you to stay until I could find someone—for a fee, of course."

"Since I have been working here, I have not had opportunity to find another position." Elias's voice was solemn. "I was going to ask if you would consider allowing me to stay on until I could find other employment—for a fee, of course."

Such was the understanding between the two men that nothing more needed to be said.

"Elias, I will be needing an early bath today. Prepare the tub."

"Will you want me to read to you from the scrolls this morning?" Elias asked.

"No, not today. I have a lot on my mind this morning. I need time to think." Loukas glanced into the mirror once again. "Why do I feel a thousand years old?

Elias gave no answer. None was expected.

Loukas stepped into the tub and gave a deep sigh as the warm bath began its soothing work. The water cradled his aching bones like a soft blanket welcoming a tired child for its nap.

As Elias started to withdraw from the room, Loukas raised his hand to stop him. "I need to talk to you about some matters of grave importance. Then we need to make sure everything is ready for the sacrifice and wedding feast. This may take awhile, so please be seated."

Lydia entered her father's textile shop one morning just as he was receiving a message from Nathan Ben Kobath, a jewelry merchant well known for his excellent workmanship and high prices. An early customer stood fingering the finely woven materials displayed on the counter. A buxom matron draped the loose end from a bolt of blue linen across her body to determine the suitability of texture and color.

As soon as the messenger departed, Loukas took his daughter aside and asked quietly, "Would you like to go with me to the house of Nathan Ben Kobath?"

"To his house?" Lydia questioned. "Surely he is right up the street at his shop."

With a sideways glance at his clerks, Loukas lowered his voice even more. "Today Nathan is at home. Since my visit concerns you, why don't you come along?"

"What could possibly concern me at the house of a Jew?" Lydia chuckled. "Are you about to become a proselyte, Papa?"

"No, no. Nothing like that." Loukas sighed. "Of course, if you don't care to come with me, I'll go alone."

"I'm coming. I'm coming." Lydia wondered at the conspiratorial tone of her father's voice. "I've always wanted to see one of those houses on the inside. Besides, you have my curiosity aroused."

Lydia and her father turned down a side street leading to a tree-lined avenue of modest homes. The Street of the Jews housed that segment of the population who followed the trade routes into Asia from the areas of Syria and Palestine as well as those of the Diaspora who had found refuge there.

"This is a very attractive street," Lydia commented. Even as she spoke she was not sure what she had expected to see. "I don't understand why the Jews are so disliked by everyone," she continued. "Of course, they do drive some hard bargains when one is dealing with them."

"That has nothing to do with it," Loukas replied. "All of us like a bargain. These Hebrew people are tolerated as part of the community because we need their professional and financial skills."

"*Tolerated* has an unhappy sound to it," Lydia said.

"Well," Loukas replied, "that's about what it amounts to. They hold fast to their belief in one God and refuse to give homage to the gods and goddesses who watch over our city. Right away that creates a barrier. Even if you wanted to invite one of them into your home or to a social function, they would not come. So we simply leave them alone, outside of business."

"Except for Elias," Lydia teased.

"Yes, except for Elias," Loukas answered. "How did I manage before Elias?" He did not expect an answer.

Their conversation lagged as he began to search for the home of Nathan Ben Kobath. Houses along this street were built of cut stone overlaid with gleaming white plaster, with outer walls even with the street. Loukas stopped before one richly carved door recessed into the wall. A brass gong and hammer hung by the doorpost. A small brass box hung directly below the gong.

At a quick rap of the hammer, a porter opened a small sliding partition. After a brief inspection he opened the door and bowed a welcome. Lydia slipped her hand into that of her father as they followed the porter across a tiled entrance hall. A servant immediately appeared, carrying a bronze basin of water, a long towel girded about the waist of his sleeveless tunic. Loukas and Lydia were seated on a bench by the door, and the servant knelt and deftly removed their sandals.

One by one he held their feet over the basin. Lydia sighed with pleasure as he dipped water in his hand, letting it run down over her dusty foot before drying her skin with the towel. When this process was completed, he gave the guests a pair of soft sandals to wear while in the house. Their own sandals were placed by the door where they could find them on their way out.

The porter conducted them to an inner courtyard, where flowers bloomed in profusion around a fountain. A striped canvas awning protected a low table from the bright morning sun.

Nathan Ben Kobath came from an inner chamber to greet his visitors, a long fringed shawl draped around his shoulders. Two leather thongs held a small leather box bound to his forehead and another one strapped to his left arm. Both boxes were replicas of the brass box Lydia had noticed on the outer doorpost.

Lydia quietly observed that Nathan tried to conceal his surprise at seeing her with her Father. She was aware that it was not the usual practice for a woman to be on the street in the middle of a busy day. She looked curiously at the shawl around his shoulders and watched as he removed it, taking time to fold it carefully to keep the long fringes from becoming tangled, before handing it to a servant.

"Good morning, noble Loukas. You are up and on the streets early this morning. My wife and I have just finished our morning prayers to Yah-weh." He started to add, *the one true God,* but held his tongue. Maybe later.

Lydia followed her father as Nathan gestured toward a bench by a small oval table. He waited for them to be seated before lowering himself to a position across from them. "Will you join me in a bit of breakfast?"

Not waiting for an answer, he clapped his hands. A servant came with a basin and towel. The three dipped their fingers into the water and dried them. Another servant entered, bearing a platter of fruit and eggs and various cheeses along with an excellent wine. Lydia had not realized she was hungry but the food was delicious.

"We didn't mean to intrude upon your worship of the gods," Loukas said. "I, too, have been to the temple this morning, as is my custom." Lydia thought his voice sounded a bit smug, as if he intended to convey the superiority of worshiping the gods publicly, over a god worshiped in the privacy of a home, as if one could not bear the light of public display.

"You did not intrude," Nathan said with a smile. "But you are mistaken. We both worshiped, but with a difference. You worship a statue of marble and we worship the one true living God."

He inclined his head toward Lydia. "I see you noticed the phylacteries on my arm and forehead." He opened the lid of one of the boxes to reveal a tiny scroll inscribed with Hebrew writing. "The words written on these scrolls were given to my people by the Lord God Himself."

Nathan quoted the words from memory. "Hear, O Israel: the Lord our God is one Lord: and thou shall worship the Lord thy God with all thine heart, and with all thy soul, and with all thy might."

"We are instructed to wear these words on our foreheads, near to our minds, and on our left arm, near to our heart. We have them on the doorposts of our houses. Then, as we go in and out, we are reminded to keep our laws and to worship our God." Nathan did not give his explanation boastfully or in anger. He simply answered Lydia's questioning look.

Loukas gave a short laugh. "Ah, yes, the living God. But then, all the gods are living. Or so the priests would have us believe. You were brought up to believe your god was the most powerful. I was reared to give sacrifice to the gods of my fathers. I wonder...will we ever know who is *the* god?"

Nathan opened his mouth to speak but Loukas held up his hand.

"Let us not argue, Nathan. You must know that Loukas the weaver did not leave his shop in the agora and come to your house at this hour to argue about the gods, or to enjoy breakfast with you, as pleasant as this has been."

"You are right," Nathan answered. "I know what you have come to see."

Lydia listened to the exchange between her father and Nathan with great interest. She often heard the men around her father's table discuss the gods, but she could not remember ever meeting someone who actually worshiped one god. And a living god at that.

She did not understand her father's expression of doubt about his own worship. Furthermore, she wondered what had they come here to see. And why all the mystery?

She was still thinking about these things when the servant returned with small silver finger bowls filled with scented water. They all rinsed and dried their fingers on linen napkins before Nathan invited them inside.

Lydia thought the house rather plain. There were no statues or decorative paintings. Colorful rugs on the floors and tapestries on the walls kept the rooms from being too austere. She did not see Nathan's wife but heard the sound of soft singing coming from some inner room. An air of serenity and contentment seemed to fill the house. She wondered if her father had the same impression.

Nathan escorted them into a small room, bare of furnishings except for a table and four chairs in the middle of the floor. A black velvet cloth covered the table. Lights flickered from oil lamps placed along the walls.

Loukas and Lydia were seated. Nathan dismissed the servant with instructions that they were not to be disturbed. Lydia watched with fascination as their host withdrew an ordinary looking box from a drawer in the table. She felt she was observing a ceremony as she observed his deliberate movements.

If he was trying to create an atmosphere of suspense, he certainly was succeeding.

"Come, Nathan," Loukas said. "Keeping me waiting won't get you a *sater* more for your pains. I only hope you have been successful in getting what I ordered."

"Judge for yourself," Nathan replied. "How will this do for a wedding present?" He pulled a soft deerskin pouch from the box and opened it. With a flourish he spread a gold necklace on the table.

Five medallions hung suspended from an intricately crafted chain. Encased on each medallion was an open rose holding a gold topaz in its center. Each rose was intertwined with three leaves of dark green emeralds to complete the design.

Lydia gave an involuntary gasp at the magnificence. The necklace had to be worth a fortune! This was an elaborate gift, even for her father.

"Let me help you try it on." Loukas fastened the necklace around Lydia's throat. Each way she turned, the lights picked up the soft glow of the gold and the reflection from the stones.

"Take it off for now," Loukas said. "This is to wear on the day of your wedding."

Lydia reluctantly allowed her father to remove the elegant necklace, but continued to turn it over in her hands. Nathan looked at Loukas. "Did you want your other purchase now?"

"Yes," he replied. "I may as well give it to Lydia today. The fewer people who know about this next gift the better. I would rather not draw attention to it among the servants."

"Another gift?" Lydia was astonished. What more could he possibly give her? And why must it be a secret?

Nathan replaced the necklace in its leather pouch and put it aside. When the table was clear once more, he handed Loukas a nondescript-looking small wooden box. To Lydia it looked no different from one her father used in the store to keep copies of his sales transactions.

When Loukas opened the box, a puzzled expression crossed her father's face. Lydia peeked inside and saw a plain gold bracelet, the kind any shop girl in the city could purchase. Even her personal slave, Myia, could afford a bracelet like this.

Lydia glanced from Nathan to her father. Surely Nathan was playing some kind of joke. This could not be what her father had ordered as a present for her.

"This is, of course, a very ordinary-looking bracelet," Nathan said. "There is nothing of real beauty or apparent value about it."

His stress on the word *apparent* aroused Lydia's interest.

"A robber would not bother to take this because he could not turn a profit from it," Nathan continued. "He would be looking for a valuable piece, perhaps one with stones set in it. A slave would not bother to take it because he would think the same thing. Therefore, you can wear it anywhere or leave it at home without fear of it being stolen. It is linked in such a way that you can wear it on your ankle if you do not wish to display it on your arm."

"Why would I wish to wear it at all?" Lydia asked. "I have several bracelets more beautiful than this. Someone would think I had borrowed it from a slave."

Lydia was not a mercenary person, but she was at a loss to see why her father would give her an exquisite necklace and then such an ordinary bracelet.

Nathan smiled knowingly at his guests. "Let's try it on." As he lifted the bracelet, he turned it so that a tiny catch embedded on the inside was visible. "Perhaps it needs a bit of adjustment. Suppose you move that little catch all the way to the left and see what happens."

Lydia obeyed, then gasped with amazement as a tiny hidden spring released the top portion of the bracelet. A hollow depression held three flawless diamonds that reflected the light like stars imprisoned in a dark cave.

She did not know what to say. She could only stare in stunned silence. Again she looked from Nathan to her father.

Loukas nodded with satisfaction as he closed the secret compartment of the bracelet and slid it onto Lydia's arm. "You will never go hungry or be in want as long as you keep this bracelet."

Loukas held Lydia's trembling hand. "It is my wish that you wear the bracelet always. You are going far from me. The way to Philippi is full of many dangers, and even the power of Rome cannot always protect you. It will make your leaving easier for me if I do not have to worry about you."

Lydia interrupted her father's speech to give him a hard embrace.

"You must promise to tell no one the secret of this gift," he continued. "Not Myia, not even Menalcus. If he should ask why you always wear the bracelet, tell him it is a reminder of your childhood."

"I promise."

Lydia could not find words to express the feelings welling up within her heart. Her agony over leaving home and her father conflicted with her love for Menalcus, the handsome courier in the Roman Army that would soon be her husband. But at the moment, the overriding emotion was one of gratitude for her father's love all the years of her life. She hugged him once more.

"Suppose you return home now," Loukas suggested. "I have sent for a servant to accompany you. It would not do for you to lose your jewels on the very day you receive them. Do not take any chances with your lovely necklace or your not-so-lovely bracelet."

"Aren't you coming with me?"

"No. I must stay here and pay for our purchases. I will have to argue half the day for a fair price from this camel dealer."

Nathan laughed as he escorted Lydia to the door, where her servant waited.

No doubt he and Loukas would bargain long and hard over the price of the necklace and the bracelet, but Lydia knew they each expected that. In fact, they would have it no other way.

A heart-rending cry and uncontrolled sobbing woke Lydia from a restless sleep. She felt tears on her face, and with a start she realized the cry had come from her own throat.

In the first confused moments of waking, she tried to remember what she had been dreaming. She sat up, trying to separate dream from reality, but in the bright light of early morning, the dream kept eluding her. She had felt a deep, urgent sense of need, so real she could still recall the sensation. Someone or something had abandoned her. With outstretched arms she had cried out for help.

That was all she could remember, and she would have quickly dismissed the dream if it were not for the fact that this same thing had happened before. She would wake up experiencing a sense of desperation or deep need, with no one to come to her assistance.

But this was not the day to dwell on morbid things. This was her wedding day! She clapped her hands. Her personal slave, Myia, entered the room, ready to assist with the morning bath.

Lydia stepped into the tub and quickly sponged her body with warm water. As soon as she was finished, Myia briskly toweled her dry. Later in the day she would enjoy the more elaborate bathing in preparation for the wedding festivities.

"Is my lady troubled this morning?" Myia asked. "Your eyes show signs of weeping."

"No, Myia, I am not troubled. I simply had a bad dream." Lydia paused. "You are very discerning this morning."

"I just want today to be a happy day for you. And I would not want to displease the gods by sending forth a tear-streaked bride."

Lydia laughed. The ominous sense of unease produced by her dream vanished.

Myia took careful pains in preparing Lydia for the day. A loose tunic of pale blue, held in by a corded belt, reached to Lydia's knees. Slippers of softest leather completed her morning wardrobe. Later in the day the bridesmaids would arrive to help prepare her for the time of sacrifice and the wedding to follow.

Lydia must remain within the doors of her father's house until that time. It would be an offense to her reputation and to her father if she appeared in public before the proper sacrifice had been offered.

As she waited for Myia to finish binding her hair into an attractive bun with a ribbon the exact shade of blue as her dress, Lydia grew restless. "That will be enough for now. You can outdo yourself this afternoon. Bring my breakfast to the balcony and then leave me."

Myia stepped to the door and gave orders to the slave standing there. He soon returned with a tray of fresh figs, cold sliced breast of chicken, and an amphora of watered wine sweetened with honey.

Myia carried the tray to a small table on the balcony, then obediently left the room.

As Lydia nibbled at her morning repast, she felt a wave of appreciation for her personal slave. Myia was a slight girl, only a year or so younger than Lydia. Her face was dominated by large, luminous eyes, so dark as to appear black. Her milky white complexion, with a rather broad nose over a cupid-bow mouth, was sparingly sprinkled with freckles. A cap of close-cut black curls hugged her head and covered all but the tips of her ears. A ready smile revealed small, even teeth, white as pearls. Had Myia been born to better circumstances, she could have been a reigning beauty.

As it was, she managed to make enough of a stir among the slave population to keep her occupied. More than one gentleman visitor to the house of Loukas looked at her with speculative eyes.

An orphan with no memory of parents, Myia had been born with a deformed foot. Soon after her birth she was abandoned on the path leading to the temple of Pallas, the goddess of wisdom. Leaving a crippled child within the temple proper was a grave sacrilege. Perhaps her parents, lacking the courage to destroy her, had left her nearby in the hope that someone would find her or that she would mercifully die from exposure.

Loukas chanced to see her there, and having a daughter near the same age, had pity on her and ordered his slave to bring her home. When the slave allowed a look of disapproval to show on his face at the sight of the filthy child, Loukas cuffed him aside and picked up the frail little cripple himself.

At that precise moment, the hoot of an owl was heard. The owl was the bird of Pallas. Its voice was considered to be a blessing of the goddess herself. The hoot brought instant terror to the soul of the slave. He tried to make amends by bowing before the child and holding his arms out for her.

"Never mind," Loukas stated coldly. "I'll carry the poor little creature myself."

And carry her he did—right into his house.

The careless slave was sold at auction the following week. This served as a lesson to the other slaves that while the master was kind, obedience was expected, without comment or question. It was also a warning that Myia was not to be mistreated.

As she grew up, Myia's ready smile and sunny outlook won a place in the hearts of the entire household. She became especially adept in copying the latest hair styles. The most stubborn locks yielded to her agile fingers, and the slave women were constantly asking Myia to arrange their hair.

When she was old enough to assume responsibility, Myia became Lydia's personal slave, a gift from Loukas to his daughter.

Lydia ordered a special shoe to be designed to hide the sight of Myia's withered foot. Though slaves were not to wear shoes of any kind, none dared question Lydia's command. With the help of a crutch, Myia could get about as quickly as any of the slaves who had two good feet. And woe to the one who encountered her displeasure. She had been known to use the crutch as an extension of her arm, to ward off any who made unwelcome advances or made fun of her.

Myia had a happy disposition and would not allow troubled thoughts to disturb her for long. When Lydia had explained to her that, as a slave, she would never be allowed to have a wedding of her own, a look of wistful longing had crossed her face. She had sighed with regret at being sent from Lydia's presence on this most festive of days, but then immediately put a on a smile, determined to enjoy vicariously the pleasures of her mistress.

Left alone, Lydia looked at the food on her breakfast tray. Nothing appealed to her. She selected a plump fig and rose to lean against the balustrade.

I'm not ready. Time is passing too swiftly. After today my life will never be the same. I'll be married, owned by Menalcus.

The idea of being completely at the command of another person, even one as delightful as Menalcus seemed to be, perturbed Lydia. Loukas was the only authority figure she had ever known. For as long a she could remember, Loukas had taken her to the marketplace with him. When he made his rounds at the weaving looms and dye works, she was his shadow.

She recalled her younger years, when Greek ladies were not supposed to be seen outside the house. Loukas made sure she remained indoors under the tutelage of Old Anna, his most trusted slave, long enough to learn how to manage the slaves and to give orders necessary to maintain a home suitable for a prosperous shop owner. She would always be grateful Loukas thought it necessary that she learn to read and write, something not many girls knew.

The odious task of learning to inventory supplies and order meals seemed to last forever, But soon Lydia was accompanying the steward to the market to make sure he picked the freshest vegetables and that he did not get cheated by the venders of meat and poultry. She followed the household slaves around to make sure they did not neglect any duty. As a result of her diligence, the house of Loukas became known for gracious hospitality and spotless elegance.

She had been overjoyed to be back with her father as he inspected the dyes squeezed from the tiny shellfish native to this area, or haggled with caravan merchants for bolts of silk, or watched with careful eye as lengths of material were submerged in the dye vats. She was always fascinated to see the sun-bleached materials disappear into the huge vats of red, purple, green, yellow, and deep blue. When the newly dyed material was spread to dry, the cloth resembled a giant rainbow.

Lydia trained herself to spot weak places in the weaving or uneven patches in the dyed material. Her watchfulness kept the workers producing their best work. She loved the sight of the shuttles flying back and forth in the hands of the weavers as they worked at the big looms. The woven material coming from the looms was sometimes handed to other workers to embroider with vivid designs that never failed to excite her.

She spent hours imagining the person who would use this or that shade of blue, or that stripe of green. It especially pleased her when the caravan or traders from faraway places came to buy the rolls of cloth. Lydia felt as if part of her family went to these distant cities to be used and admired.

Now she was going to live in a strange city. There would be no looms or dye works for her to visit. She would be the mistress of a household, responsible for her husband and his comfort. What would it be like? How would she pass her days? What would he expect of her?

She reached out to lay her hand against the warm marble railing of the balcony as if to imprint the touch of home against the coming days, when she would know this place only in memory.

Lydia had never known the love of a mother. But Old Anna, her nurse, loved her as her own child. Most of her friends were raised by a retinue of slaves more than by their actual parents. She had not thought her childhood as anything unusual or less than it ought to be. How could she, when Loukas loved her so much?

Now, however, she felt a deep longing to talk with her mother. Someone who could tell her the things she would encounter as a bride in a new land—as a bride in any land. She looked down at her clenched hands. She was working herself up into a good case of nerves.

A slight movement of the beaded curtain by the doorway into the men's apartments below caught her eye.

Poor Papa. He is as restless as I. I'll go down and talk to him. This may be the last opportunity we will have to be together.

Leaving her tray on the table, Lydia scurried out of her room. Myia, waiting in the hallway, followed near enough to be called but not close enough to intrude.

When Lydia reached her father's room, she saw him standing just within the archway, deep in thought. She hesitated and considered turning aside and retracing her steps to her own quarters. But when her father looked up and saw her, he beamed a welcoming smile.

"Are you coming to visit your old papa on your wedding day, little Lily-belle?"

The use of her childhood name erased the reluctance Lydia had felt about coming to her father. "It's been a long time since you called me that."

"It's been a long time since you came hunting me with a woebegone face. What is troubling you on this most happy day?"

Lydia sat on a low stool in her father's sparsely furnished room. Sheets of snowy linen covered a simple cot, padded with cotton. A table resting on carved lion's heads and clawed feet, the top inlaid with bands of silver, held a silver pitcher and a matching stemmed goblet with an exquisitely wrought cluster of grapes and leaves engraved around the lip and a banquet scene depicted on the bottom of the pedestal.

Her fingers traced the carving on the goblet while her eyes followed a frieze of Lydian gymnasts carved in bas relief along one wall. A bust of Loukas's father stared from a pedestal. Lydia used to imagine he was trying to tell her a secret but could not break the power of the stone that imprisoned his lips.

"There's really nothing bothering me," Lydia replied. "It's been a long week with all of the festivities and parties. Now it's my wedding day and I can't seem to do anything to pass the time until the hour of sacrifice."

"I thought you would be getting your hair fixed or whatever girls do to make themselves beautiful," Loukas teased.

"There's plenty of time for that after the bridesmaids come. If I could get the horses and go riding, I would be fine." Lydia shot a sideways glance at her father's face. "I don't suppose you'd want to risk your reputation and sneak out with me for a quick gallop, would you?"

"Why not? It will give me something to remember in the long nights when you are away."

He softly clapped his hands. When Elias appeared, he gave orders for their horses to be made ready and led to the back gate of the villa. Loukas and Lydia put on loose-fitting brown cloaks that amply covered their figures. A deep hood, pulled down until their faces could not be recognized, completed their costume.

They walked their horses sedately through the less traveled side streets to avoid the crowds going to and from the marketplace. They approached the gates to the city and rode through the Triumphal Arch out onto the main highway, leaving the city behind them. Lydia had ridden since childhood and managed her little mare with the hands of an expert.

The trail soon left the much traveled thoroughfare and led past the vineyards and olive groves on into the foothills. Stands of giant oaks, hoary with age, towered on each side of the road. Lydia thrilled to the sunlight, the blue sky, and the spirited horse beneath her. Throwing back her hood, she let the mare have her head. Her father followed suit. They were soon through the trees and far out on the plain, with the wind and the green earth to enjoy.

The riders pulled their horses down to a steady walk. Loukas's black stallion seemed eager to race on, but under the firm rein of his master, he stayed beside Lydia's mare. The mare tried to nuzzle the stallion's neck, but he snorted and blew, pretending to ignore her.

Lydia noticed a gray pallor to her father's face and the way he kept one hand pressed to his thigh. But she was too preoccupied with her own thoughts and feelings to contemplate the cause of his distress.

When they reached an outcropping of trees, they drew rein and dismounted to sit and enjoy the shade.

"Now, Lily-belle." Loukas took her hand and stroked her fingers as he had done so many times in the past. "What's troubling you? Have you changed your mind about marrying Menalcus? You don't have to go through with it, you know."

"Oh, no, it's not that," she assured him.

"Then what's the problem?"

"I'm not really sure. I had a bad dream last night. I guess that set the mood. It was a ridiculous dream. I can't even recall it to mind, but I was crying when I woke up. I had this dreadful feeling of searching for something I had to have, but I don't know what or why."

She stood and walked a few paces, picked up a stick, and picked at its bark, like a woodpecker hunting for insects. She darted a glance at Loukas every now and then. He was waiting patiently for her to provide more details.

Finally she threw the stick away and returned to her seat. "Until this morning I had not thought beyond the moment of the ceremony. I have given no consideration to what comes next. Papa, what will Menalcus expect of me tonight? How will I know if he is pleased with me?"

Loukas sat in silence. He started to speak several times, only to close his lips. He reached for Lydia's hand and spoke in a low voice. "Lydia, these are the things a mother should talk about with you. I will tell you how it was with us. I'm afraid that's the best I can do."

Lydia moved closer until she could rest her head on her father's knee. He stroked her hair as he told her of the thrill and joy he had felt on his own wedding night. His voice became vibrant with remembered emotion and then soft and calm as he went back in memory to that long-ago day when gentle Judith came to him as a bride.

"My daughter, Menalcus will only expect you to be yourself. He will delight in teaching you the ways of a man and woman. You must let him be your lord and master in every area. His word must be your command."

The idea of being under the complete dominance of another person, and especially of being "commanded" to do things, brought instant protest to her lips.

"Shh." Loukas restrained Lydia with a tender hand on her shoulder. "It does not have to be the way it sounds." He chuckled. "There are ways of being submissive without being dominated. If you really love Menalcus, and trust him to care for you, you will want to please him. And if Menalcus truly loves you, he will be eager to fulfill your every wish. Real love is wanting the best for your partner, even when it is something you do not like."

Lydia passed this off with a toss of her head and continued to frown.

"You will know when Menalcus is pleased with you by his actions," her father said. "You will also know when he is displeased. You must learn to avoid those things that will drive Menalcus from your side and cause him to seek pleasure elsewhere."

Lydia jumped to her feet. There would be no "pleasure elsewhere" in her marriage!

Loukas continued before Lydia could interrupt him. "A man notices the way a woman smells, the way she combs her hair and wears her clothes, and how she smiles. He likes a clean house and well-behaved children. Find things to talk about that interest him. Ask his advice. Don't whine and complain about your day. If you can do these simple things, you will not have to worry about who is master. Your love for each other will decide."

Lydia sighed. This was not exactly what she had wanted to hear. She wanted to find out about the physical side of marriage. She had heard the gossip of her friends, one of whom had recently become a bride. Her description of her wedding night had both horrified and fascinated her circle of listeners. Lydia decided right then that whatever took place within her bedroom walls would remain there.

The reluctance of her father to discuss that part of marriage with her was certainly understandable.

Poor dear. She had put him on the spot with her sighs and her questions.

Tired of her somber mood, Lydia pulled her father to his feet and made ready for the return ride home. When Loukas was mounted, she caught his reins for a brief moment.

"Papa, thank you for this ride. I will always remember it." Tears welled in her eyes and spilled down her cheeks. "And now…on with the wedding!"

With a touch of the heel, their mounts charged down the trail. Workers in nearby citrus groves paused to watch them race by. A wave of the hand and a smile marked their passage.

The morning of Lydia's wedding might have been slow in passing for Lydia and her father, but certainly not for the rest of the household. They returned home to find the house filled with activity.

Flower girls from the country arrived with baskets of flowers, picked in the half-light of early morning, the dew still standing on some of the petals. Green boughs from the nearby mountainside adorned the walls of the hallway. Garlands of ivy and myrtle wreathed tall columns. A chaplet of flowers crowned each ancestral bust.

Myia took full command as she led Lydia to her apartment. She declared that Lydia would be the most beautiful bride in Thyatira. She began by submerging the young woman in a luxurious bath and sponging her skin with delicately scented oils. Then she sprayed her with perfumed water, followed by a gentle toweling to leave her skin a warm pink.

Lydia reclined on a couch covered by a huge towel while Myia massaged warm oil into her skin until it glowed. The two laughed and talked about funny things that had happened in their years together.

A slave entered the room to announce the arrival of the bridesmaids to help with the dressing of the bride. Lydia greeted the girls with a happy smile, and Myia promptly assigned them their posts of service.

Lydia sat in a chair with her feet on a low stool while Myia prepared her hair. A bridesmaid stood in front of Lydia, holding a hand mirror of polished steel in which Lydia could follow the progress of her toilet. Another girl held a box of perfumes, eye and lip salves, rouges, ointments, and spoons for applying the same. Other boxes on a nearby table contained earrings, ribbons, necklaces, and assorted jewelry.

A slave stood to one side, wielding a long-handled fan so no drop of perspiration would spoil the preparations. If the fan slowed the least bit in its rhythm, a sharp look from Myia was enough to set it going again.

Myia's fingers seemed to possess a magic of their own as she combed Lydia's hair straight back from her face. She wove an intricately fashioned gold band into strands of Lydia's shiny blonde hair and drew the entire mass into a bun at the crown her head. A tiara of filigreed gold, set with pearls and emeralds, was securely fastened in place.

Like a master artist, Myia tinted Lydia's eyelids with the faintest hint of lavender eye salve. She did not outline the eyes in black or slant the brows upward, as the Egyptians did. Lydia's lashes and arched eyebrows did not need the accent of cosmetics, she claimed. A slight blush of rouge and lip salve completed her make-up.

Lydia stood, and Myia draped a tunic of sheer white linen from her shoulders. It hung in loose folds to her ankles. The skirt was decorated in tiny geometric patterns created by drawing certain threads in the material.

Another bridesmaid presented a silk tunic of pale lavender, which she slipped over Lydia's head to fall in soft lines just below her knees. A wide girdle of deep purple, lavishly embroidered with gold threads and tiny seed pearls, was clasped around her waist.

Gold lace medallion earrings, with a large pearl in the center and a fan of twined gold from which three pendants of emeralds and pearls was suspended, drew sighs of admiration from everyone.

Then the necklace Loukas had given her was carefully fastened around Lydia's neck. The bridesmaids clapped their hands in wonder and delight.

Myia placed the last adornment, a ring from Menalcus consisting of one giant pearl set in gold, on Lydia's forefinger. It seemed to pulse and glow with a life of its own.

A bracelet of gold studded with emeralds and pearls, which had belonged to Lydia's mother, graced her left arm. The beauty of her mother's bracelet certainly overshadowed the plain gold one Lydia insisted on wearing, much to Myia's surprise and dismay. The bridesmaids did not understand. But when one asked if it was a token to one of the gods, Lydia did not argue.

A bridesmaid slipped brocade satin slippers, adorned with a wide lavender bow and fastened with a pearled clasp, onto Lydia's feet. A veil, reaching to her waist and weighted at each corner by a square gold coin, set with an emerald as large a pigeon egg, completed the dressing.

The bridesmaids and Myia chattered the entire time Lydia was being dressed. It was a good thing their comments and remarks did not require her attention. If she had paid attention to all the innuendoes and sly remarks, her composure would have fled for sure.

Finally, Myia stepped back to view her creation. They had finished just in time. The music of the flutes and tambourines coming through the open window announced the approach of the wedding procession. The litter bearers would soon be at the door to carry Lydia to the temple for the sacrifice preceding the wedding ceremony and feast.

Lydia tried to think only of the wedding. It was no use. She could not picture herself taking part in some of the crude activities she had heard a few of the slaves joking about from time to time. Neither could she imagine the physical contacts her friends described in such languishing and romantic tones, which sounded more like some of the cattle she had seen mating out in the pasture than something people would do. Surely Menalcus would not expect her to… But if he did?

She sighed with relief when it was time to join the procession. At least she would not have any more time to think. She determined to enjoy this day to the fullest. After all, how many times did a girl marry?

The townspeople had gathered early in the morning outside the city gates to take part in the wedding procession of Lydia, daughter of Loukas the weaver. The streets of the city were crowded with throngs of poets, musicians, artists, workers, and even school children.

First came a band of flute players and dancers with tambourines, followed by a company of infantry and cavalry from the garrison. Next, six priests led a white bullock, horns gilded with gold, to be offered as sacrifice. A garland of myrtle and roses hung about his neck, and his varnished hooves glinted in the sunlight.

Next in line were the men of the city, merchants and store owners—contemporaries of Loukas. Each had a retinue of slaves who bore costly gifts to be offered to the goddess on behalf of the bride.

The matrons and maids of the city made up the column of women. Each woman was dressed in her best, wore garlands of flowers in her hair, and carried flowers to be tossed along the way. Behind the women a group of workers from each of the trade guilds stepped proudly along. The guild master carried gifts representing the best work of each craft. These would join the other offerings to the goddess to secure blessings on the prosperity of the bride and groom.

The procession wound through the streets, gaining more and more followers until it reached the street of Loukas. In the street outside the house, slaves lowered a flower-draped litter to the pavement. The music of the flutes and tambourines became a soft, coaxing melody, which led into a happy chant that traveled the length of the procession.

The *pronuba*—a wealthy lady chosen to be the head matron, who would oversee the rituals of the wedding—knocked on the front door. The porter opened it immediately.

Loukas descended from the doorway and mounted his black stallion, especially groomed for this occasion. Ropes of ivy and myrtle, intertwined with flowers, decorated the highly polished harness. His richly embroidered robes spread over the rump of the stallion. At his signal the procession moved forward a few paces. Household slaves made an archway of green boughs from the doorway to the litter. Flowers were tossed in profusion upon the steps so the feet of the bride would not touch the pavement.

When Lydia appeared in the doorway, the flutes and tambourines played an accompaniment to the laughter and shouts of the crowd. She paused to survey the laughing faces of her friends. The merry sounds of the musicians and the blending of flowers with the bright costumes of those in the procession blurred for a brief instant as she realized the finality of this moment. She had the uncanny impression of standing outside of herself, observing what was taking place as if she were watching a play on the stage.

The excited laughter of the bridesmaids as she took her place on the litter broke the spell, and she gave herself up to the full enjoyment of the moment. The pronuba led the way, followed by the litter surrounded by Lydia's bridesmaids. The procession moved ahead to the accompaniment of the music.

The party bringing the bridegroom approached the temple area from another direction. As the wedding procession began to ascend the acropolis, Lydia glimpsed the perfectly groomed horses of Menalcus and his company. A special troop of Roman soldiers in full uniform, their plumed helmets carried on their left arms, marched behind the groom in perfect cadence. Their progress was timed so the two processions met at the first flight of marble steps leading to the temple area.

Lydia looked at the circular temple nestled deep in a shady grove of silver poplar trees, whose leaves seemed to whisper the secrets of the deity in the slight breeze. A double row of fluted ionic columns reached from the marble floor to the ceiling. Golden sheaves of wheat and corn, symbolic of the fertility of the land, decorated the capitals, and elegant clusters of grapes wound in and out of grape leaves, peaches, pomegranates, and other fruit to decorate the entablature that curved above the stately marble columns.

Her eyes traveled to the center of the temple and the statue of Cybele, patron goddess of the city. Gleaming white marble mirrored back the slightest glimmer of light. The reflection of candles, placed around the goddess's feet by the priests, seemed to give life to the statue. Lydia heard the murmur of the townspeople as the priests offered prayers. Many swore the statue breathed and the folds of her garment swayed in the breeze.

Lydia raised her eyes to study the stone face of the goddess. *Please, please, let my marriage be a good one. Let me be a good wife. Let us live together long years and have many strong children.*

This was the prayer she knew she must say. But the true cry of her heart was, *Help me. Help me know what to do and what to say. Help me to please Menalcus, and don't let him see how scared I am.*

The groundwork of Lydia's trust since childhood, like that of every faithful Greek, was to believe the gods were the guardians of mankind and the avengers of evil. They observed the hearts and minds of men, honored the upright, regarded the faithful, and heard the voices of supplication. She also knew the gods were capricious and often played with the lives of mortals to satisfy some whim or to vent their own feeling and desires.

Lydia sighed. The stone eyes of Cybele remained lidded as if half asleep.

The two parties came together before a series of white marble steps used only by the priests. Twenty white-robed men, assisted by many priestesses, were in attendance. Just before the pronuba assisted the bride from the litter, Lydia was able to sneak a look at her husband-to-be.

Short black curls hugged his ears and accented his well-shaped head. The outline of a dark beard that would need shaving every day covered his face. Heavy black eyebrows, a rather sharp nose, and firm lips blended into a face most people would see as handsome.

Yes, decidedly handsome!

The pronuba received a scarlet veil from Menalcus's groomsman, which she fastened over the bridal veil.

Menalcus stepped forward. He tried to see through the veil covering Lydia's face as they moved toward the altar. Lydia relaxed a little as she caught a half-smile playing around his lips.

The sudden silence as the music ceased brought their attention back to the ceremony.

The slow, muted beat of the temple musician's hands on the drums signaled the time for the sacrificial offering. The townspeople parted to make a passageway for the magnificent white bullock being led to the altar.

The high priest motioned for silence. Two priests sprinkled the neck of the animal with salt and consecrated barley. Swiftly, but with a ritualistic grace, the knife descended to let out the creature's life.

Lydia could not restrain a shiver of revulsion as the knife descended. Nor could she help but wonder how this shedding of innocent blood had anything to do with her future happiness. The high priest held a golden goblet in which he deftly caught the first spurt of blood, which he drank before handing the cup to a lesser priest. Each priest in turn drank a portion of the blood of the slowly dying animal.

She closed her eyes as the high priest stood with bloody knife extended over the feverish activity at the foot of the altar. Four priests were designated to separate the entrails and parts of the bullock to be burned on the glowing altar. Two priests removed a stone slab in the floor, revealing a trough designed to carry away the excess blood.

As each piece to be burned was dissected, it was laid on the smoldering coals. The pronuba urged Menalcus and Lydia closer to the altar as the smoke began to rise. The bridesmaids and groomsmen fanned the smoke toward the couple in the belief it would make them fruitful. The townspeople raised their hands in prayer and made fanning motions as if to draw the smoke into their own lungs. They believed inhaling the smoke of the sacrifice made them a partaker of the power of the deity being worshiped.

Lydia tried not to cough as the acrid smoke burned her throat and eyes. She was glad when they were allowed to step back into cleaner air.

The remainder of the bullock was swiftly removed from the temple proper to be dressed and roasted over a slow fire.

After the bride and groom finished saying their prayers, the priest pronounced many incantations, followed by responses from the people.

The workers and guild masters stepped forward to present their gifts. Each gift was carried to the altar and received by a priest, who held it up to the goddess for her blessing before placing it at her feet. The giving and receiving of each gift called for a toast to the bride and groom by the donor.

By the time this long ritual was completed, it was late afternoon. Loukas signaled the end of the festivities by offering a sheaf of consecrated barley to the high priest. After several sing-song incantations, the priest placed it at the feet of Cybele. As he stood with both arms lifted toward the ceiling, the pronuba removed the red veil from Lydia's head and handed it to a priest, who placed it over the barley sheaf to assure the goddess of Lydia's virginity.

Loukas descended the steps of the temple, and the ceremony was over.

Menalcus led her to his meticulously groomed horse, whose rump was covered by a beautifully embroidered blanket that reached to the ground on both sides. Garlands of flowers encircled its neck and were plaited into its flowing mane and tail. Lydia blushed when Menalcus lifted her onto the back of the steed.

The music of flutes and the singing of gay songs conducted the bridal party to Loukas's home. Menalcus walked beside the horse and responded with smiles and laughter to the good-natured greetings and sallies that marked their progress.

Normally Lydia and Menalcus would have gone to the home of the bridegroom, but because Menalcus lived in a barracks, they were going to stay with Loukas for two days, when they would be leaving for Philippi.

At the entrance to the house, Menalcus lifted Lydia from the horse. A slave advanced, bearing a small container of perfumed oil. Lydia anointed the lintels of the door with oil and then twisted small bands of woolen material around the doorposts, to bring blessing and prosperity to the new household.

Before she had time to think about the many happy days she had lived in this house, Menalcus took her in his arms and, to hilarious laughter and much unwanted advice, carried his bride across the threshold. A very old superstition declared it an evil omen for the bride to stumble when entering her home for the first time.

The wedding party and several invited guests, about twenty men and as many women, followed Loukas into the house. Those who remained returned to the temple area to partake of the feast Loukas's workmen had prepared, the main course being the roasted bullock.

The guests were more than ready to refresh themselves. Loukas and Menalcus led the way to the men's apartments while the ladies went upstairs with Lydia. They bathed and perfumed themselves, a welcome relief from the heat and activity of the procession and temple ceremony. Everyone dressed in fresh garments brought by servants for this purpose.

The grand table in the main hall was prepared for the men of the party. Lydia would be the only woman allowed to dine at this table, seated between her father and Menalcus. As soon as the initial part of the meal was over, she would join the women dining in the *gynaceum*, or women's quarters.

First, she knew, all the male guests would gather around the grand table, which was covered with pure white linen delicately embroidered in rich designs.

They would sing a song and exchange salutations.
Loukas would pour a wine offering to the gods. The
men would recline on couches, spread with fine
matching linen for this occasion, and lean against
cushions of intricate drawn work. Menalcus would
be seated in the place of honor.

When it was time for Lydia to appear, she came
into the main hall, dressed in a rich lavender gown
that reached to her ankles. Dainty ruffles of snowy
lace covered the bodice from neck to waist. A heavily
embroidered apron in threads of gold, red, and blue
was secured at the waist by a broad belt of matching
design. She took a chaplet of flowers from a tray carried by a slave and crowned each head, beginning
with Loukas and ending with Menalcus.

Another slave appeared, bearing a mound of
snowy linen napkins on a tray. Lydia placed these
embroidered squares on the breasts of her guests
and personally handed each one a fresh cup of wine.
These napkins would be carried home as a gift from
the bride.

The youngest and most handsome of the slaves
served the meal. A spoon was laid before each guest.
Lydia directed the placing of platters heaped with
fresh-roasted pork, veal, chicken, and venison, cut
into bits. The men filled their plates from platters
of broiled fish, oysters, crabs, and eels, followed
by trays of cheeses, steaming bowls of peas, beans,

squash, rice, and heaping bowls of large white onions.

All manner of fruit covered the center of the table: luscious purple grapes, golden oranges, tangerines, pomegranates, and plums. Long loaves of bread, golden brown on the outside and fluffy white inside, were passed from person to person, and each guest tore off what he wanted. Slaves constantly stepped forward with bowls of scented water and fresh towels of immaculate linen for the guests to clean their fingers. Bones and scraps of food were tossed under the table to be cleaned up after the meal was over.

Seeing that all was progressing well, Lydia rose from the table. With glasses raised to her health, she left the main hall to join the women, where a similar feast was spread. Myia placed flowers on the heads of all the women and draped garlands of myrtle and violets around their necks.

Some of the guests raised their eyebrows when Myia assumed the place of honor next to the bride. Families often became personal friends with their slaves, sometimes even adopting them into their family. But for a slave to occupy the seat of honor at the table was unheard of. However, Lydia was not influenced by the social mores of the day. Myia was her best friend and she wanted this honor to be hers.

After dinner the tables were cleared and spread with fresh linen. Lydia invited the ladies to come into the main hall, where more singing followed. The servants brought honor to their master with a special dance they expertly performed to the delight of their audience. The wine cups were filled many times.

The men would continue their celebration far into the night, for they loved companionship and the opportunity to talk. To sing songs, recite poetry, and enjoy the delight of elevated emotions was the essence of pleasure. But as soon as the dance was finished, the bridesmaids led Lydia to her room to prepare her for the marriage bed. With all her heart Lydia wished they would leave, but she realized this was the most cherished part of their duties.

Much giggling and droll conversation went on as Lydia was placed in the center of her dressing room. Each piece of her attire was carefully removed and handed to a slave. Myia supervised each step of the process.

After this Lydia was again lowered into a tub of warm water, fragrant with scented oils. A brisk toweling and rubbing with a sharp-scented astringent completed her toilet.

A simple linen gown, plain in every detail, was slipped over her head. It fell in soft pleats to her feet. Again Myia carefully dressed her hair. The work of the morning was slowly undone, and after a gentle brushing, Myia drew the hair into a loose plait and fastened the end with a white ribbon.

Much laughter and advice filled the few minutes it took the excited bridesmaids to assist Lydia into the bed. Their final act was to scatter rose petals over the covers as they said good night and lowered the thin curtain around the bed. She would not see them again before her departure.

Lydia could not stop the tears that came. These girls were not intimate friends, but she had grown up with them, had attended their parties, and had helped in weddings like her own. Now she was saying good-bye to her childhood. After tonight she would not be free to giggle and play the innocent games of virgins. Tomorrow she would be a matron.

Lydia restrained the impulse to call Myia back on some pretext. She could hear the singing and laughter of the men still in full sway through the shuttered doorway. They were certainly enjoying the evening.

She stared at the rose petals strewn over the covers surrounding her. Lydia had never shared her bed, and she was not sure she was ready to share it now.

Whether it was the result of her warm bath or release from the activities, Lydia suddenly felt exhausted. She shifted her position several times to try to stay awake. She was not sure what she was to do next, but she knew sleeping was not it. In spite of her efforts, her eyelids refused to stay open. The last sound she heard was of someone reciting an ode to the god of the hearth.

Lydia tried to turn over in her bed, but something was weighing her down. There seemed to be a heavy bar across her chest. She twisted again but the weight was still there. She reached to move whatever was holding her down and was shocked to feel a warm, hairy arm draped over her body.

Fully awake, she looked down to see a tanned masculine arm, and with the sight came the memory of the day before. She turned her head to meet the deep brown eyes of Menalcus. Startled to see his face so close, wide awake and staring at her—no, laughing at her—she froze.

"Good morning, dear wife."

"Good morning," Lydia muttered. She dropped her gaze and tried once again to turn over, to no avail. Why didn't he move his arm? If she could sit up, she could collect her senses.

Menalcus did not move.

"I'm sorry," she managed to stammer. "I fell asleep. Did I... Did you... Did we...?"

Menalcus raised himself on one elbow but made no attempt to move his arm flung across her tense body. Her heart was pounding. Small beads of perspiration were starting to form on her upper lip. The more he stared at her, the more stiff her body became. A warm blush heated her face.

"No, my dear wife." Menalcus traced the outline of her cheek with his hand. "I'm afraid I enjoyed one song too many and emptied the cup a bit more than I should have. Even if you had not been sleeping so prettily, I fear my performance would have been lacking."

Lydia was relieved that she was not totally responsible for the fact that her marriage had not proceeded beyond the ceremony. She lifted her eyes to look at Menalcus. He was not smiling, yet there seemed to be a hint of a twinkle lurking in his eyes. And his hands were moving.

She quickly closed her eyes as she felt his hand at her throat. Then one finger slowly moved over her breast, down her side to the inside of her thigh, to the knee, and back up the other side in the same manner. She was amazed at the feelings stirring through her. Although she had not moved at all, warm waves of a strange desire welled up within her.

She turned toward Menalcus, wanting him to touch her again, wanting him to kiss her. And he did—on the forehead, gently, as he might have kissed a sister.

Before Lydia could sort out these strange new feelings, Menalcus threw his legs over the side of the bed and sat up. Accompanied by a light tap at the door, Myia's voice reminded the couple that it was time for the final ceremony connected with their wedding.

Lydia could not believe Menalcus had risen from bed without touching her again. More surprisingly, she could not believe how much she wanted his touch! What kind of man had she married? Did he think her such a cold fish he did not want to bother with her? Cold fish indeed! She would remedy that misconception quickly. He would learn right at the beginning that she intended to be his wife, fully and completely. If he thought he could play with her emotions and walk away, he had not reckoned correctly.

She flung the curtain aside and strode into the dressing room. Menalcus had his back to her. She stripped her nightgown from her shoulders and kicked it into a corner. Even as she reached for his shoulder to turn him around, she admired his slender waist, the way the muscles rippled across his back.

Menalcus turned at her touch. A look of astonishment shone in his eyes.

"Did you intend to shame me before my family and friends, Menalcus Romalius? Did you expect me to go to breakfast still a virgin, to be the butt of jokes by my guests and servants? Am I so undesirable that you could not bear to become my husband?"

All the time Lydia was talking, she was pushing Menalcus in the chest. With each push he stepped back a little until his back was against the wall and he could go no farther.

"Wait! Wait!" He grabbed her wrists. "What are you so upset about? What do you mean, shame you?" He was half laughing, but when he realized Lydia was serious, he stopped smiling. "I was only trying to give you some time to get used to the idea of being married. I was… I thought… I didn't want to frighten you."

"Then why did you make me feel the way you did?"

"How did you feel?"

"I wanted you to keep touching me, to hold me, to—"

Lydia got not further because Menalcus put his arms around her. "Silly goose," he murmured, then he kissed her.

An explosion of emotion coursed through her body. Without conscious effort, her arms slipped around his neck. He began to do all the things she desired. Those strange feelings returned, this time stronger than ever.

Was this love? She was not sure, but she never wanted it to end; never wanted him to release her; never wanted him to take his lips from hers.

As he lifted her and carried her to the bed, she kept her arms tightly circled around his neck and covered his face and neck with her kisses.

When Myia again tapped at the door, Lydia stirred and reluctantly started to rise. Menalcus held her, closely fitting his body to her own.

"Are you ashamed now, my wife?"

Lydia rolled over until she was directly on top of him and could look directly into his eyes. "There's not a shamed bone in my body." She gave a delighted giggle. " Nor is there one in yours."

Several kisses later, she released him and proceeded with her morning bath. Myia answered her summons and quickly helped her dress and arrange her hair. Lydia slipped into a simple tunic of light green linen, with small flowers embroidered along the hem and a matching girdle. Myia placed a closely fitted cap of white lace, cut away over the ears so it resembled a skull cap, on her head.

Lydia descended to the wedding breakfast to receive the official recognition of her role as a proper wife. She greeted a few of her father's closest friends, already seated in the main hall. Then she served breakfast as if she were an ordinary servant. At the close of the meal, she personally carried the finger bowls with scented water to each guest, along with a linen towel to dry their fingers.

When she came to Menalcus, she wanted to lean over and kiss the top of his head, but she did not dare. A quick glance into those brown eyes saw a sparkle of laughter. This time she was sure he was laughing with her and not at a her. Her face felt so hot, she was certain it must be red as a turnip!

The regular table servants were sent to clear the table and replenish the wine cups. An oblation was poured out to the gods, and then another cup was raised in a toast and blessing from Loukas.

Lydia stood by the door as the guests prepared to leave. She presented each one with a large linen handkerchief, which she had made by drawing some threads to create a border design. The men would take these home and present them to their wives, if they were married.

The ceremonies were over. All the rituals had been observed. Lydia was now the matron of her home. Surely Cybele was pleased with their offering. Why else would Lydia feel so happy?

The day of departure arrived quickly.

Lydia stood quite still in the early-morning air. The low foothills of the Tarsus mountain range were still shrouded in deep purple shadows. The approaching sunrise streaked the sky with pink and gold, pushing the dark shadows of night aside. Another day was making its debut in Thyatira. She could barely distinguish the outlines of the courtyard below. It was hard to think this would be the last morning she would view this scene.

Already the stillness of the air and the absence of clouds gave a foretaste of oppressive midday heat.

A loud crash reverberated through the stillness. Somewhere in the murky distance an early-rising worker had dropped an iron pot on the cobbled street. The echo had no sooner died than, as if on signal, the city came to life. She listened to the bustling sounds as workers in the street passed and called greetings and invoked the blessings of the gods on one another.

Lydia loosened the cloak she had thrown around her shoulders before stepping onto the balcony. Behind her the even breathing of her new husband continued undisturbed. She turned her head to look at him for a moment. A helpless, almost childlike expression marked his sleeping features.

As if he could sense her gaze, Menalcus stirred, turned over, and continued to sleep. Lydia withdrew into the corner of the balcony. For some unexplained reason she did not want Menalcus to know she had been watching him.

A movement below caught her eye. Myia stood in the courtyard. Lydia crossed the room on noiseless feet and quietly slipped into the wide hall and down the stairs. She clapped her hands softly, and soon Myia was at her side. Motioning for her to be quiet, Lydia led the way into the large bathroom, usually reserved for the men of the house.

Lydia whispered instructions to Myia, which brought a frown to her pleasant face. But she deftly dressed Lydia's hair and helped her into a short tunic such as the kind she had worn when helping Loukas in the dye yards. Lydia pulled her cloak loosely about her to further disguise her figure.

The two women slipped out of the enclosed courtyard into the city streets. Only then did Lydia permit Myia to ask why they were sneaking away from the house without telling anyone.

"Milady, you should have waited for your father." Myia was apparently not quite ready to include Menalcus in the family group. "You know he has forbidden you to go outside the house without an escort. He won't like it."

Despite protests and dire warnings, Lydia pushed and pulled Myia along the street. They blended into the hurrying throng and soon reached the city square.

Lydia placed Myia on a bench overshadowed by a statue of a bull's head on one side and a lion on the other. "Wait here for me. If I stay too long, you can come and get me."

"Come where?" Myia asked, but Lydia was already nearly out of hearing. She paused once to glance back at the small cloaked figure. Myia had pressed herself as far into the corner of the bench as she could. No one seemed to notice her.

Lydia had known for a long time she was leaving Thyatira to make her home in faraway Philippi. She had pushed that knowledge aside as if she could postpone her departure. Now it was time. There could be no more delays. She wanted one last walk through the city that had always been her home. She wanted to remember Thyatira in the morning.

The last fingers of bright sun touched the white marble buildings and statues with a gentle glow, accenting the black veining. She looked at the statuary on the street corners and the arches decorated with carvings in bas relief leading down the main thoroughfare to the northern gate. She strolled up and down the streets, past the district where craftsmen displayed their wares, past the agora where her father's shop was located. Beneath her feet, washed stones from the sea made mosaic patterns to complement the marble buildings.

On her way back to Myia, Lydia stopped in the park and touched the mane of the big marble lion outside the library. She thrust out both arms to feel the spray falling from the high third tier of a marble fountain. She paused to watch slave girls take turns drawing water from the well by the bath house, gracefully balancing the full pitchers on their shoulders. She packed into her mind and heart enough sights, sounds, and smells to last the rest of her life.

All too soon she returned to the bench where Myia waited. She did not mean to frighten her, but when she placed her hand on Myia's shoulder, the poor girl reacted with such a start, Lydia had to grab her elbow to keep from being swatted with Myia's crutch. They stood with their arms around each other, laughing like two school girls.

The smile left Lydia's face as she realized she was no longer a little girl, free to play silly pranks. It was hard to leave both her home and her childhood at the same time. But she was now a young matron, with a husband who was probably wondering where his wife had gone.

"Are you going to the temple to pray before you leave?" Myia asked.

Lydia looked toward the hillside, where the top of the temple of Cybele lifted above the trees. Memories of all the times she had climbed that hill rose to her mind.

She had gone to the temple on the day before her wedding, seeking some peace for the tangled emotions that were surging through her mind. She was not sure whether it was a trick of light that played over the face of Cybele that made her feel mocked, or if it was the bold gaze in the eyes of one of the priests, which had stayed in her mind as she bowed before the altar.

At any rate, she had not found the peace or reassurance she sought. Instead she had to repress a desire to jump up and run away. She had told no one of this experience, but she thought of it a great deal during the time that followed and especially during the sacrificial ceremony.

"Not today," she said. "I'm sure we will go to the temple while we are in Pergamum and Troas."

Myia looked surprised. The slave girl was not allowed to go to the temple because of her deformity, but she had often gone to the edge of the temple grounds when she accompanied Lydia. A vague sense of unease crossed her face.

Lydia knew Myia was not enthused about going to Philippi. But she also knew she would need Myia for support as well as for the service she would render. She could not keep from looking over her shoulder toward the temple as they re-entered the busy courtyard.

The pair returned to the villa in silence. There they found servants scurrying about, performing their usual duties. The added hustle and bustle of other servants carrying trunks and boxes to be loaded on the donkeys spoke of the newly married couple's imminent departure. Lydia's wedding gifts and the personal belongings she was taking to her new home filled a wagon pulled by four horses. Loukas had twelve donkeys carrying blue and purple cloth bound for Thessalonica.

When everything was in readiness for their departure, Lydia joined her father and Menalcus for breakfast. She had persuaded them to let her ride her mare on the journey. She would ride astride, disguised as a boy. The short, belted tunic that reached to her knees was much like the one she had worn while helping her father in the dye yards. A short cape draped over her shoulder would serve to keep her warm when needed and it could be fastened to one shoulder and draped over her arm at other times. Both men had to agree that it would be more practical than trying to ride side-saddle for such a long distance. Homosexuality was so prevalent, nothing was thought about a young boy traveling with another man.

A little nest was prepared for Myia on the wagon that would carry their baggage and foodstuff. Myra was also dressed as a young boy for more ease in traveling.

Lydia tried to keep the lump out of her throat and made herself swallow the cheese and meat on her plate. The knot in her stomach caused the food to taste like stale bread.

She looked across the table at the man she had married. At this moment she hated Menalcus. How dare he take her away from her father and all she held dear! Who did he think he was to interrupt her life and carry her away like this? Hot tears stung her eyelids. In spite of all attempts to hold them back, her sobs escaped.

A quick glance at Loukas showed a glimmer of tears in his eyes as well.

Menalcus excused himself on the pretense of making a place on the wagon for Myia. Lydia was certain he understood that his new wife and her father needed some time alone.

Loukas held Lydia in his arms for several moments, tears flowing down their cheeks. Finally, without a word, he escorted her outside, where he helped her up onto her horse, then mounted his black stallion. She was glad he had decided to ride with them for a short distance.

Lydia and Menalcus and their party were scheduled to join a caravan of silk merchants from Galatia. Only yesterday they had learned a troupe of traveling players from the theater in Ephesus would be journeying with them as far north as Pergamum.

Menalcus would be carrying messages from the prefect and other important men of the city to the dignitaries in Philippi and Thessalonica. Some messages would continue on to the emperor himself. Several men of his company made up part of an army troop, which would double as an escort for the huge caravan. Travel would, of necessity, be slow with such a large group. It would be many days before they reached Pergamum, forty some leagues away.

Menalcus gave brisk orders to move out, and within minutes the caravan was lined up, ready to join the rest of the travelers at the city gate. He urged their horses forward. It was a good thing her horse did not need immediate attention, because her tear-blinded eyes could see nothing but her husband's broad back in front of her.

At the outskirts of the city, Loukas embraced his daughter for a long moment. Then he pulled his horse to one side and watched as the long caravan moved slowly forward.

Lydia turned for a final look at her beloved father. She continued to gaze behind her as the walls of the city receded in the distance. Her last glance was met with a reflection of light from the top of the marble temple of Cybele on the hillside.

When she could no longer distinguish anything but the dim outline of the city walls, Menalcus rode up close to her bowed form and stretched out his hand to her. Slowly, her hesitant hand emerged from the voluminous cloak and settled into his.

CHAPTER 2

Pergamum

Several days' journey to the north of Thyatira, the caravan climbed a tree-bordered mountain pass. The scattered provinces of Rome were connected by a system of roads built by the labor of captured slaves. Hand-quarried blocks of stone laid side by side made a highway wide enough for two carriages to pass without pulling off to the side.

The roads were less spacious when they had to cross over mountains. While not always lined with stone, each route was well laid out, with the roadbed leveled and holes filled in with crushed stone. Underbrush on each side of the road had been cut back to lessen the risk of attack from ambush.

From time to time the soldier escorts for Lydia's caravan halted to allow the heavily burdened pack animals to catch up. Lydia breathed deeply of the wood-scented air, while her sharp gaze swept along the hillsides. She wondered what tales these wide glades could tell if every lichen-covered stone and slender blade of grass could speak. A silver stream splashed down over giant boulders. Spider webs gleamed in the early morning light, each strand outlined with strings of dewdrop pearls.

Lydia's youthful spirits could not resist the beauty surrounding her at each turn of the road. The lure and excitement of adventure opening before her began to lift the sadness of leaving her father and her home.

Wild flowers hung from craggy ledges as if eager to impart some vast secret only they were privileged to understand. Broad-leafed poplars and dense strands of oaks grew beside stately pines. Yellow birds flitted from tree to bush and back again, while blue jays screeched noisily at the intruders. Bright rays of sunshine streamed between the trees as if to spotlight the carpet of fallen leaves and fragile ferns.

The stamping of her mare and the sharp calls of the drivers brought Lydia's attention back to the trail. A rocky promontory rose straight up on her right for more than a hundred feet. The trees on the left of the trail had gradually thinned and now disappeared entirely, the result of a rock slide clearing everything in its path. She turned in the saddle to ease her tired muscles. The ascent was slow, at times only a few paces at a time, while the wagons and animals rounded the curves along the mountainside.

It was approaching midday by the time the caravan reached the summit. Lydia caught her breath in wonder as her eyes followed the descent of gray, splintered cliffs to meet waving treetops on slope after slope that fell away to the valley below. The plain stretched out like a fairyland, with the road a broad yellow ribbon in the sunlight. Cattle grazing by a meandering stream in a far-off meadow looked like toys. This craggy headland marked the highest point of their journey.

A gleam of white drew her attention to the low hills beyond the valley. Menalcus drew his horse near to tell her they were approaching the end of this first leg of their journey. That was Pergamum in the distance.

"If you look closely, you can just make out the tiered seats of the open-air theater and the outline of a few buildings," he said. "The city is built on a series of terraces leading to the acropolis. I think that tallest building almost in the center is the temple housing the altar to Zeus. We'll find time to worship before we leave."

Lydia tried to follow Menalcus's pointing finger. She looked long and hard at the spot designating the temple of Zeus. Surely this greatest of all gods would be able to satisfy the curiosity of her mind and the longing of her heart.

The caravan came to a halt about a league farther along the trail. The stop was a welcome relief. Before Menalcus could reach Lydia's side to help her dismount, she was out of the saddle. It was just as well, since she was supposed to be maintaining her disguise as a young boy. She was beginning to get used to the short tunic.. Her main problem was to keep the cape draped over her arm in such a way as to hide the bracelet she had promised to wear. Menalcus had suggested that she pack it away until the trip was over but she stubbornly refused. She hoped her fellow travelers would become so used to seeing it, they would pay little attention to it. She was comfortable on the outside but every muscle in her body called out for relief.

The respite lasted only long enough to eat a quick meal. Nearly everyone ate standing. Pergamum was still a long ride away, and they would have their fill of sitting before they reached their destination.

Several hours later the party emerged from the last wooded area onto a low headland within sight of the approach to the city gates. The caravan leader held the caravan there for the night. Experience had taught him, he explained, that it was not wise to bring loaded pack animals into the city after dark.

Daylight was beginning to wane by the time camp was made and the evening meal prepared. Lydia gazed in awe as the city blazed red and gold while the sun seemed to pause over the far western hills that served as a backdrop to the city. Long fingers of crimson light beamed across the area, reflecting back into the clouds. Every passing moment brought a transformation, each one more spectacular than the one before.

One by one the clouds changed from crimson to gold, from gold to delicate pink. The white marble walls and columned buildings, nestled against the hillside, mirrored back the last faint glow before the sun disappeared from view.

Lydia watched lights begin to blaze in the town. Moving globes of light indicated torches being carried along the streets. A bonfire outside the city gates seemed to served the dual purpose of knocking the chill of evening for the guards and providing light for inspecting the few late-arriving travelers hurrying through the gates before they closed for the night.

As the campfires of the long caravan began to die down for the night, the weary travelers sought their beds. Even the excitement of entering the city the next morning did not keep them awake after the leagues they had covered that day.

Just after dawn they crossed the bridge over the Caicus River and traveled the remaining three leagues to the gates of the city proper. Once the Roman capital of Asia, Pergamum was still one of the great cultural centers of the continent.

After waiting for several silk merchants and a theater group to enter the city, Menalcus ordered his men to the nearby garrison. Then he led his own party down a side street to an inn. Trustworthy slaves were put in charge of their goods, while Lydia and Myia placed their few necessities in a room Menalcus secured for them. Then Menalcus left to deliver several messages to the army post.

When he returned to the inn, he found his wife eager to begin exploring. Lydia insisted that Myia accompany them. "You might be very much at home moving about like this," she said, "but this is a totally new experience for me." She needed some remnant of the familiar with her, and she sensed that Myia needed the reassurance of being together as much as she did.

They made their first stop at the Aesculapion. Menalcus, their self-appointed guide, informed them that this hospital was known throughout the area as one of the finest in the Empire.

"Why do you want to go where there is nothing but sick people when there are so many other things to see?" Lydia protested.

"Because, my love," he answered, "I have an important document to deliver. It is addressed to a doctor believed to be visiting in this vicinity. I was told I would most likely find him here."

They entered the wide archway of the hospital and wandered down corridors with rooms opening on either side to reveal couches holding people too sick to be treated at home. Rows of cubicles used as offices for doctors and dentists were busy places, with slaves carrying basins and pitchers of water. In another corridor mothers waited with sick children. Young doctors were observing older doctors.

The threesome hurried past one room where a doctor held a potion of some kind to the lips of a man who appeared too weak to drink it. Sweat stood on his brow, and he shivered and moaned. Lydia had heard of the dreaded swamp fever and wondered if that was the young man's condition.

Menalcus led Lydia and Myia to a bench in a small alcove with instructions to wait while he tried to locate the doctor he was seeking. Lydia felt a chill as she watched him leave, but steeled herself to be brave.

A man of medium build, wearing a plain white toga belted with a gold chain, entered the room across from where the two women were seated. Lydia watched him move with quiet dignity from one couch to another. Those in attendance greeted him with a great show of courtesy. He did not interfere or try to give directions to any patient, but merely observed here, touched a brow there, or raised a dressing to look at an injury.

Lydia's attention was held by the calm assurance the man seemed able to communicate to the patients as well as to the attending doctors. His close-cropped black hair looked like it wanted to curl. Full lips and well-marked brows above a straight, thin nose pointed to his Greek parentage.

He stroked one young man's arm with a gentle hand, as a mother might quiet her child. Lydia overheard the attending doctor introduce him to a colleague as Luke, a physician from Antioch of Syria. Obviously he enjoyed a reputation of some note.

When he turned to go to the next couch, his eyes met Lydia's gaze. She found herself looking into blue eyes that were probing and compelling. Lydia felt as if this man knew all of her life, both past and present, and that he was a person she could trust without reserve. He smiled, causing little crinkles at the corners of his eyes. His smile dipped at one corner, giving her the feeling that he joked easily and could laugh at himself as well as with others.

Lydia was surprised to see an attendant, followed by Menalcus, approach the Syrian doctor. Menalcus bowed in greeting and, after a few words, handed over a thick packet he had been carrying. The two men shook hands. The doctor's friendly smile appeared again as Menalcus excused himself and returned to her side. The man turned and walked away, reading his message as he went.

"So, are you ready to visit those 'other things' you are so anxious to see?" he teased as they walked away.

Lydia nodded with enthusiasm.

On their way out of the hospital, they passed a room containing a statue of the god of healing. A priest stood on one side to receive gifts from supplicants in the hope of securing divine favor and healing. Some patients brought carved replicas of the part of the body they wanted restored to health. All bowed low before the god who held all of their hope.

Menalcus and Lydia started down the road when suddenly she realized that Myia was no longer with them. They retraced their steps and found the slave wistfully gazing at the statue.

Menalcus gave her a coin to present to the priest. "I don't see how that will help the girl," he whispered to Lydia as the slave girl scurried away. "But if it makes her feel better, what harm can it do?"

The couple entered an adjacent courtyard, where an open colonnade led to a public library consisting of four massive halls. "At one time this was one of the largest libraries in the world," Menalcus informed her. "But Antony took more than two hundred thousand volumes from here to the library in Alexandria for Cleopatra."

"And still there are so many left," Lydia observed. She stood in the marble forecourt, looking at row after row of scrolls stored in small reading rooms where those learning the practice of medicine could study. Other rooms were filled from floor to ceiling with scrolls containing the learning of centuries. Here she found copies of Aeschylus, Sophocles, and Euripides.

They walked past room after room where, Menalcus explained, scholars were paid by the state to engage in research and scholarships of various kinds. Reading areas were open to the public. A great arched doorway led to a large room used as a lecture hall, where the citizenry could come to listen and learn.

Lydia's mind seemed unable to comprehend the vast amount of knowledge and the life work of the thousands of scholars whose findings and visions were housed in this one building. The realization of her limited knowledge made her feel small and insignificant.

Had all this learning brought peace to the scholars who wrote it, she wondered. Did they find the answers to the deep questions of their hearts? Would she be able to find the answers to her seeking in their legacy of knowledge? Was anyone ever able to find that completeness of self, that fulfillment and wholeness as a person, which she wanted to experience?

Myia joined them, and Menalcus called Lydia from her reverie to continue their walk.

The last room in this building was guarded by a priest standing before a door with a bronze bar across the entrance. One wall of oblong niches contained the scrolls of the wills of many prominent citizens. This room also contained copies of the sacred books relating to the worship of the many cults that existed in Pergamum. As they walked past the door, Lydia wondered if those scrolls could tell her which god was the right one to worship, or if one were better off worshiping many gods so as not to offend any?

It felt good to get out in the sunshine again. The road from the Aesculapion was laid out in terraces, culminating at the acropolis. It wound around the side of the hill, then branched off at the entrance to a great open-air theater.

Menalcus grabbed Lydia's hand and swung her around to face him. "Let's go in," he said, his eyes bright with excitement. "We'll be the cast of the latest drama, 'From Country to City in Three Easy Lessons.' We might even sing a song. You may never have this chance again!"

He danced around her, ending with a sweeping bow. When he straightened up, he showed a face that looked dolefully tragic and sad. Lydia stared in amazement as he instantly changed his countenance to one of great laughter and gaiety. He stood before them, alternating his expressions, until all three collapsed in laughter.

Hand in hand like naughty children, Lydia and Menalcus skipped down the stone steps to the stage floor. Myia followed more slowly. She found a seat a few feet from the entrance in the horseshoe-shaped theater.

Menalcus and Lydia spoke to her from the floor where the orchestra or chorus usually performed. At first, they called with loud voices, but the acoustics were so good, they found they could use a normal tone and Myia could hear every word. She applauded as they struck poses of various characters, from a pompous Roman general to a squabbling fishmonger at the agora.

Menalcus walked over to the *skene,* where the stage backdrops were stored. There he found a derrick for raising and lowering scenery or actors and a rolling device for changing scenes. He tried the door to the dressing hut and found it open.

"Menalcus," Lydia shrieked. "Don't go in there. We'll get in trouble!" Lydia felt like a child about to be discovered in something forbidden.

He waved her away and stepped inside. Larger-than-life-sized masks, made of linen and plaster, hung on a wall. The masks identified characters as old or young, male or female, happy or sad. Thick-soled boots and robes with padded sleeves would give the impression the actors were large people. Funnel-shaped mouths could be inserted in each mask to act as a megaphone in projecting voices.

Menalcus selected a two-sided mask of an old woman and returned to the *proskenion,* while Lydia took a front-row seat carved out of white marble with armrests. These seats were usually reserved for priests, officials, and the highly privileged, Marcus had told her. The ordinary citizens sat on stone benches recessed into the hillside.

Lydia and Myia applauded Menalcus's performance, jeering and booing while he did an exaggerated routine of imaginary scenes. By turning back and forth between the happy side and the sad one, he was able to show the character in every conceivable mood. Lydia could not remember ever laughing so hard.

When he finalized his show with an elaborate bow, clapping and cat-calls echoed all around Lydia. She turned, startled to see some members of the troupe of actors who had traveled with them from Thyatira.

Surprised by the arrival of an audience, and having exhausted his limited repertoire of portrayals, Menalcus returned the mask to its place and carefully closed the door to the hut. Lydia joined him on the stage, and they pranced to the center, where they curtsied and bowed to their unexpected audience.

Waving good-bye to the real actors, they climbed the steps to join a wildly clapping Myia.

Three tired young people made their way back to the inn for a supper of fish, cheese, olives, and black bread, washed down with sweetened wine.

A buxom waitress leaned against Menalcus's shoulder as she placed the food before them. She rubbed her ample breasts against his upper arm when she placed the *oenochoe* of wine before him.

Lydia glared daggers at her. She was about to speak when a nudge from Myia restrained her with a nod toward her attire. She knew there would be times when she would miss the long flowing dresses she was used to wearing and this was certainly one of them. Not only did she appear to be a boy but her tunic was getting very stained from the constant travel and she knew she badly needed a bath.

The laughter in Menalcus's eyes did nothing to soothe her feelings. Common sense told her he had done nothing wrong, but she wanted to trip the girl and pour the wine from the *oenochoe* in her face.

By the time they had finished their supper, other travelers began to enter the dining area. Menalcus ushered Lydia and Myia to their little cubicle of a room. Myia excused herself to see to the welfare of the other slaves, wisely leaving the newlyweds alone.

Menalcus teased Lydia about the waitress and her charms, but she did not respond. Instead she flounced to the other side of the room, turning her back to him and tugging at the neckline of her uncomfortable tunic.

"Come on, Lydia. What did you want me to do? How was she to know you were a girl, let alone my wife?" he added. "Honestly. Sometimes you behave like a very spoiled little girl instead of a grown woman!"

Lydia whirled around to rebuke him. But when she did, she saw Menalcus's mouth drop open. He stared at her in disbelief, then his face contorted in a toothy smile. Lydia followed his gaze and realized she had managed to twist her tunic in such a manner that her breasts had become partially exposed.

Menalcus whooped with laughter.

Lydia sauntered up to him in a mimicked portrayal of the waitress. As she strolled past him, she leaned over enough to press her breast against his upper arm. She stopped behind him, just close enough to barely touch him.

"A little girl, huh?" she challenged, then brushed against his other arm, leaning over and giving him a sultry grin. She could only hold the pose a moment before they both dissolved in gales of laughter.

Menalcus caught her in his arms and they fell across the bed, laughing uproariously. In the process,

Lydia's tunic came completely open, the girdle hanging loosely around her ankles.

"I take it back," Menalcus said between kisses. "You are very much a grown woman...a little spoiled maybe, but very much a grown woman."

The next morning Menalcus told Lydia he had been summoned to appear before the commander of the garrison. That meant he would not be able to escort her to the temple of Zeus as planned. He insisted she and Myia would be perfectly safe if they still wanted to go. When Lydia expressed discomfort with the idea, he instructed Gaius to accompany them. She thanked her thoughtful husband with a tight embrace.

The two women strolled through the agora, stopping at several interesting stalls. Gaius stayed at least two paces behind them. The place was crowded with early-morning shoppers. Slaves bought produce for their masters' tables; wealthy citizens haggled with shopkeepers over wares they wished to buy. The smell of fresh produce wafted through the market.

Next they walked past the *bouleuterion*, where the town council met to discuss the needs of the citizenry and to hear minor law cases.

Several soldiers stood guard around the next building. Gaius explained that this was the mint, where coins with the image of the emperor were struck.

The road before them divided in three directions. To the left was the hospital and the theater. The fork to the right led to a stone building with a porch and entrance on the south side. The building was very plain compared to the ornate structures around it. Lydia noted that most of the men going into it had long beards, and many wore elaborately embroidered shawls with long fringes over severe black clothing.

"Look, Myia," she said. "It's a synagogue, almost exactly like the one in Thyatira. Why do you suppose anyone would want to visit such a small temple when a few more steps would carry them to the grand temple of Zeus?"

"The people who attend this synagogue would not think of entering the temple of one of our gods," Gaius explained. "They call our gods 'pagan.' In fact, they do not consider Zeus a god at all, only a statue of stone."

Lydia turned to look at Gaius. He was staring at the men going into the synagogue with a great longing on his face.

"Are you one of them?" she asked.

"No, milady. I am not a Jew," Gaius replied. "I'm what they call a God-fearer. I come from the land of Gaul. When a Roman legionnaire captured my father in battle, I became his property as well. I was presented to Menalcus as a birthday present."

"What does it mean to be a God-fearer?" Lydia asked. "Doesn't everyone fear the gods?"

"Yes," the slave replied. "Everyone I've ever known fears the gods they believe in. The difference is, the Jews believe there is only one God, and they claim He is a living God, not simply gods of stone and plaster like Apollo, Diana, Minerva, or Zeus."

Lydia trembled. "If I really believed Cybele and Athena and Zeus were actually alive, I'd certainly be afraid."

Gaius gave her a curious stare. "Are you saying you doubt the gods are immortal?"

"No." Lydia began to walk ahead. "I didn't say that—not exactly. I'm not sure."

I'd like to be sure. I need to be sure. Little furrows wrinkled her brow as she walked along, lost in thought. Gaius's words reminded her of the conversation between her father and Nathan Ben Kobath. He had insisted there was only one "living" God.

Who was right? Was there only one god? If so, what was he like?

The road ahead led upward to the acropolis, overlooking the town. Lydia put her questions aside as the three of them became part of a throng of people whose eyes were drawn to several gleaming marble structures, magnificent in the morning sun. Lydia felt a surge of anticipation as she gazed at the great temple of Zeus. Even from this distance it seemed to proclaim the might and majesty of the father of all gods.

Lydia stopped to catch her breath before ascending the last curve in the broad thoroughfare. She could feel the linen of her tunic beginning to stick between her shoulder blades. By noon the heat would be extreme. She quickened her steps, hoping to return to the inn before then.

Some worshipers stopped to rest on benches in the shade of the trees. Lydia found a place for Myia, who would not be permitted to enter the temple proper. She often thought some of those who entered the temples were more deformed on the inside than poor Myia would ever be.

Gaius continued on with Lydia, staying respectfully behind as she advanced to the temple.

The great temple rested on a base of five gleaming marble steps. On each side of these steps rose a huge base at least ten feet tall and four hundred feet long. A great frieze of carved, life-size figures covered the sides of these bases. Lydia had never seen such detailed work. She felt compelled to draw near and at the same time felt dwarfed by the immensity of the scene before her.

Gaius spoke over her shoulder. "The son of Attalus I, ruler of Pergamum about two hundred and fifty years ago, had this altar built to commemorate his father's victories in battle against the invasion of my people."

Lydia turned to stare at this slave who seemed so knowledgeable about the things of this city. Like most slaves, Gaius wore a simple, short tunic that ended above the knee. It did little to hide his well-developed body that suggested strength and power. His hair was cut short and stood in bristly shocks above a deeply lined face with a long nose that hooked slightly over thin lips. Intense blue eyes gazed calmly back at Lydia.

"And do you know what these figures represent?" she inquired. She could not stop looking at the carvings that seemed so large when one was standing close to them. Deeply undercut in such a way as to seem detached from their background, Lydia thought at first that they were free standing.

"Yes," Gaius answered. "You can see a mighty battle being waged between the gods and the giants of the earth. Of course, the gods are triumphant. The victory of the gods is supposed to represent Attalus. The defeated giants represent the Gauls who had the nerve to try to invade Pergamum."

Lydia could detect no note of derision or sarcasm in this statement of fact. A quick glance, however, detected a slight twist to the thin lips that might have been interpreted as a grin.

She circled the huge base, gazing at each figure, marveling that such detail could be extracted from cold stone. The battle depicted before her seemed to rage with terrible intensity. Clumsy giants looked up at the victorious gods in a frenzy of agony.

The heavy, muscular bodies appeared to rush at one another. The beating wings and wind-blown garments seemed to involve her in the action. Strong accents of light and dark added to the powerful impression.

Athena was clutching one of the giants by the hair, forcing him to the ground. Mother Earth gazed appealingly to Athena. Victory came carrying a crown. Writhing movements were manifest in the entire design, down to the last lock of hair.

The physical and emotional violence portrayed by the figures before her almost overwhelmed Lydia. She had the feeling the scene was going to explode and the battle spill over onto the steps. Her strength left her. She wanted to turn and run down the hill. *Why hadn't she waited until Menalcus could come with her?*

For a brief moment, the look on the face of one of the giants who was trying to defend himself

expressed a feeling she had known before. His outstretched arm, straining for help, brought back the
ache in her own arms as she had reached for help in
the terrible dream she had experienced on the eve of
her wedding. The feeling was so strong, she looked
at her arms, surprised to see them hanging by her
side instead of being stretched out in supplication.

It was several moments before Lydia could tear
her gaze away. Finally she turned to climb the monu-
mental flight of steps that rose between the duplicate
bases with their battle scenes.

The altar proper occupied the center of a rect-
angular court surrounded on three sides by an ionic
colonnade whose vaulted columns rose at least sixty
feet to support a richly decorated stucco ceiling.
Large wreaths of flowers and greenery adorned the
base of each column. Small bronze tables with con-
tainers of smoking incense placed at intervals along
the walls filled the court with a pungent scent.

Lydia watched as Gaius presented a waiting
priest with the generous offering Menalcus had given
to honor the great god on behalf of his household.
Lydia added an offering of her own, asking blessings
for herself and Myia.

She ascended a flight of steps leading to a colonnaded walkway around three sides of the wall. She
joined other visitors who peered over this balcony
to watch those who came to offer sacrifice.

The altar itself was taller than a man and was inlaid with figures of gods and goddesses depicted in pink, blue, and green marble. A high priest, dressed in a black hooded robe over a white toga, stood to one side. His assistants, in brown robes, stood ready to receive the animals to be sacrificed.

The largest pig Lydia had ever seen, along with a large, curly-horned ram, were to be the sacrifices today. The beasts were handsome specimens and perfectly groomed. The pig wore a garland of flowers around its neck. An attendant holding the slack ropes led the animals forward. They were not to be dragged or goaded but must appear to come of their own accord.

As the procession toward the altar began, the high priest stepped forward and poured a wine offering and an offering of incense into the fire. An expectant hush fell over the crowd as he raised his face and hands to the sky in the direction of Mount Olympus, home of Zeus. He paused dramatically until all noise ceased. Then he intoned a prayer in a loud, expressive voice.

"O ye deities who live on Olympus! Our fathers believed in you and so do we. Ye are gods and we are men. Ye are greater than we, and we have reason to fear. Let us be at peace with you. We offer our prayers to you. We also bring our gifts, our offerings, and our sacrifices. We bring these to please you. We know you are always victorious in your contests with mortals. It is useless for men to try to win over you.

"We beg you to look on us as friends. Protect us. Guide us in the courses we undertake. Keep evil from us and let all evil fall on our enemies. We worship you. We are your friends. You have been our god for a long time. Accept our offerings. Give us plenty. Make us strong. Keep our houses from burning. Protect our ships at sea."

At the conclusion of his prayer, the high priest lowered his arms and turned back to the waiting worshipers. Lydia had a fleeting suspicion that he would bow if applauded. He again poured a wine offering into the fire. Then he sprinkled the pig and ram with wine and coarsely ground, salted meal. While his colleagues gathered to hold the animals still, the high priest quickly, and with skilled precision, slit the throat of the pig and then of the ram.

Lydia wanted to looked away, but found her gaze glued to the sight.

The first gush of blood was caught in golden basins and poured on the fire; then the basins were refilled with more blood. The priest took the basins and sprinkled the blood on the hands and foreheads of those who brought the sacrificial offerings. The remaining blood was tossed into the fire while the priest, the worshipers, and some of the spectators—Lydia among them—raised their faces and palms to the sky and chanted together, "Accept our offerings; grant our requests; be our friend."

People turned to leave. Lydia felt nothing. There was no sense of worship, no feeling of satisfaction, and most of all, no peace. She walked down the steps into the court of the altar. Most of the worshipers had joined the families who brought the sacrificial animals and were carrying the pieces of slaughtered meat away to be prepared for the feast. Soon the court was empty except for Lydia and the high priest. Attendants came with large vats of scalding water to clean the area before the time for the next sacrifice.

She watched as the high priest washed his hands and prepared to leave. He stood for a moment, looking at the fire as if trying to find some omen in the flames still licking at the pieces of burning flesh. Then he turned to look toward the clouds hovering over the mountains to the west. Lydia noted the sag of his shoulders and the drained expression on his face as he left the court.

Did he believe in the gods to whom he prayed? Did he believe what he prayed? Or did he perform the rituals out of fear? Was he afraid not to believe, or was he afraid because of what he believed?

One thing was clear. She was no closer to finding what she was searching for than she had been back in Thyatira. Her heart was still empty except for her love for her father and Menalcus. Was that enough? She could not even put what she was seeking into words. Would she know when she found it?

The journey to Philippi would be resumed at daybreak. Lydia decided she would spend the afternoon resting in their room at the inn. It was too hot for much else. She stretched out on the lumpy bed and closed her eyes but sleep evaded her. Two blue-green flies kept buzzing from one corner of the room to the other. She tried to pretend a cool breeze was blowing, but all that rose before her mind's eye was the face of the high priest as she had last seen him. She finally fell into a half-sleep in which she struggled with giant figures in flowing robes. She was searching for something but their robes obstructed her view each time she was about to glimpse what was eluding her.

It was a relief when Myia entered to wake her. Myia's face was flushed as if she had been running.

"Where have you been?" Lydia asked her slave.

"Only for a walk, milady. Did you need me?"

"No. But why would you go for a walk? We walked all morning. Where did you go in this heat?"

"Please, milady. I'm fine. I didn't go far, and Gaius was with me."

Lydia sat up, wide awake. "Myia, stop stalling. Where have you been? I demand an answer!"

Myia confessed to Lydia that one of the slaves had carved a replica of a foot for her. "I thought if I could place the foot at the altar of Aescupulis…" Tears came to her eyes and she could not continue.

"Myia." Lydia held out her arms for her friend to come and be comforted. The two girls sat for some time without speaking. Lydia realized again how much being crippled bothered her little slave. "Myia, do you really believe that will restore your foot?"

"I don't know, milady. I just know I want to walk like everyone else. If there's the slightest chance… Don't you see? I have to believe!"

Lydia looked at this girl she had known as long as she could remember. Had she really known her at all? She had assumed Myia was happy to be her slave. How magnanimous she had felt having a shoe made for her! As if hiding a crippled foot made up for not being able to walk and run like other people.

Lydia sighed. She was not the only one who had unresolved fears and longings with no answers in sight.

CHAPTER 3

Troas

Lydia paid little attention as they rode through the gates into Troas. It had rained the entire day. She hunched her back against the slanting drizzle that had plagued them. She was soaked to the skin. The great hooded cloak had kept her dry for a while, but now it dragged against her thighs and shoulders, heavy and wet. She looked forward to dry clothes and some warm food.

Menalcus walked his big stallion past several places of business and finally reined him to the left and led the way to an inn that fronted on a sidestreet.

Even though Myia had ridden on the wagon that hauled their baggage and food, she was as wet as Lydia. Menalcus lifted her down from the wagon and signaled Gaius to see to their belongings while he ushered his little party inside.

Lydia and Myia stood shivering just inside the door to the common room while Menalcus made arrangements with the innkeeper. A huge fireplace almost filled one wall of the room. A long wooden table with benches down each side sat in the middle of the room. A few chairs were scattered here and there around the room. The rain streaked down the small panes that allowed the gray light of early evening to enter the room. The smell of roasting meat coming from the kitchen reinforced the gnawing of Lydia's stomach.

"I don't know which I want the most," Lydia whispered. "Dry clothes or something to eat. How about you?"

When Myia did not answer, Lydia turned and found her slave leaning against a table. Sweat stood out on her forehead and upper lip. She gazed up at Lydia with eyes that appeared to have difficulty focusing.

Lydia's cry alerted Menalcus. He half-carried Myia toward their room. Her cry also alerted the innkeeper who seemed a bit apprehensive about letting them have a room now. Sickness could spread quickly. His business would suffer if it became known that his establishment housed someone who might have something catching. He nervously rubbed his hands back across his bald head and started to follow the pair.

Menalcus kept walking toward their room, all the while reassuring the nervous innkeeper that Myia was simply overtired from their trip.

They entered a small room with a large bed and a couch on one side. A table held a metal basin and pitcher of water. A low stool at the foot of the bed completed the furnishings. The room was clean and had a window opening onto a garden. Lydia closed the door firmly behind them, almost hitting the agitated innkeeper in the face.

Menalcus placed Myia on the couch. While Lydia changed into dry clothing, he stripped Myia of her bulky traveling cloak and wet clothes. Myia's body shook uncontrollably and her teeth chattered. Even a dry tunic and blanket did nothing to stop her from shivering.

"She's burning with fever," Menalcus said. "I've seen this with my soldiers."

As mistress of her father's house, Lydia had learned to care for many illnesses and accidents in their household. Fever that came on with such swift intensity often proved fatal. She poured tepid water into the basin with trembling hands and bathed Myia's face. Then she pulled all the covers from the bed and draped them around the sick girl, tucking them tightly around her shoulders.

Menalcus stepped to the door and ordered a waiting slave to bring cold water. Then he returned to Lydia's side. "I'm going to go find a doctor. I'll be back as soon as I can."

Her heart began to pound as she remembered the patients in the hospital in Pergamum. She pushed the thought of death away. If she refused to let the idea enter her mind, maybe she could keep the reality away. This was not a stranger or an ordinary slave. This was Myia!

"Don't worry." He tried to sound reassuring, but his eyes revealed his worry. "Bathe her down and keep her covered as much as possible. She'll be on her feet in no time." Even as he said the words, she wondered if he believed them.

"Go," she said. "And please hurry!"

After Menalcus left, Lydia followed Menalcus's instructions to continue bathing Myia and keeping her covered. She began talking, as much to herself as to Myia. The sound of her voice kept the panic from engulfing her, but only barely. "O gods," she said aloud, "if you have any mercy, please don't let anything happen to Myia!"

The girl moaned and began turning from side to side, pushing the covers from her. Big drops of sweat stood out on her arms and face. Lydia mopped her forehead as best she could, praying desperately for Menalcus to return quickly.

Menalcus inquired of the innkeeper where he might locate a doctor. He did not want to alarm the innkeeper unnecessarily but the need for quick relief for Myia could not be ignored.

"I can't imagine what might have caused the young lad to faint." The innkeeper's eyes held a hint of anger. Apparently, he did not like the high-handed way Menalcus had taken charge of the situation and refused to answer his questions about Myia. "If, as you said in the beginning, your friend is merely tired, you would not want to disturb a doctor tonight."

"I would like to secure a potion to ward off any evil spirits that might be active," Menalcus countered. "You see, I am on business for Emperor Claudius and I must not delay my journey."

"A good night's rest is sometimes the best medicine." He looked at Menalcus with a bored expression. Clearly, he did not intend to give his guest any help.

"Very well," Menalcus stated with all the authority he could muster. "I'll go to the garrison. I know I will find a physician there. I think the commander of the fort will be interested in those who are helpful to his officers. I'll need a torchbearer at once."

The innkeeper shifted his weight from one foot to the other while smoothing his mustache between his thumb and forefinger. "Sir, a physician rushing in here at night would arouse much curiosity. It would make my guests very nervous."

Menalcus shrugged as if tired of this senseless haggling. "I wonder how nervous they will become if I suddenly yell, 'Plague!' "

The innkeeper's eyes darted from side to side to see if anyone was within hearing distance. "You wouldn't dare!" He tried to sound confident Menalcus could see perspiration forming on his brow.

"Perhaps I can be of some help."

Menalcus and the innkeeper turned to see who had spoken. Menalcus could scarcely believe his good fortune. Standing at his elbow was the distinguished doctor to whom he had delivered his last message while in Pergamum.

"Thank the gods," Menalcus stuttered as he recovered from his surprise. "I don't know why you are here, but by the gods, I am happy to see you. Could you come with me?" He urged the doctor down the corridor, explaining as they walked.

Lydia turned as her husband came through the doorway. She was so astonished at seeing the doctor with those compelling eyes that she could do little more than motion toward Myia.

For the second time she witnessed the calming influence of this man. Myia quieted, clutching the doctor's hand as if he were her link to sanity.

Luke gave a quick examination of the patient, then stepped to the door and gave the awaiting slave orders to fetch his bag of medicines from his room. The slave hurried off and soon returned with a bag of packets and vials.

The doctor mixed a powdered formula with water, then tenderly lifted Myia to a position where she could swallow the mixture.

Lydia sagged against Menalcus's strong arm. Together they watched Myia begin to relax. The low moans gradually ceased. In a few moments she fell into a restless sleep.

"She will be very weak for a few days," the doctor said, "but she seems to be a fighter. Unless something unexpected turns up, she should be ready to travel on a cart in three or four days." He gave further instructions for her care and gave Lydia a vial of the powder with instructions for administering it.

Unwilling to leave Myia's side, Lydia asked Menalcus to have the innkeeper send her meal to the room. He agreed and made arrangements to have dinner with the doctor.

The next day found Myia free of fever but very weak. Once Lydia was sure Myia was out of danger, she agreed to take a tour of the city with Menalcus.

They were pleasantly surprised when Luke decided to go with them. They were happy to learn, he was a frequent visitor to the city and proved to be an excellent guide.

"Troas is a colony of Rome. You would be hard pressed to find a more strategically located port. It is situated on the trade routes between Macedonia and the northwest branch of the Taurus Mountain range."

Lydia marveled at all the trading ships in the harbor. Menalcus pointed out a grain ship from Alexandria. It looked very cumbersome.

"That ship will carry about twelve hundred ton of cargo," Doctor Luke informed them, "and still have room for two hundred passengers. Not the greatest of accommodations, mind you, but it will get you to your destination."

"Will we ever see the day when ships will carry only passengers?" Lydia asked.

"I suppose it will come someday," Luke answered, "but I doubt it will be in our lifetime. The cost of operating one of those ships, plus the risk of the open seas, would make the price of a ticket out of the reach of most."

"But they look so awkward. Are they safe for travel?" Lydia's mind raced ahead to the trip they would soon be taking. More and more she liked the feel of solid earth beneath her feet.

"There are many mishaps and losses," Luke replied. "We have much to learn about traveling the open water."

"Don't worry, Lydia," Menalcus said. "We'll be sailing in a trireme, a ship of Rome's Imperial Navy."

He directed their attention to where a row of ships stood, their leather sails slack in the still air. "Each one has 170 rowers seated on three levels. Fourteen-foot oars propel the ship through the water when the square sails fail to catch the wind. The crew on each ship consists of thirty men, plus ten to eighteen soldiers. A metal-tipped ram protrudes from the front for the purpose of ramming a hole in an enemy vessel."

They were certainly not ships of beauty, Lydia thought. But their appearance did indicate the strength of Rome.

"Ordinarily passengers would not be allowed aboard these military ships," Menalcus continued. "But because I am a courier for the emperor, my party is an exception to the rule."

A short distance beyond the wharf they came to the city wall.

"Those walls are six leagues in circumference," Luke informed them. "See those high arches ahead? They support an aqueduct that carries fresh water from Mount Ida to the town."

Lydia shaded her eyes against the bright sun. She could make out high arches of huge stones leading back to mountains in the hazy distance.

"This aqueduct is at least twenty leagues long," Luke continued. "It drops an average of one foot for every two hundred feet in length. The channel that carries fresh water is covered with concrete. I guarantee these aqueducts will stand for hundreds of years."

Lydia grinned at the obvious note of pride in Luke's voice.

"That's a real engineering feat," Menalcus said. "Rome has made our world a wonderful place in which to live. All is not perfect, but as long as Caesar is honored and obeyed, life is not so bad."

They walked on past strolling musicians. A piper blew shrill notes while a fat man with castanets on his fingers swayed to the sound of the pipes and the incessant beat of a large, flat drum held in the hands of another fat man.

A closer look revealed the two men were twins. A silver band entwined in their hair revealed identical markings. The music rose and fell as their sandaled feet beat out the rhythm. At the end of the song, the piper pushed a basket forward on the pavement. Another song began, with the twins gyrating to the movement of the music.

Luke and Menalcus both flipped small coins into the basket. Then the threesome moved along, their steps leading down streets thronged with soldiers from the garrison, traders and travelers from distant lands, slaves carrying produce from market, and country folks heading toward stalls in the agora with their wares. Shops along the way offered rugs from Carthage, cheeses and pork from Sicily, ivory from Ethiopia, glass from Egypt, perfumes from Arabia, and city-manufactured pottery and jewelry.

The trio found their way back to the inn, where they enjoyed a lunch of leeks, olives, cheese, and fish, accompanied with a warm wine.

After their meal, Lydia and Menalcus returned to their room, where they found Myia sleeping. When she stirred, he helped her to sit up and lean against his shoulder while Lydia fed her broth ordered from the kitchen.

Luke stopped by to check on his patient. He seemed pleased with her progress.

Myia managed a weak smile for him. The simple task of eating had exhausted her.

"You must be very careful for a few weeks," he instructed Lydia. "See that she gets plenty of rest and fresh fruit. This fever will return again and again unless you guard against it diligently."

"What do you think causes so much fever among our people?" Menalcus asked.

"I wish I knew." Luke replied. "Perhaps the change in climate from the high mountains to the muggy, low swampland of the coast. Perhaps the bugs, rats, and flies that hang about our cities. Maybe the mosquitoes and gnats that swarm up out of the lowlands. Our medical knowledge is growing every day. Conceivably we will have better answers in the future."

"In the meantime, " Lydia suggested, "why don't you two gentlemen go to the baths to wait out the heat of the day? Myia is not the only one who needs some rest."

"I guess we know when to leave." Menalcus laughed. The two men left, carrying clean garments over their arms.

The Roman baths, center of the social life of the city, ranked second only to their temples in grandeur. Those in the larger cities were as commodious as were the marble palaces of Caesar's and those of other officials. Menalcus had seldom seen one to equal this *thermae* of Troas.

When Luke and Menalcus approached the *thermae*, a *balneator* received the piece of money each bather must pay. Luke nodded to several acquaintances as they entered the garden. Parties of men holding philosophical discussions lounged in shaded alcoves. Luke was invited to join more than one of these discussions, but declined with a wave of his hand. Menalcus was pleased that Luke, obviously well known and respected, preferred to spend the afternoon with him.

They entered the building itself, which was supported by tall ionic columns covered with detailed drawings. A beautiful mural patterned in varicolored mosaics encircled the entire building. Scenes of gods and goddesses at play were depicted in rich blue, gold, and green bits of tile. Carved foliage entwined with fruit and flowers wound around the ceiling and decorated the capitals of each column.

The men entered the large central *tepidairum*, a warm lounge filled with couches upon which they could relax. A slave helped divest both men of their robes. The moment Luke and Menalcus had reclined on couches, other slaves stepped forward to massage their bodies with warm oils. Menalcus relaxed to the point of falling asleep.

He opened his eyes to find Luke had preceded him into the *caledarium*, a room filled with steam. Men reclined in various positions on marble seats in tiers of four and six rows. The higher the row, the hotter the temperature. Luke sat on the second row, a towel draped around his head. Menalcus climbed to a vacant seat behind him.

An obese man on Luke's left was having a discourse with a tall man with a mop of black ringlets and a long beard, equally as curly. He answered to the name of Silvanus. Something about his manner caught Menalcus's attention. Perhaps he had seen him before.

Sweat began to pour down Menalcus's body. He mopped his face from time to time to keep the water out of his eyes and the corners of his mouth.. Even so he could taste the salt of his own sweat. It was easy to understand why this was called the hot room.

The fat man began questioning Silvanus about a remote area of the empire called Palestine; in particular, about the political situation there.

"Palestine has always been a hotbed of conniving and unrest," the stranger said. "The Jews believe they are a chosen people, called by their God to receive special favors. I guess they think Rome should be slaves to them instead of being their rulers."

"Claudius is a good ruler," answered Silvanus. "He is trying to give our people all the freedom he can, but there are always those willing to use religion as an excuse to make trouble. As for our God, He has called all of us to be His people by giving his son to die for us."

Luke roused and addressed Silvanus. "You said, 'our God.' Are you a Jew?"

"I am of Jewish parentage," he answered. "Born in Caesarea. I have lived in Jerusalem for much of my life. Recently I have been traveling throughout the cities of Galatia and Lydia."

"Are you a merchant?" Luke inquired.

"No." Silvanus turned his large, dark eyes fully upon Luke. "I am a traveling companion of a great man, Paul of Tarsus. He has been called to be an apostle of our Lord Jesus Christ and to bring his message to all people who will hear him."

"I have heard of this Paul. I believe the Jews call him Saul. He is a great rabbi among his people, is he not?"

As the conversation between Luke and Silvanus continued, Menalcus could not help but notice how this stranger held Luke's undivided attention. He himself had not heard anything intriguing. Apparently the fat man agreed, because he left the room without a backward glance. What could be so important about this Paul, or Saul, or whoever he was? And who was this Jesus Christ? Another god? Silvanus had better not let too many people hear him call anyone Lord except Claudius Caesar.

Actually, Menalcus was a little piqued that Luke was spending so much time with this Silvanus. He found the doctor to be a well-traveled, stimulating conversationalist and looked forward to more of his company.

Menalcus became so hot he couldn't stand it. He had to get some relief. He excused himself and entered the next room, where the air was still warm but not steaming. He eased himself into a hot tub, using the marble ledge around the edge of the tub, and immersed himself to the shoulders, then fitted his head back into a scooped-out curve and relaxed. A little flicker of annoyance crossed his mind as he noted Luke hardly marked his going.

He allowed his gaze to take in the beautiful surroundings. Artistically decorated arches led into other areas of the *thermae*, eventually leading to gardens stretching in all directions. How refreshing the green shrubs and flowering plants were to his senses.

After what seemed a long time, Luke had still not appeared. Menalcus climbed from the tub and beckoned for a towel to drape around his loins. As he strode past the entrance to the *caledarium*, he saw Luke and Sylvanus moving past the open peristyles to the *frigidarium*.

The cooling room had a line of cold showers that sent the blood rushing to the surface of the skin. The more hardy bathers immersed themselves in large vats of ice-cold water, encouraged by the belief that this procedure would increase virility.

Menalcus knew he was being childish, but he wished Silvanus would leave. He was eager to pursue his friendship with Luke. He walked through the showers and would have passed by the two men without speaking. But as he came abreast of them, Luke put out his hand and drew Menalcus to his side.

"My friend, where did you go? Silvanus has been telling me some of the most amazing things I have ever heard. Tell me, in your travels as a courier, have you ever heard of Jesus of Nazareth? He was crucified by the authorities when Pilate was prefect of Judea. That must have been about thirteen or fourteen years ago."

"I may have heard the name." A frown wrinkled Menalcus's brow. "But out of the thousands of criminals who are crucified, what makes this one so special?"

"Silvanus believes he is the son of God."

"Which god?" asked Menalcus. "Zeus? Mars? Baachus?"

"No, no," Silvanus interjected. "The son of the one true God, the living God of Israel, the God who created the universe!"

Menalcus looked around to see who might be hearing this strange conversation. He would not want anyone to think he believed any of it.

"Must not have been much of a god if he allowed his son to be crucified like a common thief. Why all the excitement anyway? Surely there are enough gods to go around. I'm not so certain any of them care about us mortals." Menalcus muttered this last part half under his breath. It was more a reflection of his own thoughts than something he intended to say aloud.

Silvanus announced that he had to leave. Ashamed of his pettiness, Menalcus tried not to show his relief. Luke made arrangements to meet Silvanus the next day. "I must hear more of this Jesus and of Paul of Tarsus," he said.

After moving to a long pool that was open to the skies, Luke flicked Menalcus on the backside with his towel. "Last one in is an old woman!"

Both men dove headfirst into the water and with swift strokes swam to the far end of the pool. Menalcus flipped over on his back and floated while he regained his breath. Luke continued swimming until he reached the spot where they had entered the pool. Someone threw a ball, and a rough-and-tumble game of water ball ensued.

Laughing and exhausted, the two men climbed from the pool. A slave immediately approached and toweled them dry. They donned fresh togas, then enjoyed a glass of wine and some cheese served on platters of beaten silver.

Strolling arm in arm around the promenade, they paused on the west side to view the enormous library with hundreds of scrolls lining the walls. Many men sat at tables reading or taking notes. Students from the nearby school of law were studying the ancient laws and interpretations of bygone generations as well as the present laws of the Roman Empire.

Luke led the way toward the open peristyles. Lovely ionic columns stood ten feet in the air, each topped with the head of one of the gods or goddesses. At the end of the peristyles stood a column of gleaming marble holding the bust of the emperor. Every Roman citizen who passed this way was required to salute. Not many even broke stride as they smote their breast with a clenched fist and said, "Hail Caesar!" It scarcely interrupted what they were saying.

Their walk continued past a series of lecture rooms where philosophers and teachers of Greek, mathematics, and science held classes. When they arrived once more at the entrance, Luke excused himself on a matter of business.

Menalcus wandered through the garden to the doorway of the stadium, where he watched gymnasts try their various forms and runners raced around an indoor track. Wrestlers grunted and strained as they tried to beat one another. Menalcus recognized one or two men from the garrison who were participating. Others were wagering their month's pay on their favorite competitors.

A small gate led to the busiest part of the *thermae*, the part that made the beauty and comfort of the rest of the building possible. Huge stone reservoirs held many ephahs of water. Several slaves were charged with the task of keeping the water in these tanks at a certain level. Heated water traveled in underground pipes the length and breadth of the building. This water served the steam rooms and the hot tubs, and kept the floors of the building at an even temperature all year round.

Slaves by the score were working as fast as they could, sweating and heaving fuel into the gaping maw of several furnaces. Other slaves bent over under the loads of wood they carried to keep this process going.

Poor devils, Menalcus mused. *Our luxury comes at a high price. Next to serving at the oars or the mines, stoking the furnaces of public buildings must be the worst fate for a slave.*

He was glad to return to the inn, eager as he was to see Lydia. She had known little rest since Myia became ill. Perhaps she had enjoyed a long nap while he was gone.

Myia was not yet able to join them for her meals. So Lydia ordered a special platter of fresh fruit and wine and a piece of broiled fish sent to her before joining Menalcus and Luke for a festive dinner.

When a few of Menalcus's friends from the garrison entered the inn, they quickly accepted his invitation to join their party.

Pleading fatigue, Lydia excused herself. Luke bid her good night, saying he hoped they might have another pleasant day tomorrow.

But such was not to be. During the early morning hours, a messenger arrived, announcing that Menalcus was to come to the garrison at once. There he was told to prepare to travel immediately. The officers of the triremes had received orders to sail at first tide. They must be aboard as quickly as possible.

If the wind held, they would be at Samothrace by noon the next day, and hopefully in Neapolis in another two days.

CHAPTER 4

Samothrace

Lydia's eyes sparkled with delight as she watched the prow of the ship cut through the cold waters. The sea was fairly smooth, and the wind carried them along under a sky of intense blue that held only a few clouds. She turned her head in all directions, but as far as she could see, there was no living thing. Their ship was like a tiny cup floating on a vast plate of blue. It had seemed so large when it was docked in the harbor, but was now dwarfed by the immensity of the sky and sea surrounding them.

She loved the feel of the wind and the sun on her face and arms. Although she would have liked to stay on deck the rest of the day, Myia still needed her assistance.

As soon as she entered the cabin, a low moan claimed her attention.

"I'm so sick," Myia whispered.

No sooner had the words left Myia's lips than she began to heave and retch. Lydia held the miserable girl's head and tried to keep from throwing up herself. As fast as one of the slaves emptied the basin, Myia needed it again. Her face was pasty, her lips blue, her eyes sunk back in her head.

Lydia bathed her friend's forehead and smoothed the hair back from her temples. She stayed by her side until Myia finally dropped off into a fitful sleep.

At a touch on her arm Lydia turned to see Menalcus motioning her to join him.

"Poor Myia," Lydia said, following Menalcus out of the room. "She is so sick. I'm glad we will only be on board a short while. I don't think she could survive a long voyage, especially with still being so weak from the fever."

"We will be in Samothrace soon," he assured her. "We will anchor there for two nights. Perhaps some time on dry land will help her feel better. But come, I want to show you something."

Menalcus led her to the side of the ship and pointed down to the water. Lydia was amazed to see the water turning from the deep green of the open sea to a dirty gray. As the ship progressed, the water became almost black. She looked across the rail and saw they had come within sight of the coastline.

" What makes the water change color?"

"Behind those mountains is a great inland sea that has no tides. Large rivers flow into that sea from both sides, carrying the rich black soil from the mountains and valleys. The water from that sea comes between those two points of land."

Lydia looked in the direction Menalcus pointed and saw a break in the coastline. As she peered more intently, she saw water swirling out of the pass with unbelievable force.

"We're lucky not to be traveling any later in the year," Menalcus said. "In the wintertime, the great northern winds rush through that pass. The water drains into the sea with such force that huge waves make sailing very hazardous. Most ships are not built to withstand the gales experienced here."

Lydia shivered as she tried to imagine what it would be like to be on such a large expanse of water with heavy seas and gale-force winds. She felt all the more grateful for the day's sunshine.

Near dusk, the helmsman shouted that they were approaching the island of Samothrace.

"Menalcus, can we go ashore tonight?" Lydia asked. "I think it would give Myia a chance to gain a little strength."

"I'll ask the captain if someone can row us ashore. There is an inn there. Hopefully it is not filled."

After receiving the captain's assistance, Menalcus helped Lydia and Myia into a small boat, and in short order they were on dry land. They hurried to the inn and soon had the little slave girl tucked into bed, grateful that it did not move.

The next morning the two of them walked through the town, past a long stoa with small shops leading to a cross street, on which was located the shrine of the Cabiri, twin gods of Phoenician origin. Two temples, one on each side of a wide avenue of white crushed stones, marked the entrance to the Sanctuary of the Great Gods.

Eight feet tall, of white Parian marble, Nike was portrayed as if descending to rest her foot on the dark marble prow of a ship. The white marble seen against the blue sky was reflected in a pool of water. Marble slabs with a rippled exterior just under the surface of the water gave a sparkling and shimmering effect, creating the impression of moving water. Mammoth boulders stood in a second pool edged by a deep gorge separating the statue from the ground where Menalcus and Lydia stood.

The immense wingspread of the statue gave the impression the Niki was peering out to sea, waiting to set foot on the deck of a ship coming into the harbor. An impression of a strong wind molded a thin, belted garment against her figure, shaping every fold of the delicately carved drapery. Her right leg pushed forward against the wind-blown skirt gathered around and between her legs, giving the illusion of movement.

Lydia felt tears sting her eyes. The statue was so beautiful! To think that one block of marble could be made to look like folded, pleated cloth over living flesh was beyond belief. She stared at the figure with such concentration that it seemed to actually breathe. She would like to know an artist of such great talent. Surely this was a gift from the gods.

Menalcus asked Lydia if she would like to consult an oracle about her future. She did not put much stock in such things, but she saw that Menalcus was serious. He explained that an oracle of highest reputation lived in a cave on Samothrace. Pilgrims from all over the empire came to learn what the gods had in store for them

Though she was skeptical of anyone who tried to foretell the future, curiosity got the best of her. She agreed to go if Menalcus would go with her.

They followed a well-paved road leading to a cave in a bare granite mountain that ran the length of the island and towered almost a half league into the air. Other visitors were on their way to listen to the oracle as well.

They entered a dimly lit cave and waited for their eyes to adjust from the bright sunlight. Menalcus found a place for them to sit in one of the niches that had been carved along the frescoed walls of the cave. Lydia sat close to him as she looked around the large room.

She noticed a raised seat near a crack in the cave wall where gasses escaped at intervals. The chair was elaborately carved, the legs ending in a lion's head. The entire chair was gilded in gold.

Lydia saw a young girl, not even as old as herself, perched on the elegant seat. For some reason, she had expected to see an old woman, stooped with age. The only thing about this girl that looked old was the mournful look in her eyes. Her shoulders sagged as if the messages she must tell were dragging her down with their fateful meanings.

A priest stood directly behind the oracle's chair. His head was covered and only part of his face was exposed.

Attendants and inquirers stood or sat near the oracle. Some buried their heads in their arms. Others had their robes pulled completely over their heads.

For one brief moment the oracle's eyes met Lydia's. Despite herself, Lydia drew back, a feeling of unease causing her to take several deep breaths before she could compose herself. She was glad Menalcus was seated next to her.

What was behind the strange look directed at her? Was she reacting to her own imagination, or was there something for her to discover?

Suddenly, the melodious and mysterious whisper of a harp came from some unseen portion of the cave. The oracle received a golden goblet of spiced wine. She lifted it in both hands toward the roof of the cave—first to the left and then to the right—before drinking the entire contents.

The strumming of the harp became a little louder, and Lydia heard the added beat of a tambourine. The oracle covered her face with her long hair. She brought a cloak up around her shoulders and draped it loosely around her head. An attendant lit small bowls of incense in each corner of the cave.

The oracle began to bob her head from side to side in time to the music, which was becoming louder and faster. A hissing sound warned of escaping gas, which began to fill the cave. Without warning a geyser of steam rose from a small opening to one side of the room. The smell of sulfuric gasses became almost overpowering.

The oracle swayed faster and faster. The music sounded louder and wilder.

Suddenly the oracle sprang to her feet and threw the cloak from her, causing Lydia to jump. She brushed the hair away from her face, waved her arms over her head, and then intertwined them before she began to speak.

Low guttural sounds came from deep within her throat. Head thrown back and arms extended, she spoke several sentences in rapid succession. The priest leaned forward so as not to miss a word.

The oracle dropped her arms and her body jerked uncontrollably. As quickly as it began, the quivering stopped. She slumped back into her chair, limp and exhausted.

The gas stopped escaping from the fissure in the rock. The steam evaporated. The music ceased. In the silence that followed the priest stepped forward and delivered the message uttered by the oracle in a flat monotone.

"There will be much happiness and a great tragedy. One unknown to you will bring a life-changing message. Your heart will cry out, full of questions. Look deep into your dreams. The gods will answer your questions with much power and you will doubt no more."

Lydia thought about the message the priest had delivered. In one sense it was general enough to fit anyone's life. Still, she wondered if the oracle knew about her dreams and the feelings of terror they carried. Would the gods be merciful and answer her search for peace? She felt as if a cold hand were squeezing her heart.

The oracle had not moved while the priest was speaking. Her face was drained in color. Her eyes remained closed.

One by one the seekers filed out of the cave into the open air, past a stony-faced priest who stood beside an intricately carved box at the entrance. Each one who passed in or out of the cave was expected to place a coin in the treasury. If a supplicant wanted a further word with the priest, an extra coin gained admittance into a simple marble temple standing at the right of the entrance to the cave.

Before leaving the cave, Lydia glanced back at the oracle and saw her being lifted by two attendants and carried out of the room.

The sun had never looked so good or the fresh air smelled so sweet. Lydia breathed deeply in an effort to lighten the tense feeling in her chest. When she grasped Menalcus's arm, he covered her hand with his own and gave her a tiny smile.

Menalcus was glad to be out of the cave. He had decided to visit the oracle more from curiosity than from any desire to know his future. His opinion of soothsayers and oracles was about the same as his thoughts on religion. He would trust his own strength and his own intelligence to stay ahead of the game. He needed no crutch to help him.

He believed every person was responsible for his own place in life. It was up to each one to be on the alert, take every advantage, seek out opportunities to make life pleasant and happy. It was more important to please your commanding officer, and thus the emperor, than to worry about pacifying unseen gods.

The emperor and his officers had power over life and death. The gods, if there were such beings, were too busy with their own affairs to be concerned with men.

CHAPTER 5

Neapolis

The ship bustled with activity as they sailed into the lovely bay of Neapolis, port city of the trade routes. This seaport was a vital link between landlocked Europe and the commerce of Asia.

Lydia had strained her eyes for the first sight of the city. She refused to leave the ship's rail, even for breakfast. Soon she began to see the red-tiled roofs of the villas half hidden among the vineyards on the slopes. Giant granaries, which were the lifeblood of the empire, stood on the left of the pier.

Myia, still pale but excited at the prospect of soon being on land, joined Lydia. They both returned the waves of the men aboard passing fishing boats heading out in their quest for tuna, anchovies, and sardines.

"Why don't they catch all these fish we can see right below us in the water?"

Menalcus explained that these commercial fishermen ignored the schools of mullet they could see in the clear water, leaving them for the youths casting their nets further down the beach.

Lydia's gaze returned to the sailing vessels unloading their cargo. The deep waters of the bay permitted large ships to unload their wares directly onto the pier. Squat granite posts, spaced close to the edge of the water, lined the marble-paved piers that jutted out into the Aegean Sea. Rowboats carrying patrons on pleasure excursions moved along the stone quays. Far down the beach Lydia could barely discern slaves panning for salt from the sea.

The captain of their trireme nosed their vessel in between two merchant ships. Once his duties were done and the ship safely docked, he stopped a few moments to explain about the two ships on either side—one bringing gems, spices, and other rarities from Ceylon, India, the Nile, and Alexandria, and the other from Persia, bearing rugs and silks from China. Porters were loading most of these goods onto donkeys and forming caravans to proceed overland to Thessalonica and on to Rome.

Menalcus explained to Lydia, "This is the same route your father's cloth, and that of the silk merchants who traveled with us to Troas, will take as soon as the ship carrying their merchandise arrives."

When it was their turn to disembark, Lydia practically ran down the gangplank, eager to take in a new world of sights and sounds. Bales and bundles were strewn about, waiting for porters and slaves with carts. Menalcus gave orders for Gaius to take care of Myia and then caught up with his wife. He followed her pointing finger and did his best to explain what she was seeing and at the same time help her keep her footing in the hurrying throng.

A young girl held crusted loaves of bread for sale. Behind her, two older women shoved more of the wheel-shaped loaves into an outdoor oven. Two youths crossed the broad street and studied the baked loaves lying on a sun-bleached cloth spread on the sand. A sailor on his way aboard ship broke open a loaf, then wolfed down the steaming white bread as he walked.

Menalcus guided Lydia past racks of octopuses stretched to dry in the sun. Although people were buying this favorite food around the Aegean, Lydia thought they resembled inverted monsters, awaiting their prey.

They walked past people eating their mid-day meal on the breakwater while watching a juggler perform his act in exchange for coins. Nearby, two fishermen mended their nets while discussing their catch for the day.

Menalcus placed his hand under Lydia's elbow and guided her away from the waterfront. They passed the public baths, a theater, and two temples. Brick apartment houses many stories high were built against the hillside.

They looked into shops on the street, where overhanging balconies shaded customers from the hot sun and at the same time provided a place for the owners, who lived on the second floor, to enjoy the cool sea breeze.

A broad public way led to the bazaar, a plastered concrete vault covering a complete line of shops. Daylight from overhead windows streamed into the cool, dark niches where coppersmiths, metal-workers, and sellers of perfumes, jewelry, and other luxuries displayed their wares. The air was fragrant with the smell of lavender and thyme. Menalcus purchased a bunch of lavender for Lydia to carry.

Near the entrance, eggs, cheeses, oranges, figs, melons, grapes, and olives were displayed in rounded piles, tempting their appetites. They purchased some grapes and figs to eat as they walked to the open end of the long edifice.

Every street boasted an inn of some kind. Menalcus stopped in front of a modest-looking place called The Inn of Three Maidens. He made arrangements for rooms before leaving to show Gaius where to bring Myia, after which he said he must make a brief stop at the garrison, promising Lydia he would be back before supper.

After they had eaten their fill, Menalcus and Lydia climbed to the roof of the inn. From this vantage point they could see the outline of the trireme at the dock. The town was spread below them like a stage. An evening breeze rustled the palm leaves, filling the air with the smell of the sea. Up here on the roof, the odors of the street and the animals were not so overpowering.

Breakers rolled in lazy sequence to the moonlit beach. The rhythmic sound of the surf whispered gently in their ears. Stars sparkled like huge diamonds in the night sky. Everything was still and peaceful except for a loud laugh now and then punctuating the noise from the street. Distant singing from some celebration was a muted finale to a busy day.

Menalcus put his arm around Lydia's soft waist. She leaned against his chest, the hardness of his muscles a reminder of his manhood as well as a reassurance of safety and protection. He caressed her cheek with his lips.

Lydia turned to him, and he kissed her long and fully on the lips.

She felt as if fire were growing in her legs, up into her loins and on into her breasts. She pressed against Menalcus but could not get close enough.

She tried to melt right into his body, not wanting this embrace to ever end.

Menalcus was holding her so tightly she could scarcely breathe. But not for all the gold in the world would she have him loosen his grip. He picked her up and carried her to a pile of rushes lying in one corner of the roof.

Lydia turned on her side and drew the linen sheet over her shoulders. The damp air coming through the open window penetrated the light cover. From the drowsy depth of half sleep, she realized she was cold, but was reluctant to move. The persistent cold refused to let her sink back into a sound sleep. If she could just lie still...

Through closed lids, she became aware of daylight entering the room. She turned, searching for the warmth of her husband's body, but the bed was empty.

One more minute, she told herself, now wide awake, *then I'll get up.*

She wondered what her father was doing this morning. Did he miss her? One thing was for sure, he would not be cold. The climate here by the sea was very different from the arid heat of Thyatira. Heat would come to Neapolis later in the morning.

A wan but cheerful Myia appeared to help her get dressed. Lydia found she was ambivalent about going to Philippi today. Maybe it would be best if Menalcus went ahead and she stayed here until both she and Myia were fully rested. On the other hand she could hardly wait to get to her new home.

Menalcus had already eaten by the time Lydia appeared for breakfast. There was no time for her to discuss her feelings. The dreamy mood that had accompanied her while she was dressing quickly gave way to the task at hand.

By the eighth hour they were on the road for the ten-league journey to Philippi.

CHAPTER 6

Philippi

Menalcus and his party joined the other travelers who rode their horses out on the Apian Way in the light of early morning. Myia was back in the wagon but Menalcus and Lydia were glad to be in the saddle again. Lydia had persuaded Menalcus to allow her to finish the journey in her boy's disguise. Ten leagues was a long ride. She could not see any point in riding sidesaddle in a hot dress or in a litter when she could ride her horse in comfort.

The mist that had settled over the seacoast during the night was rapidly disappearing under the blazing sun. It would surely be scorching by midday.

Lydia shifted in her saddle to take a last look across the sea toward her homeland. Once she lost sight of that wide expanse of water, she felt the last ties with her home would be gone. Tears threatened to fall in spite of her determination to adjust to the new life ahead.

Menalcus was laughing and joking with some of the Roman troop accompanying them. Myia was being carried on a litter by four runners. Lydia was glad to have these few moments to herself.

Menalcus dropped back to ride beside her. "Would you believe this very road connects the whole Roman Empire? It took years to have all these huge squares of stone cut and laid.

"Where does the road go from here?" Lydia wanted to learn all she could about this new country she was entering.

As Menalcus told of the cities and territories tied by this road, a note of immense pride in his country crept into his voice.

Lydia paid close attention as he shared his experiences. She was beginning to realize she really knew very little of this man she had married. She knew even less about his work.

"Menalcus, will you be traveling to those places again?" At his nod she then asked, "And how long will you be gone?"

"I'll go whenever and wherever my orders take me" was the somewhat vague and discomforting reply.

Lydia tried to quell the little alarm bells that sounded in her head. She had known Menalcus would be traveling some, but she did not relish living in a foreign country where she did not even know the household slaves. What would she do if he was away for long periods of time?

The journey here had been a grand adventure. A slight blush stained her cheeks as she recalled the times of lovemaking and laughter. Would that continue? Did those times mean as much to Menalcus as they did to her? He had been so many places and done so many things. Surely she was not the only girl he had known.

But I am the one he married, she consoled herself.

It was a gorgeous day. The distant mountains loomed gray-blue, fading to a deep red as they drew nearer. Oak, maple, and pine on the mountainsides gave way to cedar and scrub pine where the valley began. Menalcus told of the wild animals that roamed there: bears, wolves, boars, lynx, and wildcats, not to mention jackals, foxes, and wild goats.

The sun climbed higher. Clouds vanished, leaving only blue sky to magnify the heat waves dancing in the clear mountain air.

A halt was called for the noon meal. Lydia was hungry and glad for a chance to walk about and stretch her legs. By the time the journey resumed, the fierce heat had abated somewhat. She looked forward to reaching home.

In the middle of the afternoon, the little group topped a small incline, and Lydia saw Philippi spread out before them. She caught her breath. She had not expected the city to be so large, or so beautiful. She had thought Pergamum a great city, but that place paled in comparison with this city that was to be her home. Sun reflecting from the white marble buildings hurt her eyes.

The city was laid out after the Roman way, with the streets in an orderly grid pattern. But the buildings reflected the influence of the Greeks who lived there.

The horses moved ahead. They rode through sizable orchards of citrus trees, pomegranates, and apricots. Fig trees grew everywhere. Vineyards of small grapes and currants stretched before them. Closer to the city walls, peasant farmers tended long neat rows of vegetables in market gardens.

To the right, near the outskirts of the city, was a huge amphitheater, capable of holding up to twenty thousand people. On the left, far outside the city gates where the smell would not be so overbearing, were the wool-processing plants and fuller mills, tanneries, and poultry houses. Menalcus pointed out a pig farm in the far distance.

A swiftly moving river flowed past the walls of the city. Green lacy branches of willow trees trailed the ends of tender fronds in the cold water as they leaned out from the river banks.

The city gate opened onto a wide, stone-paved street. At each side of the gate was a statue of a battle hero.

They rode through a triumphal arch inscribed with the feats of Philip, son of Alexander the Great. The main street led straight through town to a mighty temple dedicated to the goddess Athena, patroness of the city. Other temples to Isis and lesser deities were located throughout Philippi.

Lydia only caught a glimpse of the forum, where a large public building housed the many functions of city life. Tall Corinthian columns supported the two-story colonnade that extended around the square. She was surprised to see two or three hotels that could house as many as fifty guests. One had a garden for dining out of doors.

They trotted their horses past the Palestra, an exercise yard where youths were training to compete in races, wrestling, and many kinds of sports. Their naked bodies glistened with sweat. Unlike Lydia, they did not seem to mind the hot sun that browned their skin.

Freshly killed chickens hung from the outer eave of the roof of a poultry shop located next to a partially covered food market. Chickens, ducks, and geese, waiting to have their heads lopped off and their feathers plucked, lay in wire coops on the ground. They lay very still in the hot air, mouths agape, only occasionally hissing or quacking out their discomfort.

Thermopoluims were located on every block. Their L-shaped masonry counters displayed food and wine for the passersby. Large wine amphora were recessed in holes in the counter to keep them from being overturned. Some of the bars had kitchens and served heated wine and hot stew. Others had back rooms where one could sit and talk. Lydia was tempted to ask Menalcus to stop but knew he was too close to home to take the time.

Brothels were prominent on every street corner, some two stories high. Signs depicting what went on inside were chiseled in stone above the doorways. Lydia remembered what her father had said about "pleasures elsewhere." Perhaps this is what he meant. She urged her horse a bit faster.

Menalcus guided their horses to the left at the next cross street. They turned down a narrow alley beside a fine villa. Menalcus dismounted and rapped at a wide austere door. A porter looked out of a small sliding aperture built within the door. Immediately the door swung open to admit the weary travelers.

Menalcus lifted Lydia from the saddle. "Welcome home!"

He took her hand and led her through a garden filled with rows of vegetables, some of which Lydia did not recognize. Along the back wall of the

villa were several apartments where the slaves were
housed. A low wall divided this area from a large
open-air court with a central fountain and many
bright flowers and shade trees. Every walkway was
bordered with pots of blooming plants.

The sounds of their arrival must have preceded
them into the house. Household slaves lined up to
be greeted by their new mistress. The slaves looked
from her to Menalcus and then back again.

Lydia realized they were looking at her stained
and smelly tunic. No wonder they did not know how
to act. She was sure they were wondering what kind
of wife their master had brought home.

One slave brought a copper basin and knelt
to wash her feet. When he toweled them dry, he
hesitantly brought out a pair of ornate soft-leather
sandals they had assumed would be appropriate for
their new mistress. These dainty shoes looked so
incongruous with her dusty boy's outfit, the poor fellow seemed puzzled as to whether proceed or not.

Lydia tried to look dignified but bit her lip to
stifle a giggle. She did not want to add to this slave's
embarrassment.

Maybe she only imagined it, but it seemed as
if the other slaves raised their noses just a wee bit,
certainly not enough to be noticed by their master.
She thought one of them actually sniffed.

Menalcus rescued the moment by introducing
the slaves to her, with a short description of their

assigned posts. When the slaves returned to their duties, Lydia knew she would be roundly discussed as soon as they were out of hearing.

One look at Myia's pinched little face and Lydia knew she, too, was scared. She noted how tightly Myia held onto her crutch. She tried to smile a reassurance she was not sure she possessed.

May the gods help any of these strangers who even looks like he might make fun of her, she thought.

Lydia could hardly wait to be shown to her room. Menalcus led her up an open stairway to a second-floor gallery. The master bedroom and personal servants' rooms opened from this gallery. He informed Lydia it was the habit of most married men to sleep on the first floor and visit the rooms of their wives as desired. Menalcus said nothing of *his* plans. He merely showed Lydia the other rooms for guests, or perhaps children in future years.

Lydia was delighted with the small bath/dressing room that opened off a large, airy bedroom. Menalcus demonstrated the shower by pulling a chain. A large metal tub stood in one corner, in case she preferred a good soak. Waste water and sewage were carried through large pipes to an underground system beneath the city and on to a disposal point.

After a quick kiss, he excused himself to go downstairs to another such room in the men's quarters

Myia poured perfumed oils in the steaming tub. The fragrant odors, plus Myia's stern injunction to get undressed, found Lydia hurriedly stepping out of her much-worn tunic. She laid it aside reluctantly. Once she stepped into that tub, she would no longer be the carefree tomboy, traveling companion to Menalcus. She would emerge a full-fledged matron of a Roman household, albeit in a Greek city.

While she soaked, Myia followed Gaius to the servant's quarters, where she could get a quick shower and a fresh uniform. By the time he brought her back, Lydia had almost fallen asleep.

Myia gingerly picked up the smelly old tunic between her thumb and forefinger and stepped to the door, where she instructed a slave to remove it immediately.

Lydia allowed Myia to scrub her with a large sponge and towel her dry. She relaxed while sweet oil was rubbed into her skin. The two girls discussed their life in this new place.

"No more going about in the streets when you get the urge for an outing," Myia began. "A proper matron remains indoors at all times. There are slaves to do the errands. If you must go outside, you will need to be in the company of at least two slaves, preferably in a litter carried by slaves."

Lydia sighed. "No more eating with Menalcus and a common slave at the same table."

Myia giggled. "A proper matron takes her meals in the women's dining room or in her own apartment."

Lydia tried to look dignified. "The only exception being if her husband deigns to invite his wife for a special occasion. In that event, she will only remain at table until the main course is completed and will then find a reason to excuse herself and retire to her room."

Myia picked up the instructions she had learned by rote from the slave who had instructed them while back in Thyatira. "A proper matron will not be on familiar terms with her slaves."

What had begun as a tongue-in-cheek exchange of the social mores of the time became more serious as the reality of their situation sank in. Their smiles disappeared. By the time Lydia was dressed in a simple peplos, with matching headband, silence had fallen between them.

Lydia descended the stairs and found Menalcus ready to show her the rest of the house. He began at the street door as if they were guests. The porter's room was on his right. A wide reception room allowed for the arrival of several guests at one time.

When they entered the large atrium, Lydia's first impression was of color. One entire wall was a mural of gods and goddesses in a lovely dance. Another was a landscape of trees, flowers, and a flowing river.

A third wall was covered with an imitation marble veneer.

Her eyes traveled upward to the ceiling, which was twenty-five or thirty feet high with a large opening in the middle to allow air, light, and rainwater to enter the room. Gargoyle heads, through which the rainwater could run, decorated the edge of the opening directly over a large tank designed to catch the water. Potted plants surrounded this *impluvium,* from which pipes led to an underground cistern where water for household use could be stored.

On one side of the *impluvium* was the shrine for the household gods. A libation was offered each day before this shrine for good fortune and protection, along with a portion from each meal to ensure the blessing of the gods upon this household.

A long table with several couches indicated the atrium was the main dining area of the house. Flowers were everywhere in pots, vases, and as garlands.

Menalcus guided her down a small hallway leading to the kitchen. On the right of this passageway were the men's sleeping quarters. The women's dining area and guest rooms were on the left.

The cook stood deferentially to one side, her ample figure covered by a snow-white apron, while Menalcus and Lydia examined her domain. Lydia liked the large, well-stocked kitchen. Wooden cupboards lined one side for the storing of cooking equipment, oil lamps, and the charcoal braziers used for heat in the winter. Large amphoras for holding wine, grain, oil, and honey stood on one side of the room. An opening in the top, large enough to admit a ladle, was covered with a large, flat tile.

A krater for mixing wine and water rested on a long table. Several *kylix* stood on a tray, ready for serving. Most of these double-handled drinking cups were of polished brass. Lydia picked up an elaborately decorated one of silver, used for special occasions. Drinking mugs without handles, which were for the servants' use, were kept on a shelf that held the dishes the servants ate from.

A long, narrow-necked oil flask stood by itself on a high shelf. This *lekythos* was used for those special occasions when oil must be poured slowly, mostly for funeral rites. Lydia hoped it would not need to be used anytime soon.

Smaller flasks of oil and vinegar were near the stove. The kitchen hearth was built of cement with a brick facing. The firebox was lined with tile and fed from the front. Bronze pots on the side of the hearth stood ready to be pushed over the firebox.

Lydia saw bundles of wood stacked near the kitchen door. One slave was assigned the task of keeping wood for the kitchen fires. A large pot full of boiling water was kept on the stove. Hot water for showers and laundry came from a large vat in the courtyard.

Menalcus watched as a smile began and gradually grew on the rosy face of the cook as Lydia surveyed every inch of the kitchen. It was plain to see his wife knew about what went on in this room and that she approved of what she saw. It looked like things would go well with Lydia in charge.

Lydia's head was in a whirl. What a marvelous house! Everything was absolutely wonderful. So much more than she had dreamed or expected.

She followed Menalcus out into the courtyard of the enclosed garden. A colonnaded portico with doors opening into various rooms looked cool and inviting. She could envision this as a delightful place for many of their meals. As if to confirm her thoughts, two slaves brought trays of fresh fruit and sweetened wine to refresh them.

Menalcus sat with a contented sigh, his face beaming with peace, security, and tranquility.

He smiled at Lydia as if to reassure her. "You have plenty of time. Soak up a little of the atmosphere. It will add to your appreciation for the rest of the house. Besides, the slaves need time to look you over."

He gave a stealthy glance toward a doorway, where a few of the slaves were cowering, taking turns peering at Lydia. When they saw her looking their way, they disappeared.

158 · Acts Chapter 16

She and Menalcus talked for a long time about the many things she had seen for the first time since leaving Thyatira. When her eyelids began to droop, Menalcus suggested she retire for a nap before supper. She did not have to be coaxed.

Lydia descended the stairs with hesitant steps. Would Menalcus want to eat alone or should she join him? Just as she reached the bottom step, he appeared in the doorway of the atrium.

He looked at Lydia as if he had never seen her before. She bit her lip and started to turn toward the women's dining room. Menalcus held out his arms. She ran to him with a happy laugh.

So much for being a proper matron, she thought, giggling to herself.

Lydia opened her eyes to the dim light of early dawn. For a moment she thought she was back in Thyatira. Her eyelids closed again as sleep tried to reclaim her mind for a while.

She heard the sound of muffled footsteps through the open window. The country folk were bringing produce of their fields, milk, and honey to market. Without actually seeing them she knew water carriers were hurrying to and fro from the fountains, their pitchers balanced on one shoulder.

Soon artisans and shopkeepers would throng the streets. The city began to hum with the noise and activity of industry.

Lydia turned on her back, letting her arm fall across the covers. Her hand touched warm flesh. Startled, she turned her head and met the sleepy gaze of her husband.

"Good morning." Menalcus' smile brought a smile to her own lips.

"Good morning." Lydia stretched like a cat. "Oh, Menalcus, I was dreaming. For just a moment I though I was back home."

"Do you miss it so much?" Menalcus picked up her hand. "We've been here several weeks. I had hoped…"

"Well, to be honest, I still don't feel like I belong here….not yet."

A closed look that seemed to shut her out replaced his smile. Maybe she should have lied. She was accustomed to speaking frankly. It was certainly difficult learning to live with someone you hardly knew. How could she be as intimate as she had been with Menalcus and still feel much of the time as if she were living with a stranger?

Since arriving in Philippi they had settled into a loose routine of daily living. The sweet lover who had made the journey from Thyatira such an adventure was now preoccupied with his duties as courier to the Roman Army.

Menalcus interrupted her thoughts by pushing aside the mosquito netting and making his way to the bathroom.

"Do you still miss your home so much? I considered this place my home until my grandmother died. After that my home was wherever my work took me. I never had to work at feeling "at home." I guess I am having a hard time understanding why it is so hard for you to think of this as your home."

He gave Lydia a quick kiss. With a brief wave of his hand and a frown still on his face, he left for the kitchen where he stopped long enough to break his fast with some bread dipped in wine. Then it was off for the garrison.

Lydia gave a deep sigh. Why did Menalcus take the fact that she missed her father and the things she had known all of her life so personally?

The more she thought about the morning, the more aggravated she became. Could she help it if remembrance of her father brought tears to her eyes several times a day? Or if the sight of Myia, pale and listless, caused her to remember happier times?

I will learn, she promised herself.

Well, no better time to start than the present. She would show Menalcus she was trying to adjust. She clapped her hands, and Myia came with her breakfast of fruit and warm wine.

Lydia picked up a slice of orange, looked at it, and put it down again. She pushed the plate aside and motioned for the finger bowl.

"Myia, get one of your uniforms for me. I promised Menalcus I would learn to like Philippi. I can't like something I know nothing about, so you and I are going exploring. We will get to know more about this city than the people who were born here. By the end of this day, you and I will be able to qualify as tour guides to this place."

Myia stood as if she had not heard.

Lydia took her by the shoulders and gave her a little shake. "Myia, don't ignore me. Get the clothes and let's go!" She turned Myia toward the door and gave her a playful smack on the backside. Now that she was committed to the adventure, she was beginning to enjoy it.

Soon the two of them, their long cloaks fastened at the neck, slipped out of the house. They headed in the general direction of the market place.

"The best place to learn about people is to observe what they buy and sell," Lydia stated. "Now, use your eyes and ears to learn all you can. I want to be able to surprise Menalcus tonight."

"He'll be surprised all right," Myia replied. "Maybe you could get a job as a flower girl and really surprise him!"

"Perhaps next week," Lydia teased. "Right now, let's learn the lay of the land around the agora."

The streets were full of people. The two women stepped aside for a troop of boys hurrying to school. The public market was a place of busy activity and loud noise. Built in the center of town where the main streets crossed, it could readily be entered from all directions.

Unlike the low booths that served the market place in Thyatira, Philippi had a beautiful structure with colorful ornamentation on ceilings, walls, and columns. The area served as a public promenade where friends could meet and exchange pleasantries or discuss affairs of state.

They walked slowly past stalls where the owners sold wine, peas and lentils, others fruits and vegetables, or flowers. Lydia touched Myia's arm and paused by a flower stand piled high with freshly picked wildflowers from the nearby fields.

The Greeks, Lydia learned, never ate dinner until they had wreathed themselves with flowers. Flower girls were busy from early dawn gathering the leaves and floral offerings of gardens, fields, and mountainsides.

The two women watched young children fashion myrtle, ivy, and silver poplar into artistic forms and place them around wine vases, cups, plates, and serving dishes. Older women filled baskets to the brim with choice garlands, which their daughters would take to the larger homes to decorate doors, pedestals, and columns. When these treasures had served their purpose, guests would carry them away as mementos, perhaps to be hung on their own doors.

Lydia and Myia strolled on toward the south end of the agora, where the *basilea*, divided inside by large columns into a broad hall and two side halls, housed the courtroom as well as the banking and trading center of the city. They walked past tables where bankers and brokers transacted their dealings. Great merchants, importers, and shippers congregated at these tables. Borrowers and lenders came together in these marble porticoes. Money changers made checks, received deposits, and wrote bills of exchange. Lydia watched one old man deliver his will to a banker for safekeeping.

The girls continued past these prestigious rooms to the northern end, where the public baths, library, and guild hall were located. They laughed as they peeked in the door of the *odeum*, a small covered theater, and remembered their own stage appearance at the theater in Pergamum

Lydia stopped often to look at the graffito advertising elections and upcoming events that was scrawled everywhere.

Several prominent men walked by on their way to the baths. Slaves followed, carrying clean garments and *strigils*, used to scrape off cleansing oil and dirt. Lydia and Myia giggled at one pompous man who obviously desired recognition so much that he had his slave call out his name as he advanced down the street.

The two girls had become so engrossed in the activities they were observing, they failed to notice the passage of time until a large shaded arbor over a few tables caught their attention. The smell of freshly baked bread and hot spicy stew reminded them how hungry they were. Lydia gave Myia a coin to purchase food while she chose a seat in the shade. No point in being mistaken as other than slave girls.

The way they consumed their food fitted their disguise very well. When the last crumb was gone and their fingers had been duly licked, they reentered the street to resume their tour.

Three people turned the corner. One bumped Myia, knocking her to the pavement.

"Out of my way, slave," he growled. "Watch where you are going!"

Lydia looked up from helping Myia to see a hulking man, his oily black hair held in place by a narrow leather thong. A pointed beard accented narrow lips over broken, dirty teeth. Black eyes glittered with arrogance and anger. She looked away, aware that she must not panic or draw attention to herself.

She glanced quickly at the other two people. An involuntary gasp escaped her lips. Before her was the most beautiful girl she had ever seen. Her hair was as black as a raven's wing. It hung in curls over bare shoulders that sloped to rounded breasts that seemed ready to burst the modest peplos she wore. Her eyes were as black as her hair. A perfectly straight nose, over ruby lips that parted over equally perfect teeth, completed an example of beauty seldom seen except in the sculptures of great artists.

The man beside her was just as startling, but in a totally different way. Lydia was sure she was looking into the face of pure evil. Bulging eyes of pale gray bored into her own. Full, sensuous lips smiled without parting. An ugly scar from the tip of one ear ended just below his chin.

"Please excuse us." Lydia gave Myia a warning look and drew her back against the building to let this strange trio pass.

As they walked by, Lydia's eyes met those of the beautiful girl. Was there a plea in the blackness of that glance? Perhaps fright was making her imagine things.

Mistress and slave started on their way with a great sigh of relief. They were both more than ready to return home.

"Wait!" a high-pitched voice ordered. "Don't go!"

Lydia and Myia froze. Surely that order was not meant for them. Lydia looked over her shoulder, then stared in horror as she saw the three strangers rushing toward them. Her first impulse was to run. Myia clutched her arm, her face drained of all color.

"Wait! I must talk to you." The high, nasal voice came from the well-favored girl. But it didn't seem to suit her. A woman with the dark sultry beauty of this one should speak in soft, gentle tones, not this whining, abrasive sound.

The trio stopped directly in their path. The men said nothing, although the bully had an irritated frown on his face. Lydia looked into the face of the girl who seemed to be almost two personalities. Even as she gazed into those black eyes, a change seemed to come over the girl.

She looked straight at Lydia, but Lydia had the eerie feeling the girl was not seeing her at all.

When she opened her mouth to speak nothing moved, not even her lips, yet Lydia could still hear that thin, nasal voice. "Three are coming and you will believe. You will lose all but gain everything. You are not a servant but are served. That will change. Your heart cries in your dreams. Look deep inside. Beware of the cost."

The words stopped. The girl grew rigid as if carved from stone. Her eyes rolled back in her head and her tongue lolled out of one side of her mouth.

The two men grabbed her on either side as her body began to quiver and shake, then went into extreme convulsions, as if in a frenzy.

It was then Lydia saw the chain that bound the girl's wrist to the evil-looking man. Fear held Lydia immobile. She knew she should run but she could neither move nor speak.

A crowd soon gathered about them, drawn by the struggling of the young girl. As suddenly as the seizure began, it subsided. The girl went limp. Her face dripped with perspiration. She looked at Lydia without recognition. The two men stared at Lydia long and hard as if memorizing her features. Then they passed on, half supporting the girl between them.

Lydia and Myia lost no time returning home. They were so frightened they did not speak until they were safe in Lydia's room. Then they fell into each other's arms, sighing with relief. One thing was for sure, their exploring days were over.

That night Lydia had a difficult time getting to sleep. When she did, the strange dream returned. This time, when she stretched out her arms, begging for help, a chain appeared on one wrist. At the end of the chain was an arm that kept trying to pull her away.

She woke up, sat erect in bed, and shivered with cold, even though the night air was sultry. She was glad Menalcus did not stir. She did not want to think about her dream, let alone talk about it. If she let her mind dwell on it, she would have to recall the words of the oracle, and now this strange girl. What did it mean? Had these two very different people been talking about her dreams? Or was it merely a coincidence?

She had not had the nerve to tell Menalcus about their escapade. Maybe later...

A faint breeze whispered through the open window and touched Lydia's skin. The first light of early dawn revealed a room of ghostly forms, still shrouded in semidarkness. She held herself very still, careful not to disturb Menalcus sleeping quietly beside her. It would be time to wake him soon enough. For this moment, she needed to hold her world intact. For this moment, all was safe, all was secure.

Part of her wanted to awaken Menalcus so they might have these last few hours together before his duty took him away from her again. Another part of her wanted to hold off the reality of his departure until the last possible moment.

She turned her head on the pillow and gazed at his sleeping face. Her eyes took in every feature, imprinting every detail on her mind. She wanted to be able to close her eyes and continue to see the dark curls that crowned his handsome head. Beard stubble only enhanced the firmness of his lips and the deep cleft in his chin. Those long black lashes would have been cherished by any girl in Philippi. How soon before she would see his dear smile again and hear his soft voice in the night?

She had not expected to love him so much. Both of them had accepted their marriage as a good arrangement. Menalcus had treated her with great courtesy and kindness from the beginning of their relationship. Somewhere along the way, their mutual pleasure in each other's company had deepened into a love that grew with each passing year.

Sometimes Lydia hated Claudius and his power to order men to his side at a moment's notice. All of the years Menalcus had served in the army had not immunized her against the torture of his leaving.

The sounds of the waking household invaded the stillness. Menalcus stirred. He reached for Lydia before he opened his eyes. She moved against his warm body, her throat hurting with love for him.

"It can't be morning already," Menalcus muttered. "I just went to sleep!"

"I know," Lydia replied. "I'm not sure I slept at all. I wish... Menalcus, must you leave today?"

"Would you like to tell Claudius to forget about me for a little while? No, thank you. I don't want to leave you any more than you want me to go, but you don't argue with the emperor. Especially not Claudius."

"I know. But I'm selfish. I don't want to wait until we're old to have long evenings together. I want them now. I don't want you to be in one part of the world and me in another. I want you here beside me. I want to reach out in the night and touch you. I want to sleep with your body curled around mine, like this every night. I want to wake up and see you there beside me."

"I hate it when you are away and I never know if it will be a few days, a week or more, perhaps months. And the children miss you. I truly hate it!"

Menalcus placed one hand under her chin. "And I will be dreaming of those nights while I am away. We'll be together, no matter where I am or how far away, because we'll be remembering these times together. Every night I promise to tell you how much I love you. I'll hold your head in my hands and touch your cheeks. I'll smooth that lovely hair back from your face and I'll kiss you like this—and this—and this."

With a groan of mixed yearning and pain, he gathered her into his arms. He made love to her gently, as if he might crush something precious if he moved too quickly. His very gentleness added to the strength of their passion.

They were still locked in a tight embrace when Myia tapped on the door. In spite of her determination not to cry, Lydia could feel hot tears stinging and a constriction in her throat.

"Hey," Menalcus hollered. "Lydia, you're choking me to death. Don't squeeze so tight. I won't do Claudius any good if you strangle me, even with love. Come on, now—please don't cry. I can't leave with you crying. Lydia, I don't want to leave you. You know that, don't you?"

"Yes. Yes. I know that. I know all the things I'm supposed to say and do." Lydia spoke with her face snuggled against his shoulder. "And I promised myself I'd be brave and strong and send you off with a smile on my face. But that was last night. I hate your having to go!"

In another minute she would be sobbing. She rose from the bed and hurried to the bathroom. She stepped into the shower and let the tears flow, lost in the water cascading over her smooth skin.

I must get myself under control. I mustn't add to Menalcus's burden by carrying on like a new bride. But oh, I'll miss him! I'll miss him so much! Lydia washed her face over and over to remove the tear marks.

Myia would be coming in soon to dress her skin with oil and attar of roses. She heard the door open and close and turned to receive her towel. Instead, Menalcus took her hand and stepped into the shower with her.

"I just had an idea. If I take my shower with you, we'll have that much more time together."

Surprised and delighted, Lydia threw back her head and laughed, glad for this chance to send him off with some wonderful memories.

"You devil! Something tells me this may be the longest shower since Artiluis invented the method!"

"Yes, it just might. Now, if you wash, I'll dry. Or would you rather dry?"

Lydia looked at the tapestry panel in her lap. Without thought she pulled the needle back and forth over the design.

"Oh, mercy! One whole row done in the wrong color!"

For a moment she considered leaving it the way it was. Who would notice? *I would*, she answered her own unspoken question. She took out the row of stitches with an exasperated sigh. At this rate the panel would never be finished. Impatient with herself and her thoughts, she laid the work aside and began to walk around the garden. Her steps were measured and slow but her thoughts were racing. She was tired of doing nothing. The life of a lady was not enough to satisfy the restless energy and searching of her spirit.

Some would have laughed at her idea of nothing to do. There was much work involved in keeping the house of a Roman officer in order. In addition the years they had been together had produced three children, each one enough to keep one person busy all day. There was plenty of work, but also enough slaves to see that it was done.

That was the problem. There was really nothing Lydia needed to do with her own hands.. At the beginning of the week she went over the household accounts, decided on meals, gave necessary instructions, and the household slaves did the rest. Slaves took care of the gardens and the stables.

For each child there was at least two slaves The children were bathed and dressed by slaves, fed by slaves, taught and played with by slaves, unless Lydia wanted to do those things herself. She could see them as much or as little as she wanted and it seemed silly to feel so useless She knew she could insist on taking over their care for herself but she did not want to upset the smooth routine of the household , nor did she want slaves standing around idle.

The cry of a street vendor coming through the open window brought Lydia's attention back to the present. She pushed the thoughts about her life aside and decided to go play with the baby. *That will keep me busy for a while.*

She hurried to the nursery, only to be met by a zealous nursemaid with a finger to her lips. Lydia tiptoed into the room to observe little Krysta, sound asleep, lying on her stomach, knees drawn up, her little rear end sticking up in the air. Her black curls, so like Menalcus's, laid in damp ringlets on her forehead. Lydia leaned over to kiss her. The child stirred slightly and gave a big sigh.

Lydia walked past the nursemaid, a thin smile on her lips but inwardly she was very disheartened to realize that even her own baby did not need her care. She swallowed the lump in her throat and decided to follow the sounds of childish laughter to the kitchen.

Four-year-old Hermanus sat on a high stool at the kitchen table, swathed in one of cook's big aprons. The matron was preparing a meat pie for dinner and Hermanus had his own piece of dough. Lydia watched as he put his dough in a mound of flour on the table in front of him. First he pounded it with his fist. Then, when it was flat enough, he pushed his hand, palm down, into the dough as hard as he could. Crowing like a rooster, he shouted for cook to look. Cook obligingly examined his hand print and praised him accordingly.

Hermanus played in the flour, squeezing his dough into a ball and plunking it in the flour again and again. He rubbed his hands together before patting some flour on his cheek. Then he grasped a pinch of flour and put it in his mouth. Lydia laughed at the look of distaste that spread across his face. Such spitting and gagging! He rubbed his tongue with his apron while she brought him a cup of water.

"Would you like to come to the garden and play ball with me?" she asked.

Hermanus looked at his mother and then at the pile of flour. He picked his little piece of dough out of the snowy mound and tossed it from one hand to the other. "I think I had better stay and help cook. She's going to give me some cookies if I am good. I have to get my pie ready to bake."

He began flattening his dough again, which was beginning to look slightly gray from all the handling. He waited patiently for cook to lay down her marble rolling pin before he picked it up. It was so heavy she had to help him roll out his dough. Then she showed him how to turn it over and roll it out again.

Lydia gave him a quick squeeze. "I'll be in the garden if you change your mind."

She hurried from the room as quickly as possible but not before the tears started to fall. The realization that her son preferred the company of their cook to that of his own mother was like a knife thrust into her heart. She wanted to cuddle him and to ruffle his hair and to watch him run and laugh with her. But he didn't want to spend time with her. What was she good for if she could not be a mother to her own children?

She walked up and down the rows of vegetables in the kitchen garden and then around the flower beds with the forlorn hope Hermanus would come running out the door to play with her. But he did not come.

She could not blame the slaves, they adored her children. They adored Lydia. That was part of the problem. They thought the more they could do so that she did not have to lift a finger to do anything, the better they were serving her. She had to find something to give her life meaning.

She returned to the atrium and clapped her hands for Myia. The slave in charge of the linens appeared and informed her that Myia had gone with another slave to purchase a potion for the severe headaches she had been experiencing.

Lydia strolled listlessly back into the garden. She trailed her fingers in the cool water from the fountain. There was her needlework, right where she had left it.

I've got to find something to do.

She made herself stop those thoughts. She was home. This was her home and had been for years. It

was different from the home where she was reared, to
be sure, but still it *was* home. She unconsciously kept
turning the wedding bracelet on her upper arm.

What's the matter with me? she scolded herself.
*I've got so much to thank the gods for. Why isn't it
enough?*

She thought of their acquaintances and how the
other women spent their time. A large portion of
the day was spent at the public baths, where they
engaged in the latest gossip or speculated on events
that were taking place. More than one reputation
had been torn to shreds as the women lolled in the
warm waters or were massaged by their attendants.
One time at the baths had been enough for Lydia.
She much preferred taking care of her personal
needs at home.

Consequently her circle of friends was very
small. But Lydia did not care. She had become friends
with most of the household slaves. Many of them
were educated, talented people. They served her
with love and faithfulness because she treated them
like persons. Their desire to please her made them
diligent about their duties. They looked for ways to
keep her from having to lift a finger, not realizing
they were only adding to her problem.

In spite of her earlier determination, thoughts
of her life at Thyatira continued to intrude. How
she missed her father and the work of the dyers and
weavers. If she closed her eyes she could imagine

the clean odor of new material, envision the bolts of beautiful colors: the royal purples, the brilliant reds, and the delicate greens and yellows.

Nowhere else in the world were there reds like those in her homeland. Other dyers made red and purple cloth from the roots of mountain-grown plants. This "turkey red" was known to run and fade. Not so the purples of Thyatira, which were in great demand wherever they were displayed.

An idea took root and began to grow. *Did she dare? Could she do it successfully?*

The next few days Lydia hardly ate or slept. She spent hours scratching figures on a clay tablet and rubbing them out again. Several afternoons she enlisted Myia and another servant to accompany her on walks through the business district. They did not know she was eyeing every possible spot as a potential for a textile shop.

One day, she passed an establishment at the edge of the street where the better shops ended and the open market began. The shutters were closed, but by peeking around the edges she could see some half-empty shelves and a rude counter. The dim interior seemed to be in a general state of disarray.

A return visit the following day found the shutters still closed. Inquiry from the neighboring shop owners revealed the shopkeeper had died, and the owner of the building was looking for a new tenant. That was all Lydia needed to hear.

In the privacy of her room, Lydia removed the wedding bracelet from her arm. She turned it around and around as she recalled the scene in Nathan Ben Kobath's home when she and her father first learned the secret of the bracelet. For the first time since she received it, she pressed the hidden catch. The soft gleam and sparkle of the diamonds seemed to wink at her. She had forgotten how beautiful they were.

She placed each stone in the palm of her hand as if weighing one against the other. After replacing them with great care, she returned the bracelet to her arm. She hugged herself with delight. She would do it! She could pay for the shop out of the proceeds from the sale of one of the stones. What a gift her father had bestowed upon her! He had wanted to be sure she would never be hungry. Did he know, back then, there were other hungers besides those for meat and bread?

The days that followed were filled with messengers running back and forth. Lydia was engrossed in writing letters to be dispatched to her father. She informed him of her plans, but also asked for advice and requested that some of his goods be sent for her to sell.

A visit to a banker put her mind at rest as to her financial possibilities. She only showed him one stone. He promised to put her in touch with a gem merchant who would gladly purchase such a specimen. He questioned Lydia at great length about her plans, and she answered all of his queries in succinct detail. It was evident she had done her homework.

He seemed to find it a welcome change to do business with a woman of such intelligence. Lydia was sure of what she wanted and she knew the wholesale end of the cloth business. Her frankness and business acumen made her a delightful customer.

He took a fatherly interest in her venture and was able to put her in touch with reliable caravan owners who could carry goods to her at a fair price. The banker also acted as her agent with the shop owner.

Somewhere in the back of Lydia's mind lingered the question of what she would tell Menalcus. She probably should have waited to talk it over with him. Suppose after all this, he said no? Would he refuse to let her proceed? She resolutely pushed that possibility aside and plunged into the activity of getting accounts set up and plans drawn for the interior of her shop. The very thought thrilled her from head to toe!

Lydia's high spirits infected the entire household. Even the children became part of the fun. Dinnertime found them full of questions for their mother. She helped them understand by playing pretend. Five-year-old Diana played the shopkeeper while Lydia became the hard-to-please customer. Hermanus was a noisy camel driver bringing a load of merchandise to be unpacked. Krysta crawled around or toddled over to lean against Lydia's knee. When the game got very exciting she would throw both hands up in the air and clap them in delight. That made them all laugh. The more they laughed, the more she clapped.

As soon as the light of day made it possible to distinguish objects in the room, Lydia prepared for one of the biggest days of her life. If all went well, tomorrow morning she would wake up a shop owner. Her very own business! All she needed was for the gem merchant to come today and agree on the money he would deposit with the banker.

Menalcus's face appeared in her mind for a fleeting moment. What would he say? Would he be angry? She refused to think about it. She would deal with that when the time came.

She was careful to pour an extra libation to their god and to place flowers around all the ancestral heads. Everything must be in order when her caller came. Nothing would be left to chance. A special visit to the temple of Isis was planned to ensure the favor of the goddess on her venture.

Myia followed Lydia's orders and arranged a beautiful offering of oranges, pomegranates, and figs in a basket with ivy and wild blossoms twined around the handle. She was going with Lydia as far as the temple grounds. Perhaps the goddess would show some special favor to her as well.

They joined a line of worshipers ascending the steep marble steps leading to the temple entrance. Lydia prayed for the success of her business as she placed her offering at the feet of the large statue. Above all else, she asked the goddess to placate Menalcus so that he would not object to her plans.

She backed away from the statue with head bowed, but when she reached the portico of the temple she let her eyes travel up to the stone face. For long moments she gazed at the carved eyes and cold, hard mouth of the goddess. Her unbidden question as to how a stone statue could answer her prayers surfaced once again in her mind. She shooed it away, not wishing to anger the goddess with her doubtful thoughts.

But on the way home her mind was occupied with questions about the involvement of gods and goddesses in the affairs of humankind. Why couldn't she simply believe and take comfort in her worship? Why did she always come away from the temple with unanswered questions? Where was there peace for her heart?

The questions would have to wait. Right now she had business to transact. She would need all of her wits about her. Her banker friend had warned her this gem merchant was not above taking advantage of her. She trusted his judgment.

Lydia arrived home so preoccupied with her thoughts that she paid little attention to the flurry of activity in the courtyard. She went straight to her room. There was barely enough time to change before the gem merchant was due to arrive.

The minute she opened her bedroom door, she stopped, the blood draining from her face. Her husband stood an arm's length away.

Lydia went to Menalcus and threw her arms around his neck. She held on to him a little longer that usual while she tried to get control of her shaking limbs.

Menalcus took her by her arms and made her face him.

"What's going on here, Lydia?" he demanded. "I come home to find you out and the servants try to stay as far away from me as possible. None of them will look me in the eye!"

"Menalcus, there's nothing wrong, but I have a lot to tell you. Now if you will come over here and sit down and promise not to yell, I will start at the beginning and tell you anything you want to know."

All the time she was talking, Lydia was leading Menalcus to a chair and as soon as he was seated, she knelt at his feet. She knew with a sinking feeling that she had been wrong in going ahead with her plans without talking to him first. She could only hope she could make him understand.

Lydia stole a look at Menalcus face. He was not smiling. She took a deep breath. "I'll start at the beginning."

Menalcus stared at her as if seeing her for the first time. What was she up to? "That might be a very good place to start!"

And start she did. She begged Menalcus to understand her need for this shop. And finally she stopped, knowing there was no more to be said.

Menalcus was furious and he didn't really know why and that made him angrier still. That's when the yelling began.

"I didn't marry you to have you gone all day in some little unheard of shop like a common merchant," he growled.

"Little! Inheard of!" she shrieked. "My shop will be one of the better ones in the city. The finest people will be glad to patronize me!"

"I don't want my wife *patronized!* I want you to be home with the children where you belong."

"Where I belong?" Lydia was near tears. "I'm
not one of your slaves, Menalcus. If I were, I'd know
where I belong. I go to take care of the children and
everything's already been done. I ask the children
to come play with me and they prefer the servants.
I might as well return to Thyatira for all I'm needed
around here!"

Lydia knew Myia was probably sitting on the
stairway with her hands over her ears. She could
not help but hear the argument going on in the bedroom. In fact, the passers-by in the street probably
could hear the angry voices. The household slaves
were pretending to be busy but she knew they were
straining to hear every word. Well, let them hear.
They might as well get it first-hand.

"So that's it," the argument resumed. " You're
still homesick. After all these years you still don't
like it here."

"I didn't say that! But since you brought it up,
I did like life in Thyatira. I had work to do and I
was good at doing it. I was of more use than simply
ordering people around while I do needlework that
nobody needs!"

"I want you here when I come home!"

"Sure, when you come home," Lydia stormed.
"But what about all the times when you're gallivanting up and down the country? Am I supposed to sit
here and twirl my thumbs?"

"Gallivanting? I'm doing my job! I am a courier, Lydia. You knew when you married me that I'd be on the road a good deal of the time. I thought you liked being a wife and mother."

"I do! But that doesn't mean I have to stop living!"

Menalcus and Lydia stared at each other. Her emotions spent, Lydia burst into tears.

Menalcus's fiery eyes softened. "Now, Lydia," he said. "If you'd just stop yelling we could talk this over."

"You yell much louder than I do," she said, still sobbing.

"Please don't cry." He pulled her into his arms. "Calm down now, and we'll talk."

Lydia's tears gradually quieted as she rested in Menalcus's embrace. How warm those arms!. How strong that shoulder! What would she ever do without him?

She should have waited and asked him first. Perhaps she should forget the whole idea of a shop. It was probably a foolish notion anyway.

She slipped her arms around his neck and pressed her tear-streaked face against the warm stubble of his cheek. Then she kissed his neck, then planted a long, sweet kiss on his lips, which was ardently returned.

Menalcus sat down and pulled Lydia onto his lap. There she was finally able to tell him how the plans for her shop had come to be. He listened in respectful silence.

"I'm still a wife and mother," Lydia said. "I'll always be here for you. But with all the slaves ready to respond to my slightest command, I need to do something for myself. Don't you see? I won't have much to give to you or to the children unless I keep adding to the person I am. The more there is of me, the more I have to share. Can you understand?"

"I'm trying," Menalcus said, giving her a tentative smile.

"Besides," she continued. "What if, for some reason—may the gods forbid—you could no longer carry out your duties? Or if something happened that you could not return to me for a long, long time. What would I do? Oh, I know I don't have to worry about money—although I do expect to make a pretty profit from my shop. But I need to do this for me, Menalcus. It's what I know. It's what I love. It's part of who I am."

He stared at her for a long moment. She tried to decipher the look in his eyes, to read the thoughts that lay behind them. But she couldn't be certain what he was thinking, and he didn't seem ready to share his thoughts just yet.

"However," she said with a long sigh, "I will cancel everything rather than have you unhappy. You are the head of this house, and I will honor your wishes, whatever they may be."

Even as she said the words, Lydia knew that if she had to give up the shop, something would be gone from their relationship; something intangible and very delicately balanced. And she would always hold the dream in her heart. Oh, how could one person have so many contradictory feelings?

Menalcus thought for a long time. To be honest, he knew Lydia had a valid point. "You know I would feel better when I have to be away if I knew you and the children were safe here in this house. However, I want you to be happy. So, we'll give it a try."

Lydia had been so concentrated on her own feelings she was not sure what she had heard.

"What did you say?" She could scarcely breathe. She dared not take her eyes off of his face.

"I said, 'let's give it a try'."

Lydia whooped with joy and flung her arms around Menalcus. She wanted to laugh and cry at the same time! She kissed him over and over while profusely thanking him again and again. Had she really heard him say "we"?

"So, my little business woman, I suppose you have the financial aspects all figured out. Or do you plan to open the shop on your good looks and personality?"

Though it meant breaking the promise she'd made to her father, Lydia told Menalcus the secret of the bracelet. She watched his face carefully while she explained it to him. This must not be the cause of another argument between them.

When she released the spring and revealed the sparkling diamonds nestled within, his eyes grew enormous.

"I'm only using one for now," she explained. "The other two will be saved for dire emergencies."

She could see the stunned expression on Menalcus' face, then it quickly turned to anger. Perhaps she should have told him before but there had never been any need.

"I promised Father I would tell no one my secret until such time as I had need," Lydia explained "Not even Myia knows about the jewels. And Menalcus, you must promise never to tell this secret to anyone."

Menalcus continued to stare at the stones in her bracelet. All of this was almost beyond imagining!

"I did not think it would be fair to ask you for money to satisfy a desire that is strictly my own," she went on. "So I used one of the stones to purchase the shop."

"Well, it seems you have it all figured out. We'll have to see how it works in actual practice."

"Menalcus, there's one more thing," she paused as his expression changed again, "now don't look so apprehensive. It's nothing awful. But I have asked a jeweler to come and make an offer for the stone. He's not just any jeweler but one the banker who found the empty shop for me recommended." She hesitated once more, "He did warn me he might try to take advantage of me. Won't you come down with me when the buyer gets here? I need you to make sure I don't get cheated."

Lydia was greatly relieved to see Menalcus throw back his head and give a hearty laugh. "I'd like to see the man who could put one over on you. But, yes, I'll come down, if for nothing else than to see how you manipulate someone besides me."

Menalcus surveyed the small, thin man the porter ushered into the garden. A slight, somewhat arrogant smile did nothing to soften the glitter of the black eyes. An intricately worked gold band circled Simonos's right arm from his elbow to his shoulder. A matching band bound his forehead, holding a mass of black curls in place. A spotless white tunic complimented his appearance.

Without stopping to reason why, Menalcus immediately felt on the defensive. He motioned their guest to a low bench in the shade. The splashing water from the fountain added to the refreshment of this oasis from the oppressive summer heat.

"The coolness of your garden is most welcome." Simonos spoke with politeness, bowing low.

Menalcus inclined his head.

Lydia took a seat opposite Simonos. "I regret that you felt it necessary to come in the heat of the day when everyone else is taking a rest."

"Believe me, most gracious lady, nothing of less importance than my present errand would bring me out in the middle of the day. That sun is burning down with all the heat of a fiery furnace."

"Then we shall proceed immediately?" Menalcus suggested.

A slave appeared at Lydia's side with a tall carafe of cooled wine and a plate of freshly baked cakes stuffed with dates and slivered almonds.

Simonos, Menalcus had learned, was one of the wealthiest merchants in Philippi, a jeweler of great renown. He had arrived in Philippi as a young man with only the clothes on his back and the skill of a metal worker.

An aged goldsmith listened to his plea for an opportunity to prove his skill. It had not taken long for his artistry to be recognized. The old man saw an opportunity to increase his business and so apprenticed the young man, giving him a room in his own home. Simonos quickly advanced from apprentice to the owner of his own shop. When the old man died, he took ownership of that business as well.

Noted for shrewd dealings, he had connections with the most influential houses in the city and, it was whispered, with the less desirable elements as well. Contacts in various parts of the empire kept him abreast of all that was happening, especially in the area of trade.

Menalcus could surmise from the man's bearing and dress that he was probably accustomed to dealing with large amounts of money. He watched the way Simonos surveyed the contents of the room. *"He's probably trying to estimate how much to offer and what he can get away with"*.

Lydia opened the small leather box. She arranged a small square of black velvet on the table and placed one of the three diamonds from her bracelet. She took advantage of the light coming from the window and moved the stone in a way that caused the stone to refract the sparkle of light across the ceiling.

"If Lydia arranges displays in her shop the way she is arranging this stone, she will surely be a success" Menalcus kept his thoughts to himself but was aware that the jeweler was trying to hide his excitement at the sight of the diamond. Only a small quiver of light that glittered in the depth of his black eyes betrayed him.

He slowly picked up the stone and held it to the light. Prisms of light reflected in all directions. He turned the stone this way and that before taking the jeweler's glass to examine it further. Then he replaced the jewel on the cloth with seeming indifference.

"This stone would have to be cut, of course," he said in a flat, disinterested-sounding voice. "One can never tell how it will turn out. I might get a single useable piece from it. On the other hand, it may shatter into a million shards. I stand a chance of losing my entire investment."

Menalcus knew Lydia's father would not have given her a stone of questionable value. "What would you offer for this diamond?" he asked, deliberately sounding hesitant.

Simonos fingered his chin and frowned with the difficulty of making a decision. He held up the stone again as if undecided. "I might risk as much as half a talent—silver, of course."

"I'm afraid we are both wasting our time," Lydia answered. "I could not possibly accept such an offer. I am sure the stone is worth at least two talents—in gold."

Simonos rose to his feet, drawing himself up to his full height, "Madam, you are asking an impossible price!" He looked at Menalcus in appeal.

Menalcus shrugged. "Then I apologize for your journey here on such a warm day."

Lydia calmly picked up the diamond and held it so the sunlight touched it, revealing its hidden fire as it sent prisms of light bouncing back. Then she returned the stone to its box, closed the cover, and stood as if to dismiss her guest.

Menalcus doubted if Simonos had dealt with many women who seemed to know their own mind as well as Lydia. He was sure she would see through his little game

"Very well. Then I must bid you good day, madam. Sir." He departed with a curt bow.

Menalcus hid a smile that refused to be stifled. He was highly amused at the way his wife was out-maneuvering this experienced man of the world.

Lydia quivered inside. She knew the diamond was worth far more than Simonos had offered. However, she also knew that what he offered would be as much as she needed to open the shop. She felt tempted to call him back and reconsider when Loukas's words echoed in her mind. These stones were not to be used lightly. Nor were they to be surrendered for less than their full value, especially not for the satisfying of her wishes, no matter how strong.

As Menalcus showed Simonos to the door, a loud knock sounded and one of Simonos' competitors entered. He maintained his air of indifference as he was ushered out the gate while Lydia led the other jeweler back to the garden. She did not bother to explain that this competitor had come to deliver a silver bracelet she was having engraved as a special gift for Menalcus for his birthday.

Lydia was not surprised to have a return visit from Simonos later the same day. The two speedily agreed upon a fair price for her diamond.

The moon was still high in the sky when Menalcus joined the small group of soldiers at the city gate. His leather dispatch case carried sealed messages from the capital city of Rome for the commander of the troops in Palestine. The packet was marked "Urgent."

Precious letters from Lydia to Loukas reposed in an inner pocket of his tunic. Since he also bore messages for the captain of the guard at Thyatira, a day in the home of his father-in-law would be a welcome respite. Menalcus did not look forward to the trip to hot, dry Palestine. The soldiers would be going by ship to Troas, but he would be delivering and picking up messages at Lystra, Derbe, and Antioch before the final trip down to Jerusalem.

Will those Jews never learn? Why can't they accept the good protection of the Roman government like everyone else? Look at Philippi. You didn't hear of riots and revolts there, and everyone seems happy enough.

A warm surge of gratitude filled his heart as he reflected on his home. Lydia certainly made him happy. What a joy she had turned out to be—a capable wife, able to manage a busy household; a loving mother, seeing to the upbringing and education of two daughters and a son; and now, a business woman in charge of a soon-to-be (he hoped) successful shop in the agora.

A noisy procession of farmers interrupted his thoughts, all headed for market with carts of fresh cabbages, onions, turnips, squawking chickens and ducks. By the time the farmers cleared the gates of the city and crossed the stone bridge over the river, morning was beginning to brighten the horizon. The soldiers appeared in the gray half-light like ghosts riding out on a mysterious journey.

Lydia awoke feeling groggy. She had not rested well during the night. She longed to go back to sleep.

But the sight of Menalcus's pillow, with the imprint of his head still on it, did not allow her to rest.

She pulled a chair near the window and leaned her head against the cool marble of the casement. Most of the time she knew approximately how long her husband would be away. His duties often required carrying dispatches to nearby Neapolis or to the slightly farther city of Thessalonica. But Palestine seemed such a long distance. She had tried to hide her uneasiness about this trip, sensing that Menalcus was not too happy about this assignment himself.

The one bright spot was his chance to visit Loukas. When the orders came for this mission, they had discussed the possibility of Lydia and the children going as far as Thyatira and staying with Loukas until Menalcus was ready to return. It was only a wild desire on her part, but how she would have loved for her children to meet their grandfather! To be able to show them the house and the land where she had grown up would be a thrill beyond measure. But then common sense took over.

The shop that she had worked so hard to obtain was at a stage where it demanded her constant attention. She dared not leave it for any length of time until she could train one of the slaves to oversee its operation. She was also in the process of making plans to build her own dye yards. Perhaps another time would come when they could make the trip to Thyatira as a family.

In spite of her determination not to feel sorry for herself, hot tears splashed down her cheeks. For a few moments she gave herself over to weeping.

Never one to spend much time on self-pity, Lydia dried her eyes and prepared to meet the day. Menalcus had promised to urge her father to return with him for a long visit. With that happy thought in mind, she decided she would dress the children herself this morning.

They missed their father when he was away, especially Hermanus. They always enjoyed a break in routine when their father was home. Now it was necessary to get everyone back on schedule.

Especially me, she admitted.

This was the day the household accounts must be scrutinized and orders given for the coming week. A new shipment of cloth from Thyatira had arrived late yesterday. She must check carefully to see that all was accounted for before she handed over payment for the goods. A deep sigh escaped her.

I'm tired before I even begin.

She sprang to her feet, but the moment she assumed a standing position, she was struck by a wave of nausea. She was barely able to reach the wash bowl on her bedside table before she became violently ill. When the retching finally ceased, she fell back on her pillow, wet with perspiration and totally exhausted.

Myia entered the room without waiting to be called. She clapped her hands and gave the basin to the slave who appeared at her summons. After touching Lydia's forehead, she gently but briskly washed Lydia's face with a cold cloth and brushed the damp hair away from her face.

When she felt like she could open her eyes again, Lydia stared at Myia. The years that had passed so quickly were beginning to show on the face of her friend. A few streaks of gray in the hair, a slight stoop to the shoulders, a wrinkle here and there marked the passage of time.

"Oh, Myia, not again. Tell me, please, surely not again?"

Lydia remembered the first time she had felt this ill. It was shortly after she and Menalcus settled into this house. How frightened the three of them had been, thinking Lydia had fallen prey to the same dread sickness that almost took Myia's life in Troas. When one of the older slaves was called in to take care of Lydia, their fears had been laid to rest.

A few hours of observation and a practiced examination led to the casual announcement that Menalcus would soon become a father. Weak from relief that Lydia did not have some fatal disease, Menalcus could scarcely believe the news. When it finally did sink in, he jumped and shouted for joy. That was eight years ago.

"Do you remember the look on Menalcus' face when old Elizabeth told him he had a daughter?" Myia said.

Lydia laughed. Not only did she remember it, she also recalled her own incredulous feelings when the child was placed in her arms. Such a tiny creature!

It had taken some time to adjust to a new baby. The entire household was agog with pride and happiness.

A slave with nursing skills was called in to help care for little Diana, but many times when she was carried to Lydia for feeding, Menalcus took the infant from the nurse and sat beside Lydia until the baby, sated and sound asleep, was ready to be returned to her bed.

His pride had not abated when Lydia became pregnant again a few months later. This time Menalcus realized his dream of a son. Lydia smiled as she thought of the great sense of accomplishment and peace that washed through her when Elizabeth, the midwife, announced it was a boy! Menalcus wept for joy and treated Lydia with amazing tenderness. He named the boy Hermanus, after his father.

Krysta, now almost four years old, was both the delight and the dismay of the household. While Menalcus was indulgent with all the children, and took Hermanus with him to every imaginable place, he spoiled Krysta shamelessly.

Lydia tried to think of other possible explanations for her nausea. She had eaten nothing unusual the day before. Try as she might to deny that she was pregnant again, Lydia knew she was.

The very knowledge seemed to bring another surge of nausea into her throat. The thought of going through another pregnancy was loathsome. She knew from past experience the next three months would consist of throwing up at the slightest movement or the smell of food. Except for short periods each day, she would be practically bedridden. Lydia would enjoy the best of health for the remaining months of her pregnancy, but she refused to be comforted by that.

She loved her children, and although she had slaves to help with their care, their instruction and upbringing was still her responsibility. She took this very seriously, spending time with lessons, being at their bedside when they needed her, instructing them in the ways of life at every opportunity. They would not understand why they couldn't have as much of Mommy's attention as before. Was it so wrong not to want another child?

And what about the shop? Now it would not be possible for her to go there. Pregnant women were not welcome in the business world. She would have to trust one of the slaves to carry out her bidding. Plans for the dye yard would have to be put on hold.

Unbidden tears were threatening. Lydia closed her eyes to keep Myia from seeing the rebellion and despair that surely must be obvious there. Myia would never understand. The closest she would ever come to motherhood was in loving and caring for Lydia's children. Another little one to hold and cuddle would simply add to her love for her mistress.

Menalcus would never understand either. Weren't women supposed to tend to the household and bear children? What could be so wrong about doing what you were born to do? Especially when the end result was beautiful and healthy children such as they enjoyed. Men! They had no comprehension, no inkling of understanding of what it was like to be a woman.

For a brief moment she wanted to vent her fury on Menalcus. What right did he have to be master and lord over her very being? Was she a slave to be used and dictated to? She wished with all her heart that he was the one to be so sick every day until this child was born. That would show him!

And what about the birthing? As she thought about the time of delivery, she shuddered. Her body seemed to shrink from the recollection of the unendurable pain that had accompanied the birth of each of her children. Old Elizabeth said the pain was forgotten as soon as the baby was born, but Lydia knew differently. Furthermore, she knew Elizabeth didn't believe that either. She was merely parroting what she had heard others say, supposedly to make the expectant mother feel better. Accepting the fact that pain was a part of childbirth did not make it go away.

Lydia pretended to go back to sleep until she heard Myia tiptoe from the room. Then she let the tears slip unhindered down her cheeks.

Dimly, in the recesses of her mind, she remembered talk overheard among the servants about potions that could be taken to induce a miscarriage. There were doctors who could be secretly engaged, for a fee, to take care of unwanted pregnancies.

She had no feeling for this unknown, unwanted intrusion that had found a lodging place in her body. At this point it could not be as large as one joint of her little finger. What would it matter if it were taken away? Menalcus would never suspect. He wasn't even home. No one need know, except Myia, and she would never tell.

And me. I would know. Always, I would know.

Lydia realized she could never take that escape. She might not be overjoyed at the thought of having another baby, but since it was already a fact, she would not take steps to destroy the life within her.

Maybe I'll lose this child naturally. I am getting older. Maybe this is one of those bad dreams I keep having and I'll wake up and laugh about it.

But she was not dreaming. She might as well get used to the fact that she was pregnant. No point in moping about something she could not change.

She made a mental checklist of the things she was supposed to do today. Someone else would have to take care of them. For the first time, Lydia began to appreciate the fact that she had many hands to obey her instructions.

She waited until her stomach settled a bit and then asked Myia to summon the head steward to bring the household accounts. Myia stayed nearby to see that Lydia did not work too long.

Noon found her ready to sleep again. A slave wielded a large ostrich feather fan until she was able to drift into a troubled rest.

When she awoke, she was informed that a messenger had arrived to report that her shipment had been checked and all was as reported. The caravan owner would send a messenger for payment that evening.

A very weak Lydia walked downstairs later in the day to watch the children playing in the garden. A slight breeze carried the scent of early jasmine. She found she could drink some honeyed wine and keep it down. Myia brought brown bread fresh from the oven, and Lydia ate it a few bites at a time.

That evening, Lydia walked around the fountain, trailing her hand in the water. She watched it spout from the mouth of little ceramic frogs located around the basin.

Where was Menalcus tonight? Would he be glad to know they were going to have another child? Of course, he would be pleased. She thought about her reactions that morning. She felt a little ashamed of her rebellion.

Much later that night she drifted into a troubled sleep. Her dreams brought terror that enveloped her like a cloud. Each time she managed to return to sleep, the dream continued. When she woke, her heart was racing and her pillow was wet with tears, but she could recall only the terror of the dream.

She spent most of the morning in a chair by the window, which she found more comfortable than the bed. Once in a while a slight breeze touched her face. Thoughts of the children, her pregnancy, the shop, and Menalcus were interrupted when she saw a courier approach from the direction of the garrison. In the glare of the noonday sun she watched him pull a letter from his pouch and hand it to the porter at the front door.

Dear Menalcus. He always managed to get a message to her whenever a courier was coming this way.

As soon as the letter was delivered to her, she hurriedly broke the seal and removed the epistle, somewhat longer this time than usual. Perhaps he had news of her father.

My dearest Lydia,

I hardly know how to begin this message to you. There seems no easy way to tell you. Your father is dead.

Lydia stared at the letter. "No, no, no!" she cried. It could not be true. Great sobs wracked her body as the meaning of the words she had just read refused to be denied.

Myia came rushing into the room and found Lydia weeping, the letter lying in her lap. "What is it, milady? Has Menalcus come to harm?"

"No, no, not Menalcus." Lydia sobbed. "It's my father. He's dead. And I wasn't there. I'll never see him again. Oh, my father, my father!"

Myia let her mistress cry for a while, then began to bathe her swollen face.

As soon as her thoughts reached an uneasy calm, Lydia returned to the letter.

I arrived to find your father very ill and in much pain. He had been suffering for some time. Even so, he bid me welcome and wanted to hear every detail of you and the children.

He spoke of his great love for you and even managed a laugh as I told him of your dealings with Simonos. He was so proud of you for opening a shop and very confident you will succeed. He was even more pleased when I explained your plans for your own dying yards. He called in Elias to copy down some suggestions for your perusal.

I could see he would not be with us for long, so was able to make arrangements for a relief courier to take my dispatches for me. I wanted to spend these last days with Loukas. It speaks well of your father's standing in the community that the commander of the garrison allowed this.

He did not linger long. I will tell you more when I return. For now, be assured that Elias and the doctor did all that was humanly possible to make his last days comfortable.

When the pain was most intense, he called for Elias to read to him from some scrolls he had. He must have heard them many times before, because from time to time he would say some of the words aloud with Elias: "Though I walk through the valley of the shadow of death, I will fear no evil, for thou art with me." Then he would smile.

When the end finally came, he left us with an eager look on his face, almost of anticipation. What *could make a man die like that? I would not look forward to entering those dark shades of night.*

I stayed for the funeral. Loukas had made all the arrangements and had written down complete instructions. All was done as he wished. His affairs were in order. The house and slaves will be under the watchcare of the steward until such time as the business and property can be sold. Nathan Ben Kobath will be responsible for finding a suitable buyer.

Elias will be coming soon to be with you, dear Lydia. Even though he is free to go where he will, it was his wish to visit you and assist you in any way possible during my absence.

It is beginning to look as if my stay away from you will be longer than I first expected. I will send you word as I can."

The last lines of the letter spoke of his love for her, and he sent his ardent regards to the children.

Memories of her father flooded Lydia's mind as she recalled scenes from her childhood. One of her earliest memories was of his coming to her room when she was suffering from a stomach ache. She could still recall the touch of his big hands as he gently stroked her forehead and told her stories to take her mind off her misery.

Other memories of visits to the shops while holding his hand, walking behind him as he inspected the various vats of dye, sitting beside the tables as he watched the dyers stamp designs of vines and berries, palmettes, and frets with various lines on the material. She was always at his side as he instructed her in the business and was never happier than when she was wearing the tunic and headband of the workmen.

Lydia's memory journeyed on. With each recollection, fresh tears fell. Why had she ever left home? Why had she not married someone who lived in Thyatira? Had she been at home to look after her father, perhaps he would not have died.

Common sense refuted these arguments. She had left home to be with Menalcus. She could not imagine being married to anyone other than him.

Besides, death was as sure as sunset. Everyone must take that dreary and joyless journey over the inky River Styx. She did not understand at all what Menalcus had written about her father's anticipation of death.

She agreed with Menalcus. How could a man die like that? Such thoughts were foreign to her thinking.

Lydia wished she could have been there to see the sacred rites of sepulture. Menalcus and Elias would have bathed and composed the body and laid upon his mouth the ferriage-fee for Charon, who would ferry her father's body across the Styx to that shadowy land of death. The corpse would have been clad in white and laid in a wooden coffin with the personal ornaments he usually wore. There would also be vessels for fruit or oil, his drinking cup, a cake of bread, and beverage for the departed.

Menalcus would have hired a priest to offer sacrifice in her place at the temple of Cybele. Lydia did not find much comfort in the memory of that stone visage with its great lidded eyes.

Mourning friends would bring flowers and put on badges of sorrow. The following morning at daybreak the coffin would be carried by a procession of friends, followed by dignitaries and people from the city. Lydia pictured their faces in her mind. All of the workers and slaves would follow to the grave site. There were public burying grounds outside the city walls, but Lydia knew the exact spot where Loukas would be buried. It was his own plot under the huge oak right beside the grave of the mother she had never known.

After speeches extolling her father's virtues, the coffin would be lowered into a terra-cotta vault and covered with a slab of the same material. Friends would be invited to drop a handful of dirt over the vault, which would then be covered with a mound of dirt that would later be planted with ivy and roses. A memorial stele would be inscribed with his name, an effigy of his person, and a word of praise for his virtues with an epigram composed for his memory.

Thinking through the process of burial helped Lydia accept her father's death as real and final. But she could not dwell on these thoughts for long. Finally she allowed Myia to bring her a glass of warm wine and lead her to bed. Myia gave instructions to the other slaves not to disturb their mistress for any reason.

The slaves hurried to do what was expected when death visits a family. Fresh flowers were placed everywhere. Garlands were hung at each entrance. An elaborate wreath was placed on the doorway to the street with a badge of sorrow next to a large L, emblem of the house of Loukas. Passersby knew that death, their dread enemy, had visited this house.

Lydia tried not to be morose. But her pregnancy, Menalcus's absence, and the uneasiness she continued to feel about his journey, combined with the death of her father, threw her into despondency.

She fell into a troubled sleep filled with visions of laughing Myia as an oracle in a deep cave. A second being, with the head of Cybele, kept looking at Lydia. A third figure emerged with the face of the girl she and Myia had seen chained to the two men in the marketplace. In the dream, Lydia climbed into an immense tree to escape from these creatures. As soon as she was sure she was well hidden, the tree suddenly lost all of its leaves, exposing her to danger.

More figures in an undulating crowd gathered around the base of the tree. Demons came toward her from all directions. No matter how small she tried to make herself, she knew they could see her. She must hold on to the branches. Her arms ached with the effort to maintain her balance.

"Help me, please," she cried. "Someone help me!"

She extended one arm in appeal, but the moment she let go of the branch, she started falling, falling…

She opened her eyes to discover Myia was gently shaking her. Lydia was drenched with perspiration.

"You must wake up, milady. Come now, you'll make yourself sick. You must have had a bad dream. I've fixed a nice warm bath. Let me help you."

Lydia could not stop trembling. She buried her face in her hands for fear of seeing the creatures of her dream come to life. After a few moments, reality returned, and with it came the memory of the letter from Menalcus. Her father was dead.

"I'm glad Elias is coming," Myia said. "It will be good to have someone from home. He was always kind to me."

Lydia stared at her in amazement. "What are you talking about?"

Myia nodded at Menalcus's letter, still sitting on her bedside table. Lydia recalled reading that her father's servant, Elias, was on his way to Philippi.

Life changed with the arrival of Elias. The first few weeks Lydia asked the same questions over and over about Loukas and his last illness. She could not hear enough, though each interview brought on fresh weeping.

She did not know Loukas had given him enough money to establish himself as a tailor but believed he had come to help her because of his deep love for her father.

Money from the sale of Loukas's property brought a sizable fortune into Lydia's hands. Accepting the money was a moment of sadness for Lydia because it signified the end of her former life. She would never be able to visit her home again or share any of her past with her family. However, this money would make possible the further establishment of Lydia's dye yards and shop. Loukas would have been happy to know he had provided so well for his daughter.

Lydia and Elias entered into a partnership. Elias agreed to manage the shop. Whatever he earned as a tailor would be his own. As soon as the baby was born, Lydia would oversee the building and operation of the dye yards. This arrangement would allow her more time at home and still give her the satisfaction of going to the shop whenever she desired.

Elias was exactly what the shop needed. He knew materials, and he had a flair for matching the best colors and grades of material to each customer. He had a few sample chitons to show what could be done with a gather here and a fold there. All of the women of Greece wore this same basic style. It was formed from a single rectangle of material, draped and gathered into graceful folds, making this simplistic design expressive of the person who wore it.

The thin ionic chiton required an outer garment, a himation worn by both men and women, which was draped around the body. Small weights sewn into the corners made the folds hang properly and kept the garment in place.

Elias then fit the customers with a peplos. They choose the color and grade of material they liked. Most people used wool or linen for their ordinary garments. Lydia always carried a supply of material left in its natural color for the working class. The dull shades of green, gray, and brown were the most serviceable for them.

The wealthier clients, who were steadily increasing their patronage, wanted silk, cotton, linen, or a blend of silk and linen. Their taste in colors included rich purple, red, yellow, saffron, emerald, and apple green. The aristocracy and their imitators preferred pure white.

Elias went in early to open up. The morning hours were for business transactions. At noon the shutters were closed against the midday heat and Elias enjoyed a rest before resuming business again. In the afternoon people passed through, fingered the lengths of material, exclaimed over this or that color, then went home to think about what they wanted. It was not unusual for a slave to return to make a purchase for his mistress or to see the same person early the next morning, ready to order one or more garments.

Most days Lydia did not go in to the shop at all. But on her better days, she spent a few hours there to allow Elias time to do the needlework on the orders he received. She couldn't be more delighted with the way things were going.

Winter arrived in the mountains around Philippi. Shepherds' pipes could be heard as they led their flocks from the highlands to the valley. Donkeys loaded with firewood or harvested sheaves of grain walked steadily behind their drivers. There was a snap in the air, fragrant with the scent of lavender and thyme.

Lydia was going to the shop for the last time before her confinement. From this day on, her activities would be limited to the house and garden.

A few eyebrows had been raised when she first appeared as one of the merchants. Some remarks were made behind the hand as she walked by. She assumed she was the subject of much gossip in the baths. Many Greek women owned businesses in the town, but they did not attend to them in person. That was left to trusted slaves.

As time passed, however, the occupants of the other shops saw that Lydia kept to her business and did not mix in any of their daily routines. They soon found more interesting things to discuss than a busy lady who evidently was skilled in the buying and selling of cloth. She became especially well known for her unique purple material. So Lydia had a sign painted, in a lovely shade of royal purple, to hang outside her door: "SELLER OF PURPLE."

What a glorious day! The air was soft with the feel of cooler days ahead. She pulled a stool to one side of the entrance and, as gracefully as she could, sat down. The size of her stomach made all of her movements a bit awkward. She rested her arm across the bulge created by this new, restless being within her. A sharp little jab in her side brought a smile.

The children were anxiously looking forward to the new baby, and she had long ago reconciled her thoughts to its arrival.

Lydia adjusted the folds of her *apotygrna*. She no longer wore the ribbon girdle around her waist. It would soon be necessary to give up the peplos for the looser-fitting chiton.

She loved watching the people who passed by the shop. Water carriers hurried to and fro with their pitchers, often stopping to exchange gossip before filling their *hydriae*, returning home with the earthen vessel perched on shoulder or head as easily as Lydia would carry a measure of cloth from shelf to countertop.

Money changers notarized documents and certified the validity of contracts, issued checks and drafts, and charged commissions. They provided needed services to domestic merchants, bankers, importers of foreign goods, and some of the wealthier citizens who appeared before their benches. People passed on their way to artists' studios and the physician's stall. Loungers and gossips tarried in the shade. Clowns performed, while venders of ointments and sellers of amulets plied their trade.

A crowd congregating on the corner of one of the cross streets captured Lydia's attention. She wondered idly what new marvel or sleight of hand would coax coins from the pockets of the curious today. She soon grew tired of watching and pulled herself up, ready to return home

A sudden parting to the crowd revealed two men rapidly ushering a young girl down the street. It was the same trio who had approached Lydia and Myia on that long-ago day when they had made their first trip into the city.

Lydia stepped back into the shaded entrance. She watched, fascinated, as the odd trio paused about twenty feet away. A merchant of some importance in the city called out to them. She could not hear all that was being said, but enough to perceive that an appointment was made for a later meeting.

The three walked on, advancing toward Lydia's shop. She could not help but note the girl's sagging shoulders and the droop of her beautiful head. Lydia smiled encouragement to her. A brief light flickered in those black eyes, but was quickly replaced by a gaze of blazing anger.

So intense was that look that Lydia involuntarily stepped back. Her arm brushed against Elias, who had quietly stepped up beside her. He, too, looked at the young girl, his face filled with great pity. Lydia half expected him to reach out to her, but he did not move.

A sharp tug on the chain that bound her to the evil-looking man caused the girl to stumble. She opened her lips as if to speak, but a harsh command interrupted whatever might have been said.

Lydia watched until the three of them turned the corner. Elias resumed his work as if nothing had happened.

"Elias," Lydia questioned, "do you know that girl?"

"No," he said. "But I know the evil spirit that lives within her body."

"Oh, Elias," Lydia scoffed. "Next you will be telling me she is a reincarnation or something equally as mysterious."

"No," he said in all seriousness. "She is not reincarnated. But she has a spirit living within her that enables her to tell the future. Why do you think those brutes keep such a tight hold on her? She earns much money for them by telling people what is going to happen to them. Many men in this city profit from the things she reveals."

"What is so bad about that?" Lydia asked. "Of course she shouldn't be chained and bullied about. But perhaps it would be a wonderful thing to know what is going to happen in your life."

Elias stared at Lydia. "If you could know what lies ahead, would you be so pleased to hear it if it was bad news?"

A cold wind seemed to blow over Lydia. She remembered her dreams and the yearning of her heart for peace that did not come.

"No, I guess not. But all future events don't have to be bad."

"That's true. But would you destroy hope, anticipation, the joy of being a shaper of things to come? The way I see it, a person would soon put all their hope and faith into the one who could tell the future instead of trusting Yahweh, who holds the future."

A customer entered before Lydia could reply, demanding the attention of Elias.

At home that night, Lydia thought about the strange circumstances of the morning. Did she want to know the future? She knew what she wanted the future to be: the children grown and healthy, established in the courses of their lives; she and Menalcus growing old together in the comfort and security of their home; grandchildren around to keep them happy. Would the gods allow this to happen? Did Yahweh, the god of Elias, hold her future? Did he even know who she was, and if so, did he care?

I doubt that my future enters into the thinking of any god, unless it has to do with his own pleasure, she mused.

She failed to see how one person could make such a difference in the plans of any god, particularly one as powerful as Elias claimed his to be.

Lydia strolled to the doorway of the atrium. The house seemed unusually quiet. She had retired to the courtyard after dinner, expecting the children to join her for a time of play before bed. But they had not appeared. Where were the children? Where were the slaves? Then she heard the sound of laughter coming from the rear of the villa.

She passed through the kitchen, taking note that everything was neat and tidy, on into the vegetable garden with its rows of onions, lettuce, and beans. The wall around the villa provided shade from the lowering sun. There she saw the entire household gathered around Elias, sitting in the doorway of his room, which was located next to the stable keeper's small apartment. She had offered him a room in the house but he said he felt more at home with the other workers.

Krysta was leaning against the tailor's knee, with Hermanus and Diana, a kitten in her lap, sitting on the ground in front of him. Some of the slaves had pulled low stools into the shade. Others rested against one of the fruit trees or simply sat on the ground. Elias was speaking, and his audience hung on his every word. Evidently he was a master storyteller. No one noticed Lydia's approach, not even Myia.

The children had related to her, in their childish ways, some of the tales Elias told. She recalled one had been about a shepherd boy who killed a giant and then became king. She had tried to convince the children these stories were only make believe.

Well, she would listen to one of his sagas for herself. Then she could make sure Elias owned up to a vivid imagination instead of being the herald of truth the children believed him to be.

Elias was telling of a time when his people were slaves in Egypt, where they were abused and miserably mistreated. His god delivered them by killing the firstborn of the Egyptians. Then he parted the sea so his people could walk across on dry land.

She must put a stop to this! She could not have him putting foolish notions into the heads of her children or her slaves. Parting the sea, indeed!

The next day she spoke to Elias and ordered him to stop such idle tales.

"I beg your pardon, Lydia" he said. "I was not suggesting anything to your slaves. I merely wanted them to know there is a God who cares about all people, especially those who worship him. Often these slaves speak of their homeland, and they were curious about my people. I cannot tell of my people without telling them of our God, Yah-weh."

Lydia held her ground. "I'll hear no more of your god. We are born, we live, and we die. Little the gods care about what we do or what happens to us. I want no more stories of boys in lion's dens and fiery furnaces. Nothing more about servants becoming rulers in strange countries."

Elias did not argue.

Lydia began to notice a subtle change in Myia. It was not something she could put her finger on but she had never seen Myia so quiet and yet sort of expectant. Lydia observed that each time she sent Myia on an errand, Gaius made an excuse to go with her. Lydia did not object. She did not want Myia to be in danger. She was glad for the friendship that was developing between the apparently well-educated Gaius and the little cripple.

Was Myia in love? She must speak to Gaius. Surely he was merely offering the friendship of an older brother. Lydia avoided the thought that anyone in her presence might be in love when she was so lonely for Menalcus.

Whatever the cause, Myia seemed more…Lydia fumbled for a word to describe her attitude of late. Content? Yes. Serene? Perhaps. Happy? Yes, but there was more. Unable to define the new elusive quality in her friend, Lydia determined to speak to Myia about it soon.

After an especially tiring day, Myia helped Lydia bathe and then rubbed her aching back and legs with warm oil. Lydia was thankful when it was time to go to bed.

She relaxed against the cool clean sheets. "It will be good not to do anything special tomorrow. I don't know whose idea it was for everyone to have one day a week to rest and not worry about business, but it is a wonderful one."

Now that she thought about it, she recalled that it was a suggestion from Elias. He had talked her father into observing the weekly respite in their house in Thyatira. She tried to see that her household had no more duties than were absolutely necessary on her day of rest. Not every slave owner felt the same way. But she found her house ran more efficiently when her people had some relief from duty.

"Milady." Myia paused as if hesitant to continue.

"What is it, Myia?" Lydia closed her eyes. Perhaps the gods would grant her rest tonight. Maybe she would sleep until morning instead of having those terrible dreams, especially the ones about Menalcus.

"I want to talk to you about something."

Lydia sighed and opened her eyes. "Well, what is it?"

Myia picked at the towels and ointments from the bath. "I've been talking to Elias and asking him about his God, Yahweh." She hesitated and then plunged on. "I want to know more about him. Elias told me some of his people meet to worship every Sabbath—that's what he calls Saturday—out by the riverbank. The men meet in one place and the women in another. It seems his God made rules for the men to worship apart from the women. I'm not sure why. Anyway, I went last week."

Lydia said nothing but now she was wide awake.

"I want to go again. Gaius has gone too. We both want to hear more. Those people worship a God who cares about them, milady. He cares about the poor and the mistreated and—" Her voice dropped very low—"the cripples. He cares about everyone. It is all written down in their sacred writings."

"Myia, I don't care which god you worship." Lydia tried to keep the edge out of her voice. "There certainly are enough to go around. Why all the fuss?"

"I want you to go with me."

"What? Myia, I have no need of this Yahweh. I want nothing to do with him or with any of his followers. I'm surprised you would even ask."

"I really want you to go," Myia replied. "I know if you came, you would think differently about Yahweh. You could wear your hood if you didn't want to be recognized. You know I'm not very good at explaining things. I want you to hear for yourself what their writings say."

Lydia was astonished at Myia's persistence. "Why should I go out to the river to worship some unseen, unknown god? I can go to any number of beautiful temples to worship whenever I like." Lydia paused. "Though I admit I haven't gone to any of them lately."

Lydia sat up in bed. He stomach was so big she had to spread her legs apart and lean back on her hands in order to breathe. "What kind of god has no statue, no temple, no means of identity except for a handful of people, outcasts from their own country, who gather on a riverbank?"

Myia did not answer.

Lydia was getting angry, and that surprised her, which made her angrier still. She was not sure she believed in the gods she knew, so what was upsetting her about one more? Were any of the gods real? Did they exist outside of the minds of men?

"What sacrifices does this god require?" she asked. "Do you want me to give you something to sacrifice? For goodness sake, Myia. You know I would give you whatever you need, within reason. You don't need me to go along for that."

"I don't want to sacrifice. I want you to go with me. I need to know what you think."

"I'll tell you what I think. I think you have listened to one too many of Elias's stories. A god who cares about people? Gods care about gods and their own pleasure. We are lucky if we don't get in their way. And all the prayers and all the sacrifices in the world are not going to change that. That's what I think."

Such a feeling of desolation overcame Lydia as she finished speaking that she burst into tears. She had never put her feelings about the gods into words before. She probably never would have if she had not been goaded by Myia's insistence that she go to the riverbank. Oh, if only the gods had given her the peace her heart cried out for, or if she were not pregnant, or if Menalcus were here!

She gave way to her emotions, burying her face in the pillow. She wanted to rage and scream. Where were the gods when she needed them? Where was their protection when she was frightened? She searched for something to bolster her spirits. No matter how she tried, she could not convince her mind, or her heart, that those cold and frozen gods of marble heard her pleas. If they did hear, they did not care.

There was no one to care for her while Menalcus was away. She was responsible for everyone and everything, including herself. Menalcus had given Gaius special instructions regarding her care, but after all, he was just a slave. All depended upon her. All except Elias. He could take care of himself.

Myia put her arms around Lydia and gently stroked her back until the tears subsided. "It's all right. I didn't mean to make you cry. Sometimes you see through things that confuse me. You help me to understand."

Lydia blew her nose. "I'm sorry I was cross, Myia. I just don't know for sure what I think about the gods. I have to admit I'm not very satisfied with my own acts of worship. I have always assumed the problem was with me. Now, I'm not so sure. I simply don't know."

Myia fluffed her pillow and adjusted the covers. "I'll say good night. I hope you sleep well."

" I'll go this one time," Lydia said, surprising Myia as well as herself. "It will do me good to sit by the river for a while. But wake me up a little early. You know it takes me a little longer to get dressed these days. Maybe you had better have Gaius prepare a litter for me."

The next morning found the two women on their way to the Jewish meeting place. Gaius walked beside the chair as two other slaves carefully carried Lydia along. Along the way he explained to her some of the things he had learned about the group they would be joining.

"There is no synagogue in Philippi. There must be ten Jewish men in any city before formal worship services can be held. Elias brought the number in Philippi to eight. Even though there can be no orthodox synagogue service, the people meet to worship. They need fellowship with those who believe in the living God. This weekly time of worship gives strength for the days when times can be less than easy for these people who are different from all others around them."

"We will not be the only ones who are not Jews," Gaius continued. "Anyone who is interested in learning about this God and what he has to offer can come and listen. They may become believers. If they choose to believe and not become a Jew, they are called God-fearers, just as I am. Otherwise, they return to worship the gods they have always known."

Few people traveled the street that morning. The relative quiet was occasionally broken by the barking of a dog or the sound of cart wheels passing toward the city gates. Two soldiers on their way to relieve the guards at the gate marched past. Lydia groaned within at the sight of their uniforms.

She bit her lip and blinked to hold back the tears. *I'll not cry. I can't give in to every sight and sound that reminds me of Menalcus.*

Gaius led them past the gates and to the right along the embankment. Mist rose from the quietly flowing river and evaporated into the warm air above the treetops. Willow trees trailed lazy green fronds over the bank and down to the water's edge. A band of women, heads covered with hand-woven shawls, sat on the grassy slopes under one old giant tree. Now and then they lifted their faces to the heavens, but for the most part, their heads were bowed and their hands clasped in an attitude of prayer. Lydia saw no offerings of fruit or flower. How strange!

The slaves placed her chair near enough for her to hear anything that might be said, but not so close that she became part of the group. A man in dark clothes with a striped shawl over his head and a scroll under his arm stood.

"He is the reader," Myia whispered in Lydia's ear. "He reads to the group from their sacred scroll. They call it the Torah."

Lydia did not intend to listen. She had come partly to appease Myia, but mostly because she was ashamed of the way she had carried on the night before. It was the first time she had left the house since the seventh month of her pregnancy. What a beautiful spot! She must get Myia to bring her again when they could have the place to themselves.

After long prayers, the reader began. Lydia paid little attention until she heard again the words Elias had told the children. She sat very still as the reader recounted from the scroll the story of the exodus of the children of Israel from the land of Egypt. Somehow the reading of the words "Let my people go" had a more majestic, authentic ring coming from this man.

The reader paused and more prayers were offered. Lydia's thoughts raced. She recalled Myia's words of a God who cared about the poor, the hurting, and the crippled.

The man continued reading.

"And God spoke all these words saying,
I am the Lord thy God, which has brought thee out of the land of Egypt, out of the house of bondage. Thou shall have no other gods before me. Thou shall not make unto thee any graven image, or any likeness of anything that is in the heaven above, or that is in the earth beneath, or that is in the water under the earth. Thou shall not bow thyself down to them, nor serve them; for I the Lord thy God am a jealous God."

The women raised their hands, palm upward, and said, "Selah."

Lydia resolved to ask Gaius what that meant.

The group stood to sing, their voices frail and thin in the beginning, but as the song progressed, they gained in volume and in feeling. Lydia could not restrain her desire to join in. Of course, she did not know the words, but she hummed along under her breath.

Myia squeezed her hand.

After the reader left, she introduced Lydia to the women. The ladies welcomed her and invited her to come another time. They seemed very much at ease with Myia, which told Lydia her slave had been here more than a few times.

There was little conversation on the way home. Lydia had gone with the resolve to find a way to put an end to this heresy, for so she considered Elias's religion to be. Now she needed time to think about what she had heard. If she was to quell the ridiculous notion of only one god, she must plan her words carefully.

That was the excuse Lydia made to herself as she was carried to the riverbank again and again. She kept telling herself she must know more if she was to root out this superstition about a living god from Myia's mind. Every week she heard more and more about God's care and provision for his people. When she learned the land of Canaan, which this God had given to his people, was the same land of Palestine to which Menalcus had journeyed, she could not hear enough.

She was amazed at the difference in the way she felt as she left these meetings. Still filled with questions, but without the feelings of despair and hopelessness she felt after worshiping in the temple of Cybele or Isis. She had not realized how desperately hungry she was for something in which she could truly believe.

She continued to pay homage to their household god. It would be foolish to take a chance of offending such an important deity. Even then she could not escape the words of the reader: *"Thou shall have no other gods before me."* She sighed as if heavy chains bound her heart. Would she ever know the truth?

Elias did not mention Lydia's Sabbath day attendance at the meeting place. In spite of her determination to put thoughts of this new god out of her mind, Lydia kept remembering parts of what she had heard. Finally she asked Elias to explain the words to her.

She gave permission for him to resume his storytelling to members of the household with one exception. He was not to talk of freedom to the slaves. She could not risk an uprising in her own house.

As time for her delivery neared, she dared not venture out to the riverbank. But she found many excuses to be nearby when Elias told his stories in the evenings. So it was that she first heard the names of Abraham, Isaac, and Jacob. She head of David, the beloved king and the glory that was once that of Israel.

One day Elias told of the expectation of his people for a return to that glory when Yahweh would send a Messiah to come and once again make Israel a great nation. Lydia rejected this outright. Rome was in control of the world. No son of an unknown god could fight such power; not even the one called Messiah.

The first pain caught her in mid-stride as if a giant hand gathered all the muscles in her lower back and squeezed. It passed as quickly as it came. Lydia knew it was near the time for her baby to be born. She would be glad to be rid of the extra weight she was carrying around, walking straddle legged, her distended belly leading the way.

Old Elizabeth had kept a close eye on Lydia for the past several days. Oh—another contraction! Lydia caught her breath. This time it seemed as if every muscle in her lower body tensed and finally released.

She allowed a servant to help her climb the stairs. Myia took charge, leading Lydia to a chair and sending for Elizabeth. An undercurrent of hurry and controlled excitement put the entire household on the alert. Lydia could hear the scurry of bare feet outside the door as the children were taken to another part of the house, where they would be entertained for a few hours.

Quick hands disrobed Lydia and slipped a short birthing gown over her head.

If only it could be over, Lydia thought, dreading the next few hours with all her being. She was not brave when it came to pain, and this was such a tearing, wrenching pain. She remembered the birth of the other three children. It had taken forever, or that was how it felt to her.

Myia massaged her back. Each contraction came a little harder and lasted a little longer. Elizabeth placed a large mat on the floor and covered it with sheets of white cotton, in the middle of which she placed the birthing stool, the center cut away so that when Lydia sat down the baby could drop through the hole and she could catch it.

Elizabeth spread her equipment close to the chair: a sharp knife for cutting the umbilical cord, pads of soft linen, warm oil and wine for disinfecting. Lydia turned her head away from a pair of metal forceps lying on the mat. She prayed her baby would not need help in making its entrance into the world.

Where is Menalcus? I want him here. Why isn't he here? Did he plan it this way?

Such were the childish and unreasonable thoughts racing through Lydia's head. Menalcus had not even known she was pregnant when he left. But she didn't care. Childbirth wasn't fair! All a man had to do was romp in the bed. The woman had all the work from there on, including being sick and awkward and then giving her body over to this horrendous pain. The least Menalcus could do was to be here.

Oh! This time the pain was so intense Lydia arched her back and raised off the chair.

"By this time tomorrow, the gods willing, it will be over, " she panted.

"Yes, milady." Myia smoothed her brow. "It won't last forever. The baby will come soon."

A fresh wave of contractions brought a low moan from her lips. Myia and another of the attending slaves supported her on each side as she was seated on the birthing stool. She grasped the support rod across the front of the stool and leaned her head on both hands, but only for a second. The pain returned with a viciousness that seemed to engulf her entire being.

"Push, mistress, push!" Elizabeth directed.

"I can't! I can't! Please don't press on me."

Lydia was gasping for air, swinging her head from side to side. She wanted to scream. She had heard all the tales of women who birthed babies without uttering a sound. Well, let them! She wanted to scream! She did not have a body anymore. All she had was a huge, unending mountain of pain tearing her apart. She couldn't even stop the pain long enough to draw breath.

She struggled to get up. She had to get up. She couldn't breathe! If Elizabeth would only stop pressing for one minute so she could take a deep breath, she could endure; but Elizabeth wouldn't stop.

Why didn't Myia make her stop? Didn't she realize her back was breaking in two? She was conscious of the moans that seemed to come from her, but she did not have the strength to stop them. The moans carried the pain in waves that rode the sound to a crescendo before crashing against her back, like ocean waves crashing against a rocky shore.

Lydia could stand no more. She was no longer a human being. She was pain beyond bearing.

"Here it comes!" Elizabeth knelt.

One final surge and it was over. The pain left. Lydia felt the sharp burn as the knife severed the cord that tied her to the bloody red bundle Elizabeth placed across her knees.

"It's a boy!" Elizabeth beamed proudly.

She held the warm, flailing bundle up for Lydia to see, then handed him to another slave to bathe. A thin cry, which soon grew to a healthy wail, drew a sigh of relief from everyone.

With Myia's help Elizabeth got Lydia to bed. After the midwife's final administrations, the new mother made no protest when a warm sponge bath was given and a clean nightgown pulled over her head. It was over! She had won! The pain was gone!

"Another boy." Lydia smiled at the women. "Menalcus will be so happy. His name will be Darius. Don't you like the sound of that?"

Lydia felt like the winner of the marathon games. Why didn't someone hand her a laurel wreath for her brow? She had borne a son!

A nursemaid brought the newly bathed and oiled baby and laid him by his mother's side. Lydia unwrapped the blanket enough to check all the fingers and toes. Satisfied that all was well, she held Darius close and shut her eyes. All she wanted to do was sleep.

Although her body was exhausted, her mind raced from one thought to another. A kaleidoscope of scenes passed behind her eyes. Her wedding day, her father racing beside her on his horse, the stone face of Cybele, the little group of women bowed in prayer beside the river.

In her mind's eye, she saw Menalcus floating by. A long green frond from the willow tree trailed over his body. The river slowed its journey to the sea, but just as she reached for her husband, he floated away, and she was left holding a new baby. She tried to hold the infant in one arm and race to catch Menalcus with the other, but her legs wouldn't move. The beautiful girl from the street laughed and laughed, and then her face became that of Myia. Myia was trying to steal her baby!

"There, milady," Myia said quietly. "Let me have the wee one so you can rest. He'll be right here in his basket. The nurse will bring him again after you wake up."

Myia was trying to pry the baby from the vise-like grip of Lydia's arms. Lydia opened her eyes and glanced at Myia and then at the baby. She looked around the room. Everything to do with the birthing had been cleared away. It took several moments before Lydia could separate the dream from reality.

She began to tremble. Elizabeth immediately covered her with blankets and rubbed her hands while Myia smoothed sweet oil into her temples.

It was not unusual for new mothers to develop a fever after delivery. But it was not fever that caused Lydia to tremble. It was the dream of Menalcus floating away from her. She kept telling herself it was only a dream, but she shivered just the same.

Lydia grew increasingly anxious as time passed with no word from Menalcus. Where was he? Perhaps he was on his way home and wanted to surprise her.

Toward the evening of a chilly day, the porter admitted the commander of the garrison and sent word to advise Lydia of her caller.

Lydia descended the stairs, her heart in her throat. She had difficulty speaking. "What's wrong? Where is my husband?"

The commander did not appear surprised at her failure to extend the usual courtesies. "Won't you be seated?" The soldier's swarthy face was pale beneath the day's growth of beard.

"Please tell me." Lydia felt sick. She was trembling from head to foot. She glanced at Myia, who waited nearby.

The commander took Lydia's hand in his own. "I'm afraid I have some bad news, madam. Your husband has been in an accident. He was badly hurt. He has lost one of his legs."

Lydia clung to his hand. "You said *hurt*. Not dead?"

"No, madam. He was alive at the time of this report. But he is very ill. His horse stepped into a hole and fell on his leg, crushing the bones. The leg was badly shattered. There was no choice but to amputate. I am sorry to be the bearer of such news."

Lydia could not stop shaking. Every nerve in her body vibrated. Her teeth chattered. Menalcus was alive! What did anything else matter?

Myia hurried to her side and knelt at her feet. She held Lydia's hands to try to still their trembling.

Lydia motioned weakly for the commander to be seated. She must hear all that he could tell her.

"He endured much pain before the surgery," the commander said. "Such an operation is bad enough in one of our hospitals. This one had to be done in the field. He could not have endured being transported. Loss of blood and loss of his leg have been a severe shock to his system, physically and mentally. There is still danger of infection. Still, he is strong and full of courage. He will be on his way home as soon as he is well enough to travel."

"Where did this happen?" Lydia asked.

"The dispatch said the accident occurred about two days' journey from Jerusalem. He had delivered his dispatches to the garrison and was on his way to the coast to take passage to his home in Antioch when the accident happened. Apparently it is a desolate desert area."

"How will he manage? Who will care for him? What if he is sick on the way? How long will it take?" Lydia could hear her voice becoming louder and more shrill, but she could not seem to control it. She dared not begin to think what life would be like without Menalcus.

She could not sit here. She must do something. But when she tried to stand, her legs would not support her. As she sank back into the chair, she asked, as calmly as she could, "When will he be home?"

"The army will put him on the first available ship." The commander gazed at Lydia as if to gauge how much truth he thought she could take. "There is a great deal of troop movement right now. Troops get top priority. Winter has set in, and soon bad storms will keep our ships in port. If your husband is well enough to move within the next week or so, he should be home soon. Otherwise, it may be some time."

"I want Menalcus home so I can care for him. I can't sit here wondering if he will be home in thirty days or six months!"

"If you want faster action, you will have to do it with your own resources. But that would take money—lots of it."

"Could I send some of my people to bring him home?"

"That might be the best thing, provided you have the means for getting them there and back."

"I can get the money," Lydia said. "Will you assist me in making arrangements?"

"Of course. As a matter of fact, a ship will be leaving Neapolis in two days, bound for Troas. From there your men would have to seek the best route to follow. The ships travel only by day and they hug the shore this time of year."

Lydia saw the commander look at her several times as if he was about to say something, but then he would look away as if uncertain how to proceed. She wished he would get to the point.

"Do you have a man you can trust completely? He will need to carry a large sum of money to buy passage and food, plus more for the return trip. He will also encounter other expenses."

"You mean for bribes?"

The commander nodded his head without comment.

"Yes," Lydia said. "I can send Gaius. And someone to help him."

"May I suggest you send this man alone? He can travel faster that way. I will prepare papers for him to carry so he will not be mistaken for a fugitive."

"Suppose Gaius arrives too late to get a return ship?"

"Menalcus can by carried overland on the caravan route from Antioch if a caravan is coming this way. They could at least get as far as Troas. From there, your man might find a ship's captain willing to risk crossing the Aegean at this time of year. But even if he is so lucky, the man will charge a fortune."

"Gaius is loyal to Menalcus. He is more than a slave and he knows it. If anyone can bring my husband home, he is the one I would trust above all others. I will send him to you immediately for instructions and I will secure the money he will need by the time he is ready. Oh, please, please hurry and I thank you with all of my heart."

The commander took his leave with the promise to have papers ready for Gaius as soon as he was prepared to leave.

Alone in her room that night, Lydia removed the bracelet from her arm and pressed the hidden clasp. The two remaining diamonds winked at her as if taking advantage of the moment to display their hidden fire.

She lifted one of the stones from its hidden niche and placed it carefully in a small box lined with a rich purple fabric. The bracelet was replaced in its customary position. Not even Myia would know it had been moved.

Her first impulse was to dispatch a runner to Simonos's home, since he was the one who had purchased her first diamond when she opened the shop. On second thought she decided to wait for morning. She must appear calm and casual. If the jewel merchant suspected any of the desperation she was feeling, he would surely not give her full value for the stone. How horrible to think she might jeopardize Menalcus's safety simply because she was in too much of a hurry.

Was she wise in sending Gaius? He had commented many times about how he missed his homeland to the north. She would be entrusting him with enough money to escape if he wished.

The names and faces of her other slaves passed through her mind. Some could be trusted, but they would not know how to function in a foreign place. They might not be able to make all the arrangements necessary for her to see Menalcus again. She must trust Gaius.

She refused to dwell on how ill Menalcus might be. Instead she focused on getting him home, where she could tend him with her own hands. She would nurse him back to health.

When Myia appeared with Gaius close behind, Lydia told him the details of what must be done. Gaius listened attentively, then left to prepare for the task ahead.

Lydia filled the days following Gaius's departure with a flurry of activity, dividing her energies between time with the children and time at the shop.

She took renewed interest in the children's lessons, especially with Diana, instructing her in the management of the household. Hermanus and Krysta played together when they were not absorbed in some project of their own.

Baby Darius grew more rosy cheeked and plump, and soon threatened to replace Krysta as the darling of the servants. Gifts of terra-cotta rattles, hoops with bells and rings, and an assortment of balls were deposited with his nursemaid for the entertainment of "the wee one," as he became known.

With Elias's help, Lydia hired workers to begin building the dye works according to the plans her father had sent. She hoped to make the project profitable enough to pay wages to those willing to work. She had as many slaves as she could manage. How she longed for the day Menalcus would return to help her with some of the decisions facing her.

She refused to admit the possibility that he might never return or that he might not be able to function as he had in the past.

To her surprise, the only time she felt fully re-laxed was on the days she met with the women by the river. She was not sure if it was the challenge to her thinking or the comfort of being with friends. But she had come to consider these women her friends. She no longer stayed on the outer fringes of the group, but gladly joined it.

Each time she heard the reading from the sacred scrolls, she came home full of questions for Elias that taxed his knowledge and understanding. The more he explained, the more she wanted to know.

Today the lesson had been taken from Isaiah, the Jews' most beloved prophet.

See my servant shall prosper; he shall be highly exalted. Yet many shall be amazed when they see him—yes, even far off nations and their kings; they shall stand dumbfounded, speechless in his presence. For they shall see and understand what they have been told before. They shall see my Servant beaten and bloodied, so disfigured one would scarcely know it was a person standing there. So shall he cleanse many nations.

"Who was the writer talking about, Elias?" Lydia asked on the way home. "Who is this servant, and why must he suffer so?"

"I am not sure. I am not a rabbi."

"How can a servant be highly exalted if he is to be beaten and bloodied?" Lydia persisted.

"I don't know. I can't explain it."

Lydia continued to probe. "Do you think the writer got mixed up? I seem to recall something in the Psalms about the Messiah coming to rule as God's own regent and to make his enemies bow low before him. I was reminded of the story you told about King David. Now, there was a king! I can see how one like him could be a Messiah. I wonder who this Servant is who will be trampled on by everyone."

Elias put both hands over his ears. "I don't know! I don't think any of those men in the group know either. I heard them asking the same questions. We need someone to help us understand. Maybe a rabbi will come soon and we can ask him. I will pray for someone to come and help us."

CHAPTER 7

Palestine

Menalcus sat under the canopy of his tent, gazing at the dust cloud on the horizon. His eyes squinted against the glare of the desert sun, sweat rolling inexorably from his temples. It made little rivers down the brown parchment of his face and disappeared into his newly grown beard.

His injury had relieved him of the necessity of wearing a uniform and the rule of being clean shaven. Day after endless day spent in the confines of this little patch of shade had robbed him of the incentive to move, much less shave.

A fly buzzed around his head. At first he swatted at it with an impatient wave of his hand, but even that became too much of an effort. He glanced at the position of the sun. Two more hours until noon.

Already the heat was dancing upward in shimmering waves from the bare rocks and sand of this barren place. Surely this trackless waste must be one side of hell.

Except for the bandaged stump of his leg, Menalcus was clothed only in a short-sleeved tunic that hung unconfined over a loincloth. A loose-fitting toga lay across a nearby chair. Sometimes, when the fever hit, he had to wrap its folds around him in an attempt to draw its warmth into his chill-ridden body.

A slight breeze brought a momentary respite from the stifling, oppressive heat. He held his arm out from his body in order to feel its welcome relief over as much of his skin as possible. He raised himself slightly in the chair where the orderly had placed him. Now the air could reach his back and dry, at least temporarily, the sweat running down his back.

His tunic clung to his body in sodden blotches. He reached around to pull it free from his back. The effort brought a fresh outpouring of perspiration, which dripped from his elbows to the hard-packed sand beside his chair. He was weak from the movement. Even the hair on his head seemed to sweat. He thought he could surely distinguish every water-laden strand.

Everything around him radiated heat. The sand, the metal on the uniforms of the soldiers passing by on their way to their various duties, the very breeze was a movement of hot air. The sparse furnishings of his tent seemed to retain the heat and throw it out again.

Menalcus sank back against his chair in weary submission. He pictured the fountain in the court-yard at home. The thought crossed his mind that he might never see his home again. He tried to imagine all that would be going on there, but the unbearable heat seemed to serve as a clamp on his brain.

Menalcus became absorbed in watching the beads of perspiration form along his arms. To pass the time, he wagered with himself how long it would take the droplets to become large enough to break and roll down his arm.

Again and again he brought the water bottle to his parched lips. He longed to pour the precious liquid over his head and let it cascade over his body. He wanted to lie in it and let it soak into every pore of his stinking, sweat-washed body. But he knew he could not. He would not even have his own bottle of drinking water if it were not for his wound.

A line of weary soldiers passed by on their way to the midday siesta. Even Rome could not fight the intense heat of noon on the desert. Perhaps they had taken lessons from the lizards and desert rats that withdrew into their holes or the shade of a rock to wait out the hottest hours when nothing moved.

Little sound was heard except the cries of the wounded in the hospital tent. They called for water or, in feverish delirium, cried out for relief from the pain of their shattered bodies. The stench was sometimes unbearable in spite of all efforts to keep the hospital area clean.

The lethargy created by the mounting feverishness of his wound and the sweltering discomfort of the soaring temperature caused Menalcus to close his eyes for longer and longer periods of time. He nodded once or twice and finally lolled his head against the back of his chair and gave in to fitful sleep.

He dreamed of the rhythmic splash of water in the fountain back home. Lydia emerged from the doorway, dressed in a gown of gossamer blue that outlined her full figure. She ran to take his hand. They raced toward the ocean. He was gasping for breath, his leg giving way beneath him. Then their feet hit the surf, sending sprays of deliciously cold water into the air. With cries of delight and shouts of laughter, they fell into the surf and lay there, letting the cool waves wash over them again and again.

The water and its coolness had just covered his head when he woke up to the dreaded reoccurrence of the fever-induced chills that racked his body from time to time. An orderly was bathing his face and his temples with water.

Surely the fire in his head would soon cease; or maybe it would build and build until it exploded. Even that would be a relief. It was his leg that was injured; why was the pain in his head?

Menalcus looked up into the face of the orderly. Strange how his eyes were the exact shade of blue as the dress Lydia wore in his dream.

"Lydia!"

He could hear himself screaming and knew he should stop, but he could not. Then he fainted.

CHAPTER 8

Philippi

Almost a year had gone by and Lydia had still received no word from Gaius. She dispatched servants to the garrison every day to ask the commander if he knew anything. Every traveler coming from the east was questioned to see if he had heard or seen anyone answering to the description of Gaius or Menalcus.

Lydia did not realize how tense she had become until the sound of the bell at the outer gate caused her to jump. The porter arrived at her workroom door to announce a visitor. Lydia looked past his shoulder. With a glad cry she rushed past him to embrace the tall man striding toward her.

"Dr. Luke! Oh, Dr. Luke. Where did you come from?"

Luke held Lydia at arm's length. "I take it you are glad to see me?" he teased.

Lydia dissolved into tears. She tried to stop crying, but the harder she tried, the more she cried.

When the sobs subsided, Lydia led Luke to the garden and seated him near the fountain. What was there about his presence that alleviated so much of the pressure she was feeling? She had not seen him in more than ten years and had known him for only a few day at that time. Yet she felt that if anyone could help her bring Menalcus home, it would be this man. Surely he would know what to do.

Lydia paced as she poured out the story of Menalcus's injury and the steps she had taken to bring him home.

"I'm so worried," she concluded. "Surely by now Gaius would have sent word. Do you think he would abandon Menalcus? He did have a lot of money for a slave. What could be taking so long for us to receive some message?"

"Winter is coming." Luke said. "I doubt if Gaius would be able to get a ship at this time of year. And to travel overland would be a long, arduous journey, even without caring for an invalid. Gaius will have to match his speed with Menalcus's strength. I'm sure you will get word as soon as Gaius finds a caravan or a courier coming this way."

Lydia knew all of this, but she desperately need to hear something definite.

"I'll tell you what," said Luke. "I will dispatch some inquiries tomorrow and see what I can find out."

Tears stung Lydia's eyelids again, but her heart felt amazingly lighter. It was such a relief to have someone take charge.

"I have talked only about myself and my problems," she said. "I hardly let you in the door before I dumped all my worries into your lap. How about you? What are you doing in Philippi? What happened after we left you in Troas?"

Luke chuckled. "Which question shall I answer first?"

"Just start at the beginning and tell me all that you have been doing."

"Do you remember Silvanus, the man Menalcus and I met in Troas?"

Lydia nodded. She recalled the name in a vague sort of way.

"After I discovered, much to my sorrow, that your ship had already sailed, I went on a search of Silvanus. I was intrigued with how earnestly he spoke of his friend Paul. He sincerely believed this man was especially called of God to take the gospel to the world. I wanted to meet him."

"What do you mean by *gospel*?" Lydia interrupted.

"The word *gospel* means good news. The good news I am talking about is that God loves us so much he sent his son to suffer and die for our sins so that we might have forgiveness. He paid the penalty for all the wrongs we have done so that we can have a right relationship with God."

Without waiting for her comment, Luke proceeded to recount his adventures. "My curiosity was raised so I arranged to go with him to meet Paul. It turned out Silvanus was not only a traveling companion of Paul but also serves him as a secretary. Paul has problems with his eyes from time to time."

"Did you meet this man?"

"Oh, yes. And I am so glad I did. Lydia, you must meet him. Your life will never be the same."

"I have a feeling it will never be the same regardless of whom I meet," Lydia replied.

She invited Luke to stay the night in her home.

"I'd love to," he said. "But I'm not traveling alone. I have two friends back at the tavern."

"Let me guess—Paul and Silvanus."

Luke laughed. "Yes. And Paul is ill. He may need my services during the night."

"I'm sorry to hear that," Lydia said. "So, what brought you to Philippi?"

"That's another story," Luke said, perching on the edge of the chair. "Paul was trying to go up into the Turkish province of Asia. That failed, so we headed north into Bithynia, but we could not make the necessary arrangements there either. Winter was coming so we headed back to Troas, thinking it would be a good place to wait for spring. At least we could support ourselves there. Paul is a tentmaker and people always need my services. Silvanus is a scribe and stays busy wherever he goes.

"One night a few weeks ago, Paul had a vision. He dreamed a man was calling from Macedonia, saying, 'Come over and help us.' He seemed to be standing with outstretched arms. Around him and behind him were other arms reaching out and voices calling, 'Help us!'

Lydia's mouth fell open as she remembered her own dreams and her aching arms. Did the words of the oracle and the slave girl who told fortunes have any bearing on what she was hearing? She said nothing for fear Luke would think her demented, but she shivered just the same.

Luke continued with his account. "Paul felt that God was using this vision to tell him to come to this area. We made immediate arrangements, and here we are. Unfortunately Paul fell ill at Samothrace and is still suffering."

Lydia remembered asking Elias for an explanation of what was read at the riverbank. She recalled his saying, *I don't know the answers. I will pray to Yahweh to send us someone to help us understand.*

Lydia introduced Luke to all of the children. He greeted each one as important, especially

260 · Acts Chapter 16

Hermanus. Baby Darius was properly held, inspected, and marveled over.

"What a wonderful family you have. Menalcus must be very proud. And you, Lydia." Luke took her hand. "You are even more beautiful than your children. I am not sure Menalcus deserves all this good fortune."

Lydia accepted his compliments with a happy smile. It was so good to have him here! She did not have to put up a façade with him. She knew instinctively that her deepest thoughts and innermost feelings would be safe with him.

"Flattery will get you an invitation to talk about yourself to your heart's content. I want to hear all about every minute since we left Troas."

Luke struck a modest pose and then assumed the stance of a grand orator. This brought peals of laughter from Lydia and all the household who had gathered around to meet this stranger.

Elias arrived to discuss with Lydia the affairs of the shop, as he often did. Lydia invited Luke and him to join her for dinner.

After they had finished their meal of fish and fresh vegetables garnished with onions and olives, and their drinking cups were replenished, Lydia asked Luke to tell them more about Paul.

"There's so much to tell. I may not finish it all in one night."

"Then you had better get started."

Luke laughed. "Paul is from Tarsus of Cilicia, near Antioch in Syria. He is a Jew but also a citizen of Rome."

"That must have cost him a fortune," Lydia interposed.

"Or perhaps he was rewarded for extraordinary service in battle," Elias commented.

"You are both wrong. Paul's father was a Roman citizen. So Paul, or Saul as he is known to the Jews, is a citizen by birth. However, he takes great pride in his Jewish heritage. He can preach to the Jews from his own background and to the Romans from their understanding. He is fluent in Greek and several other languages."

" What does he preach?" Elias asked.

"That God sent his son into the world in the form of a man named Jesus Christ. This man was beaten and put to death on a cross near Jerusalem. Paul is convinced, as I am, that Jesus Christ rose from the grave on the third day after his burial, as predicted in Holy Scripture. He is alive and with God the Father right now!"

"Next you'll be telling us this Jesus actually talks to Paul." Lydia could not keep the skepticism out of her voice.

"Well, yes—he did."

Lydia could not believe her ears. What nonsense! Gods didn't talk to mortals. She started to object. Surely Luke was more stable than to believe such tales. Then she recalled one of the stories Elias had told the children. God talked to a man named Abraham and to their prophet Isaiah.

She glanced at Elias and was struck by the intensity with which he listened.

"Let me explain," Luke said in response to Lydia's expression of doubt. "Paul is a well-educated man. He left Tarsus when his parents died and traveled to Jerusalem, where he studied under the great teachers and rabbis in the temple. He spent some time in the university in Alexandria.

"Paul loved the God of his forefathers and wanted nothing more than to spend his life in God's service. Because of his wealth and his lineage, he was a member of a sect call the Pharisees."

A frown crossed Lydia's forehead.

Luke anticipated her question. "The Pharisees are a strict group of Jews who believe you must adhere to every minute detail of their law. Their rabbis and scribes have spent much time writing out how the laws God gave to their leader, Moses, are to be interpreted. Paul was such a zealous worker in the temple that he became a member of the Sanhedrin."

"What's a Sanhedrin?" Lydia wanted to know.

"That is the ruling body of our worship," Elias said. "It is made up of the high priest and seventy-two other members, most of whom are Pharisees. It is much like the senate of early Greece. They make decisions about Jewish law and can pronounce judgment, even capital punishment in cases of extreme violations. But they cannot execute the sentence without the consent of Rome. That saves the Roman government a lot of time and unnecessary hassle since most of the problems of the Jewish population have to do with religious matters."

"Have you ever been before the Sanhedrin, Elias?" Lydia asked. She suddenly realized how little she really knew about the man who was her business partner, friend, and advisor.

"No, milady. The Sanhedrin only has power in the province of Judea, which is in Jerusalem. However, I'm sure their influence can come to bear even here, if they feel a matter is important enough."

"Unfortunately, you are right, Elias," Luke said. "Fanatical Jews from Jerusalem have hounded Paul in every place he has preached."

"What is Paul preaching that is so terrible?" Lydia asked. "If he is a member of this senate or Sanhedrin or whatever it's called, why is he in trouble?"

"About seventeen years ago," Luke explained, "there was a young teacher from Nazareth going about a little area called Palestine. He was reported by his disciples to be the Messiah, the promised son of God."

Elias shook his head. "There have been many of those. Each one has proved to be false. They have caused much trouble and bloodshed for my people."

"True," Luke said. "And I'm sure this is what the religious leaders thought about this young man." He paused.

Lydia and Elias motioned for him to continue.

"The Sanhedrin manipulated the Roman prefect to give the order to crucify this man. Jesus was put to death like a common criminal. On the third day after his death, he rose from the grave. He was seen by hundreds of people during the next several days. He ate and talked with his disciples and then they saw him ascend into heaven. He truly is the son of God and he lives today. He *is* Messiah!"

Elias paced, clasping and unclasping his hands. "Do you really believe this man is the one we have been looking for so long?"

"I do. Paul has persuaded me out of the Scriptures that he can be no other."

"How does Paul know for sure? If he was a member of the Sanhedrin, wasn't he one of those who caused Jesus to be killed?

"No. Paul was not in Jerusalem at that time. But when he did become active in the temple, there was no one more zealous in trying to quench this new belief. Paul calls himself a Pharisee of the Pharisees, and he really tried to keep people from following the teachings of Jesus. He wanted them to keep the Jewish law at all costs.

"You see, after the resurrection of Jesus from the dead, many people remembered the things he said and the miracles he performed. They came to believe he is the Messiah. So they started meeting together to worship and pray. A group of disciples followed him about for three years. They met with these new believers and shared what they had seen and heard Jesus teach. One of their greatest spokesmen, Peter, preached one sermon and over three thousand people believed!

"It didn't take long for the religious leaders to get annoyed with these people because they began to question some of the policies the rabbis were enforcing. The laws of Moses had been made such a burden the people could not bear them. They were afraid this new group would stir up trouble with Rome. So Paul tried to stamp out these people.

"At that time, he used his Hebrew name, Saul. One day he was on his way to a town north of Jerusalem called Damascus. His express purpose was to put some of these new believers in jail or take them in chains back to Jerusalem for trial. That's when it happened."

"What happened?" Lydia asked.

"Paul was riding along with his guards from the temple police when all of a sudden, he was blinded by a brilliant light. They all fell to the ground. The guards heard a voice but saw no one.

"This voice spoke to Saul and identified himself as the one Saul was persecuting. Saul realized in that moment that by persecuting the believers, he had been persecuting the Lord of glory himself.

"God revealed to Saul that he was to be his special messenger to all people, to tell them of his love and his offer of forgiveness. Saul was overwhelmed! He had been so wrong. He had been fighting against God instead of for him. He was in great distress over what he had done. At the same time, in great joy and gladness he had learned the truth. Saul professed his belief that Jesus is indeed the Christ, the anointed one of God. He was baptized immediately.

"He was so awed by what this new understanding meant, he went into the desert for three years. He had to search the Scriptures for himself to learn how God had fulfilled his promise to send a Messiah.

"When Paul returned from these years of study, he was filled with the mighty power of the Holy Spirit of God to preach his message. He has given his life to telling all who will listen of his experience and what he has learned.

"Needless to say, he lost his position in the Sanhedrin and also his wealth. Everything he owned was confiscated. He now uses his trade as a tentmaker to support himself. Because he would be speaking to people from many countries, he began to use his Greek name, Paul."

"And are you one of these believers?" Lydia asked.

Luke looked at her with such joy and love on his face she could not help but believe him when he said, "Oh, yes. I have never believed anything so strongly in my entire life. I have personally experienced God's forgiveness through his son, Jesus Christ."

Elias stopped in front of Luke. "I must see this Paul and talk to him. Where is he? "

Luke put his arm around Elias's shoulder. "He is staying at the inn with Silvanus and me. Every now and then he has a bout of fever that completely saps his energy. If you can be patient until the Sabbath Day, he will surely be in the synagogue service."

"We have no synagogue here. But we meet every Sabbath right outside the city walls, by the river. It is quiet there and we are not disturbed."

"Then we will be there. You will come, too, won't you, Lydia?"

"I wouldn't miss it for the world," she replied. She could not explain the sense of excitement she was feeling.

That morning she had been so worried. Now she felt as if her world would soon be put to rights again.

"I'm so glad you came," she told him as they said good night. "I couldn't have needed you more than I do right now!"

Sabbath morning found the little band of worshipers in a ferment of excitement. They had received word of the visitor from Jerusalem. How their hearts yearned at the thought of that beautiful city! They all longed to be able to go there to worship in that sacred temple one time before they died.

Lydia, Myia, and Elias were as excited as any of the regular worshipers. After listening to Luke, how could they not want to meet this Saul, or Paul as he was now called?

Lydia remembered the experience of the oracle she had heard in the cave at Samothrace. Was Paul's vision similar to that? Did the gods actually give messages to mortals? Were they given in the form of dreams? If so, what was the meaning of her own heart's cry? Why had her dreams been mentioned in her encounter with the oracle and with the girl chained by those two men?

She shook her head. She was making too much of the strange story Luke related about Paul's vision. It was merely a coincidence. Still, she had to admit she had never been satisfied with the worship of her gods. Perhaps she would hear something today to help her know the truth.

The leader stood with hands raised as a psalm of praise was chanted. The reader read from the sacred scroll about the giving of the law to Moses and then read a passage from the Psalms.

"Oh, how few believe it! Who will listen? To whom will God reveal his saving power? In God's eyes he was like a tender green shoot, sprouting from a root in dry and fertile ground. In our eyes there was no attractiveness at all, nothing to make us want him. We despised him and rejected him—a man of sorrows, acquainted with bitterest grief. We turned our backs on him and looked the other way when he went by. He was despised and we didn't care. Yet it was our grief he bore, our sorrows that weighed him down. And we thought his troubles were a punishment from God, for his own sins!

"He was chastised that we might have peace; he was lashed and we were healed! We are the ones who strayed away like sheep. We, who left God's path to follow our own. Yet God laid on him the guilt and sins of everyone of us.

"He was oppressed and he was afflicted; yet he never said a word. He was brought as a lamb to the slaughter; and as a sheep before his shearers is dumb, so he stood silent before the ones condemning him. From prison and trial they led him away to his death. But who among the people of that day

realized it was their sins that he was dying for— that he was suffering their punishment?

"He was buried like a criminal in a rich man's grave; but he had done no wrong; and had never spoken an evil word. Yet it was the Lord's good plan to bruise him and fill him with grief.

"But when his soul was made an offering for sin, then he shall have a multitude of children, many heirs. He shall live again and God's program shall prosper in his hands. When he sees all that is accomplished by the anguish of his soul, he shall be satisfied; and because of what he has experienced, my righteous Servant shall make many to be counted righteous before God, for he shall bear all their sins.

"Therefore I will give him the honors of one who is mighty and great, because he has poured out his soul unto death. He was counted as a sinner and he bore the sins of many, and he pled with God for sinners."

When the reading was finished, the scroll was handed to a man who was asked to speak. He stood between the two groups of worshipers so that all might hear.

So this was Paul. Lydia was a bit disappointed. She had built up an image of a man much like, if not larger, than Luke. But Paul was short and growing slightly bald. A short pepper-and-salt beard framed thin lips under a beak of a nose. Viewed from the side, Lydia saw a very ordinary man, with a slight stoop to his shoulders. A scar showed white just above the right temple.

Then Paul raised his head to speak and Lydia began to understand a little of the intensity of this man. Warm brown eyes reflected interest, love, and great gentleness. Once he began to speak, she forgot his looks entirely.

He began by reciting a history of God's dealings with the people of Israel. "Men of Israel," he began, "and you who fear God, listen! The God who chose our fathers and made the people great during their stay in Egypt, with an uplifted arm he led them out. For forty years he bore with them in the wilderness. He gave them land for their inheritance and after that he gave them judges and Samuel the prophet. Then they asked for a king and God gave them Saul, the son of Kish, a man of the tribe of Benjamin. And when he removed him, he raised up David to be their king; of whom he testified, 'I have found in David, the son of Jesse, a man after my heart, who will do all my will.'

"Of this man's posterity God has brought to Israel a Savior, Jesus, as he promised. Before the Savior's coming, John preached a baptism of repentance to all the people of Israel. As John was finishing his course, he said, 'I am not he. No, but after me, one is coming, the sandals of whose feet I am not worthy to untie.'

"Brethren, sons of the family of Abraham, and those who fear God, to us has been sent the message of this salvation. Those who live in Jerusalem and their rulers, because they did not recognize him nor understand the sayings of the prophets which are read every Sabbath, fulfilled these Scriptures by condemning him. Though they could not charge him with anything deserving death, they asked Pilate to have him killed. When all was fulfilled that was written of him, they took him down from the tree and laid him in a tomb. But God raised him from the dead; and for many days he appeared to those who came up with him from Galilee to Jerusalem, who are now his witnesses to the people.

"And we bring you the good news that what God promised to our fathers, this he has fulfilled to us his children by raising Jesus. Be it known unto you, therefore, men and brethren, that through this man is preached unto you the forgiveness of sins; and by him all that believe are justified from all things, from which you could not be freed by the law of Moses. Beware, therefore, lest there come upon you what is said in the prophets: 'Behold you scoffers, and wonder and perish: for I do a deed in your days, a deed you will never believe, if one declares it unto you.'"

When Paul had finished speaking, the people sat as if mesmerized. Then a few stood and began to speak. Soon an excited babble of voices filled the air. Could this be true? Had Messiah come? Was the one the psalmist wrote about be this same Jesus? Dared they believe it?

Lydia glanced at Elias. He was rocking back and forth on his heels, his hands clasped in an attitude of prayer, his face lifted toward the sky. Great tears rolled down his weathered face. It was clear Elias believed Paul's message.

No one seemed to want to leave. Never had there been such excitement! For hundreds of years their faithful forefathers had looked for Messiah. Thousands of young women had pondered in their hearts the possibility of being the mother of the son of God. Now they were hearing it had come to pass. Could they believe it?

Paul answered as many questions as were asked, always referring them back to the Holy Scriptures they had heard over and over again. Nothing could compare with the sweetness of knowing that God remembered them.

Many asked to hear the story of Paul's conversion experience in his own words. He readily shared, recounting the story of his trip to Damascus to punish those who followed Jesus. They shook their heads in amazement as he told of his experience while on the road and the resulting orders from the Lord to take his message to the Gentiles.

The people looked at one another to see how their neighbors had received this last bit of information. They obviously wanted to believe, but this was certainly a strange story. How could they be sure? Wasn't Messiah to come to the Jews?

Two or three of the older men drew Paul aside, then held up their hands for silence.

"We must hear more of this," one said. "Our brother Saul has agreed to speak to us again on next Sabbath. In the meantime, if you would know more, he will be speaking in the agora each day. We will pray for God's guidance in this matter."

Lydia glanced across the water and was surprised at the lengthening shadows. It was well past time for her to return home. She wanted to speak to Paul. There were so many questions she wanted to ask. The men were still surrounding him. There would be no opportunity today.

Luke fell in step with Lydia. "This is the most wonderful news of all the ages, something worth giving your life for." He looked into her eyes. "What did you think of Paul?"

A commotion up ahead stopped her from replying. The men around Paul parted, revealing that he was conversing with the two men and the slave girl who told fortunes.

Paul made as if to pass, but the girl followed him, crying out in a guttural voice that didn't seem to belong to her, "These men are the servants of the most high God, and they have come to tell you how to have your sins forgiven."

Lydia winced as the evil-looking man gave the chain around the girl's wrist a vicious yank. Paul turned his gaze fully upon the man, his eyes blazing with anger. Lydia could not hear what was said, but the trio stood aside until they had all passed.

Lydia saw the girl's head droop as if in great despair. She was startled at the look of pure hatred on the face of the two men who controlled their helpless victim.

As Lydia and Myia took their places the next Sabbath Day, Lydia noted several new faces among the men, faces that looked very stern. An undercurrent of expectation filled the air.

When it was time for Paul to address the congregation, one of the visitors whispered to the man sitting next to him. This man looked around, then rose to his feet. "Sir," he stated, addressing Paul, "we accept with joy your declaration to us that Messiah has come. Our brothers from Jerusalem have told us that many thousands of Jews there believe. We also accept your statement that you want to share this message with the Gentiles." He hesitated and looked at the man sitting next to him. A frown and nod urged him to continue. "Should not Gentile believers also abide by the laws of Moses and our traditions and customs?"

Lydia held her breath. If God's forgiveness depended on keeping Jewish customs, that would leave her out. How could she abide by laws and traditions she did not know?

Paul looked steadily at the man who had raised the question. His gaze took in the man seated next to the one who had spoken. A flicker of recognition crossed Paul's face.

"My brethren." Paul raised both hands for emphasis. "This question was taken up before the church in Jerusalem. While we were faithful to the heavenly calling to take the gospel to the farthest corners of the earth and thus preached in Iconium, Derbe, Perga, and other cities on our way to Antioch, other brethren from Jerusalem began to teach these new Gentile believers that unless they adhered to our ancient Jewish custom of circumcision, they could not be saved.

"These brethren followed us everywhere we preached, stirring up the citizens against us until we sometimes had to depart from the cities at the risk of our lives. Finally some of the believers at

Antioch accompanied us to Jerusalem to talk to the apostles who had been with Jesus and the elders of the church to settle this question.

"We met with the church leaders—all the apostles and elders were present—and we reported everything that God had been doing through our ministry. Some of the men of the sect of the Pharisees, as I was, stated their conviction the same as our brother here has suggested."

Several listeners nodded in agreement.

"This was such an important issue," Paul continued, "that more than one meeting was necessary. Long discussions were held. Of all people I certainly know how hard it is to give up the convictions you have embraced your entire life.

"When everyone finished speaking and was given ample opportunity to speak their opinions, we gathered once more. The apostle Peter voiced the conviction that the Holy Spirit had been given to the Gentiles as well as to the Jewish people. The conclusion of the matter was the realization that God had made no distinction between us.

"The Gentile believers have cleansed their hearts by faith in the Son of God. It is not necessary to put a yoke upon the necks of his followers that neither our fathers nor we have been able to bear.

"James, the leader of the church in Jerusalem, gave us letters to Antioch to show the believers there.

In fact, that is how I met Silvanus, and he has been my faithful companion ever since. You can imagine the great rejoicing among those to whom I preached the grace of God through Jesus Christ when they received this news."

When Paul finished speaking of this matter, he proceeded to preach more of the teachings of the Lord Jesus. He began by telling the story of a Jewish leader who visited Jesus one evening. Jesus told this man that one cannot enter the kingdom unless he is born again.

Lydia's attention was distracted by some of the visitors from Jerusalem. They were not sitting together in a group but mixed in with the regular worshipers. Every now and then one would lean over and speak to the one sitting beside him. An uneasy stir was soon evident in the group. She was struck by the dark scowls on the faces of these men. What a contrast to the peaceful looks on Silvanus's and Luke's countenances.

Paul continued his sermon, apparently oblivious to the discord. "'Born again?' Nicodemus said. 'I am an old man. How can a man enter into his mother's womb a second time and be born again?'

"Jesus explained that we are born of our human mothers in a physical sense. To become God's child we must be born of Him. Our spirit is made alive by God's own Holy Spirit. We take on new inner life in our heart and spirit. We begin again, fresh and new, like a baby. Just as our human parents taught us to walk and talk, so our heavenly Father must teach us to walk and talk in His ways. It is a new life. Our hearts are 'born again.'"

Lydia's attention was so captured by what Paul was saying, she forgot everything else around her. These words seemed to be spoken to her as surely as if she were the only person present.

"How can one be 'born again,' as you say?" someone from the front asked Paul.

"It is very simple," he answered. "And yet not something to be entered into lightly. The cost may be very heavy, because as with all new beginnings, it means a change in your life. For many of you, it means giving up all of your false gods because God is the only true god. He is a living god, not made with any man's hands."

"Tell us how to get his new life," a man asked.

"God sent his son, Jesus, into the world for this very purpose. To be born again you must believe that Jesus is God's son. He died as the perfect sacrifice for our sins and took the punishment that each of us deserve. Because he was faithful in this task, God raised him from the dead. He lives today to be our great High Priest before God. His Holy Spirit will come to live in your heart the moment you admit that your are a sinner and believe Jesus died for you and confess this with your lips. Jesus said he came to seek and to save those who are lost. Confess your sins and be baptized to show that you accept this great gift from God!"

Paul continued to preach but Lydia heard no more. These words had been spoken for her hearing. The words of the oracle and the young fortune teller came back to her mind. The thoughts of her dreams and struggles seemed like a heavy, tangled mass from which she hopelessly struggled to escape. She definitely was one who was lost. And Jesus had found her!

Now she understood why her acts of worship did not satisfy the longing of her heart. The gods she worshiped were only figures carved of stone, the product of men's longing for something to worship. She need make no more sacrifices to appease some unknown deity that could do nothing to change her understanding or her actions.

"This is what you need in your life!" The words sounded so clearly in her heart she looked around, amazed that others did not hear them.

Tears of joy slid down her cheeks as she bowed her head. "Thank you, Lord Jesus, for loving me," she whispered. "I ask you to be my God. I don't understand much about you, but I know I have been needing you all of my life. I need you to fill the empty place in my heart and satisfy the longing of my being. I have been searching such a long time."

She could not explain the peace and relief that flooded over her mind. It was as if a strong, powerful hand took all the twisted strands of her thinking and slowly blended them into a beautiful pattern.

God had been working all along to help her understand. Elias related the stories of Yahweh and his care for his people. Myia had insisted that Lydia go to the river to hear the reading of the Torah. All the words she heard but did not understand began to take on meaning. And then Luke's testimony, followed by the coming of Paul to tell her the words she needed to hear. Even her dreams seemed to have been an expression of her longing for God's presence.

When Paul finished his sermon and asked people to accept Jesus Christ as their Savior and Lord and be baptized, Lydia forgot that she was a woman and should wait for the men to make the first move. She made her way to where Paul stood. Elias was there before her. She was not surprised to see Myia, along with several members of her household, stand beside her.

Luke and Silvanus walked down to a sandy place along the bank of the river. Silvanus continued out until the water was almost to his waist. Paul stood at the edge of the stream, assisting them one by one into the water, where Silvanus received them.

Luke helped them as they emerged onto dry land once again.

The men were baptized first. They removed their long outer garments and girded their tunics up between their legs and tucked the hems under their belts. The women laid their outer robes aside and shortened their peplos by blousing the tops out over the waistbands.

As each person came to Silvanus, he asked them if they truly believed Jesus Christ was God's only begotten Son and that he died, was buried, and rose again. When this was affirmed, he raised his face to heaven and said, "I baptize you in the name of the Father, the Son, and the Holy Spirit."

Lydia noticed the refreshing shock of the water as it flowed around her waist. She felt the firm grip of Silvanus as he held her clasped hands in front and placed his other hand under her head. As he pronounced the words of baptism, he laid her back until the water flowed freely over her head. Quickly he raised her to a standing position again.

"This baptism is a symbol to show Christ's death, burial, and resurrection. Your old life is now buried with him and you are raised to walk a new kind of life."

Lydia thought of nothing except the wonderful sense of release she felt.

Luke helped her to dry ground and wrapped his long cloak around her shoulders. Tears of joy stood in his eyes. This was the day for which he had been praying. Lydia was not only a convert who would add much to the cause of Christ; she was a special friend, the wife of Menalcus.

The new converts were gladly received by the rest of the small congregation. Even many who were still undecided about Paul's message seemed happy for them. But one or two walked away, deep in conversation with the visitors from Jerusalem.

Lydia hurried home to make sure all would be in readiness when her guests arrived. She had persuaded Luke to ask Paul and Silvanus to make her house their headquarters while they were in Philippi. He had hesitated until Lydia informed him she had witnessed both him and Silvanus discreetly scratching the flea bites on their legs and various other places.

"You are most generous, dear lady," Luke said with a laugh.

"No," she said, "as a matter of fact, I am being very selfish. Having you in the house will keep my mind off all the things that might be happening to Menalcus."

He nodded, his face immediately serious.

"I have to admit I have another motive," she added. "Just think of all I am going to learn! You have no idea how many questions I want to ask!"

"Then we will come, with pleasure." Luke bowed.

The days that followed were filled with activity. Each day Paul and Silvanus went to the agora to talk to all who would listen. Luke used the quiet morning hours to go over papers he was collecting. He spent hours writing to friends in distant places, telling them the story of Christ and his followers. In addition, he kept a journal of each day's happenings as he traveled with Paul.

Luke insisted that Paul rest at least two hours during the middle of the day. Lydia heartily concurred. She could see the toll his heavy schedule was taking on the man.

Guests began to arrive as soon as the evening meal was over. They wanted to hear more of Paul's exhortations. They also wanted the moral support of others who had accepted this new way of life.

Sometimes Silvanus delivered the main message and Paul answered questions. Slowly but surely, the basis for a church was being formed.

Silvanus spent long hours with Elias, setting forth the duties of elders and other leaders in the church. Christianity was not an easy idea to grasp. It could not be understood in one day.

Lydia tried to absorb all she could. She couldn't wait to tell Menalcus all she had heard and experienced.

Would he understand? Would he be happy that she was a believer? She recalled another time when she had gone out on her own without consulting him. The opening of the shop had caused quite a turmoil in the beginning. This was much more vital than a mere business transaction.

When she was not listening or asking questions, she was praying Menalcus would soon be home and that he, too, would become a believer. Each night she reminded her guests and Elias to pray to that end.

One afternoon Lydia came downstairs and found the three men deep in conversation. They told her that Paul was being followed everywhere he went by the young fortune teller and her owners. Just at the crucial point in Paul's discourse, she would cry out in a loud voice, "These men are servants of God and they have come to tell you how to have your sins forgiven!"

The idol-worshiping citizens murmured and turn away. They did not want to hear of any god except the ones they already worshiped. It did not take Paul long to realize the girl was demon possessed. The demon would do anything to ruin the presentation of the gospel to these people. Of course, what the demon said was true, but it was voiced in such a way as to cause those who heard to turn their backs on Paul and his message.

"So today," Luke explained to Lydia, "Paul had enough. He commanded the demon to come out of the girl in the name of Jesus Christ. That's when the trouble began."

"What trouble?" Lydia asked. "I should think she would be overjoyed to be herself again,"

"That's just the problem," Luke said.

A loud, insistent pounding on the outer door interrupted them. The porter opened the door and ushered in the fortune teller. She was out of breath and clearly frightened. An ugly bruise on the side of her face and a long tear in her peplos gave further indication of distress.

"Please help me. Don't let them in. Please!" She turned to Paul. "It's your fault. You must help me!"

Lydia took the girl gently by the arm. "No one will hurt you here. Tell us what's wrong so we can help you."

It took several minutes before they could calm the distraught girl enough to learn what had happened. Slowly her story unfolded. When Paul commanded the demon to leave the girl, her ability to make money for her masters ended. This so infuriated the two men that they beat the girl and threatened her with even more bodily harm.

"How did you get away from them?" Lydia asked.

"Some men came to the door to see my masters. They did not want me to hear what was being said, so they unchained me and locked me in my room. I was able to climb out a window."

"How did you know to come here?" Luke seemed more disturbed by this than Lydia thought necessary.

"The men who came to see my masters gave them money to find out where these two men were staying." She gestured toward Paul and Silvanus. "I overheard their directions and raced here, hoping I would arrive before my masters did. I have nowhere else to hide. Please help me!"

Lydia put her arm around the frightened girl while they discussed what to do. She learned the girl's name was Janis.

"Don't be afraid." She spoke as she would to one of her children. "We'll do our best to straighten this out so that you won't have to go back to them again. In the meantime, go with Myia and get cleaned up and into some other clothes."

While she was still talking to the girl, Lydia heard noises coming from the street. They became increasingly louder.

The porter appeared at her elbow in a state of great agitation. "Milady, there's an ugly mob outside in the street. They are demanding the presence of the two gentlemen."

Before anyone could reply, Elias came rushing in from the rear of the villa. "There's a mob coming. Those men from Jerusalem and those two scalawags with that troublesome girl have stirred up the whole town against Paul and Silvanus."

Paul and Silvanus stood. "I've been expecting this," Paul said. "Our beloved brethren have been looking for an opportunity to cause trouble. Looks like I have given them their chance."

Lydia rushed Myia and Janis out of sight while Luke helped Paul and Silvanus with their cloaks. The pounding on the door became even more persistent. The angry calls grew in volume and intensity.

Once everyone else was safely behind her, Lydia went to the door. She motioned the porter to slide the grate so she could see what was going on. Her heart almost stopped when she found herself face to face with the bully who had beaten Janis. His black eyes blazed hatred and anger so intense it was like a physical blow.

Lydia slammed the cover to the grate shut. She could not stop shaking. She ran back to where the others stood.

Luke urged Paul to hurry. For a moment it looked as if the two men would follow Elias, but Paul stood his ground and stared at the front door.

"I have done nothing but proclaim the gospel of my Lord and Savior. If I sneak away without explanation, who will believe our message? Besides, I have seen mobs in action before. If I leave they will take their spite out on this house. That is no way to repay the love and hospitality Lydia has shown us."

In spite of their protests Paul remained determined.

Lydia said nothing. She felt she should urge him to stay. Perhaps all of the servants banded together would be enough to protect him. But she was frightened. In all of her life she had never been truly afraid, at least not in the breath-stopping way she was now. But then, she had never come face to face with evil before. And this evil was directed at her!

Her mind raced. What would happen if the door gave way? What had she gotten into by inviting Luke and these men to her home? What would Menalcus say if she allowed their house to be destroyed by brawlers from the street? What if they harmed her or the children? Why didn't Paul and Silvanus just go?

Luke offered to go with them but Paul motioned for him to stay. "We may have more need of you here. If we do not return soon, speak encouragement to the believers. And pray for us."

The moment Paul and Silvanus stepped into the street, the mob grabbed them and dragged before the magistrates in the agora.

The crowd raised such a clamor the judges had to shout for silence.

"These Jews are corrupting our city," one of the two owners of the slave girl roared. "They are teaching the people to do things that are against Roman law!"

"We have noticed Paul and Silvanus in the agora," one of the judges said, "and the people who stop to listen to them to them speak about their God. But of what importance is one more god in a city already full of gods and goddesses?"

"But the charge of stirring up folks against Roman rule is another matter," a second judge pointed out. "We have no wish to incur the wrath of the empire."

Paul asked to be heard but the noise of the mob only increased.

Finally, the judges ordered Paul and Silvanus to be stripped and beaten. Paul gnashed his teeth as the lash was applied until blood flowed down his back.

Then he and Sylvanus were thrown into prison. The jailer was charged to guard them at the peril of his own life.

Paul and Silvanus were taken into the inner dungeon, where their feet were clamped into stocks. The air was fetid and smelled of urine and moldy straw.

Their supper failed to arrive, but it was just as well. Neither Paul nor Silvanus felt like eating. They talked about their situation. Paul was incensed that they had not been allowed to speak in their own defense. This was not the first time he had been in trouble for preaching in the name of Jesus. Given the sinfulness of men, it probably would not be the last.

He and Silvanus took turns repeating Scripture to each other and rejoicing over the truths revealed in them. In spite of the burning of their lacerated flesh, a measure of peace calmed their spirits. Silvanus prayed and then lifted his clear tenor voice in a hymn to the Lord. Although he would never be renowned for his singing voice, Paul joined in.

The other prisoners roused from their fitful sleep. Annoyed at first, they began marveling at the kind of men who would sing in prison.

"One of them has a right nice voice," Paul heard one prisoner say.

"Yeah," replied another. "Might as well listen. We don't have anything else to do today."

"Or tomorrow," came a reply. "Or the day after that or the day after that."

Following the departure of the mob, the silence of the street was deafening. Lydia had to sit down in the nearest chair. She was shaking so badly her legs would not support her. She felt relief that Paul and Silvanus were gone but at the same time ashamed for feeling that way. She was glad nothing had happened to her or to this house; glad those awful people were no longer screaming and yelling outside her door.

I'm completely selfish. I shouldn't be thinking of myself. What will happen to Paul and Silvanus? That evil man certainly intended to get even with them. I should be on my knees praying for them and all I want to do is fall on my knees and thank God that crowd is gone.

Luke was pacing, his face reflecting misery. "I should have gone with them."

"What good could you have done?" Lydia asked. She was relieved he was still here. She longed for Menalcus. He would know what to do. In fact, if he had been here, the whole incident probably would not have happened.

She turned to speak to Elias but he was gone. He must have followed the mob. He would find a way to help the two men if he could.

Luke stopped pacing. "Paul said, 'Encourage the believers. And pray for us.' Come, Lydia. You and I are believers. We need to encourage each other. The Lord knows I certainly need it. Let's send word to the other believers and pray for Paul and Silvanus and for ourselves."

The prospect of something positive to do calmed Lydia. She sent runners to summon the believers to her house. Elias returned to report the news of the beating and imprisonment. Lydia was devastated. Somehow she felt responsible.

Luke was outraged. "They beat and imprisoned them without a hearing? Wait until those judges find out both men are Roman citizens. They had no right to act as they did. Just like Pilate when Jesus was tried. Scared of the mob!"

"Scared for their jobs, more likely," Elias commented.

Luke reached for his medicine bag. "I'll go and dress their backs. At least I can do that much."

"It's no use," Elias said. "You won't be allowed near them. The judges threatened the jailer with his life if they get away. You can be sure he will take no chances with letting them have visitors."

Lydia did not expect the believers to come that night. Certainly they would be afraid of being arrested. The Jewish believers knew what it was to be persecuted for their beliefs. This would be just one more in a long list of such abuses.

Much to her surprise, not only did the regular worshipers come, but some who had been undecided about Paul's message came also.

"We must pray for them," one said.

"And for each other," chimed in another.

"And for those judges," suggested yet another. "The good people of our city would not do such a thing. It was the rabble who have nothing to do but cause trouble. I'll wager half of them never heard of Paul or Silvanus before."

After the last person had gone home, Lydia went to bed but not to sleep. She tried to think only of the things Paul had taught them, but the eyes of the man at the door, the sight of Janis's bruised face, and the memory of her own cowardice kept intruding. An involuntary shiver convulsed her body. She pulled the coverlet high around her neck.

Why wasn't she as confident as those who had come to the prayer meeting that night? After she was baptized she had been sure she could face anything, yet now, only a few days later, she felt as if she had betrayed her friends. Where was the strength the Lord had promised?

Paul had shown no fear, even while being dragged down the street. Neither had Silvanus. Why was she so fearful?

She was not used to dealing with fear. She had never had reason to experience the paralyzing clutch of terror that dried her throat and turned her bones into jelly. This was a different kind of fear from her childhood memories of bad dreams because she had always had Loukas to reassure her.

It seemed to Lydia she had embarked on a great battle, and what she had experienced today was just the beginning. Vague shapes and faces seemed to appear just beyond her line of vision. She did not want to see them. She was afraid, and her fear made her more tired than she had ever been. Still, she could not sleep.

Where was Menalcus? It had been months since she received the word that he had been injured and she'd sent Gaius to fetch him. Luke's inquires revealed that Gaius had arrived at the port of Caesarea. He immediately journeyed by horseback to the camp on the other side of the mountain range, where he found Menalcus. A courier had included the message with his army dispatch that the homeward journey would begin as soon as Menalcus gained some strength.

Lydia read all kinds of meanings into that brief statement. Why hadn't Gaius said straight out how things were? The fact that he did not gave rise to her suspicion that something was terribly wrong.

She pulled her pillow down and wrapped her arms around it, trying to pretend she was clasping Menalcus in her arms.

"O God," she prayed, "please let Menalcus get home. Help Gaius have the strength and knowledge to know what to do. Let Menalcus know I love him. Bless Paul and Silvanus and help them tonight. Thank you for Luke and Elias. Please, Lord, help me to be faithful to you and to guide this household."

The more Lydia talked with her heavenly Father, the more she was able to relax. Peace returned to her heart and she drifted off to sleep.

Sometime during the night she was awakened by a faint rumbling in the distance. Was it a thunderstorm? She became aware that her bed was shaking beneath her. A jar on the bedside table teetered and crashed to the floor.

She threw back the covers and ran to the window. There was no sign of a storm. The rumbling sound had ceased. A torch in the courtyard below showed Elias up and about. He was soon joined by other servants.

Lydia ran to the next room, where Darius was sleeping soundly, the edge of his blanket clutched in one hand. A quick look in the other bedrooms assured her the children were asleep, except for Hermanus.

He joined her in the hall, eyes round with excitement. "What is it Mama? What's happening?"

"I don't know, Son."

Lydia allowed him to follow her downstairs. She met Elias and several others in the kitchen. A broken *oenchoe* and a *hydra* lay in pieces on the floor. A thin line of wine trickled across the floor and disappeared near the stove. Luke came in from the atrium.

"What happened, Elias?" Lydia tried to make her voice calm. The servants were agitated enough without her adding to their concern.

"One of the men who has lived here a long time seems to think there has been an earthquake somewhere nearby," Elias said. "He claims it happened before, many years ago."

"An earthquake?" Lydia had heard dire stories of such happenings from her father. "What should we do?"

"There doesn't seem to be any damage except for a few things that were broken. The house is secure. No one was hurt. Unless it happens again, I suggest we all go back to bed." Elias motioned for the servants to leave.

They looked to Lydia for her instructions. She nodded for them to obey.

"Come, Hermanus," Luke said to the boy. "How about you spending the rest of the night in the men's quarters with me? Tomorrow you can help me look around and make sure all is well."

Lydia gave Luke a grateful look. He had not missed the way Hermanus clung to her hand and must understand how hard it would be for Hermanus to return to his room and be alone in the dark, not knowing what might happen next.

Hermanus looked at his mother. At her smile of approval, he exchanged his grip on her fingers for the warm clasp of Luke's big hand.

Upstairs, it seemed Lydia had no sooner closed her eyes than she heard men's voices coming from below. One of them sounded like Paul. But that couldn't be. He was in jail!

Then she heard Elias and Luke. Someone was running up the stairs.

She was half out of bed when Hermanus burst through the door. "Mama! Mama! Paul and Silvanus are downstairs! You've got to come!"

Lydia tried to quiet her son so he would not wake the rest of the children, but it was too late. Darius cried out in protest from his room. The girls were calling back and forth and demanding to know what was going on.

As soon as peace was restored, Lydia descended the stairs and found the house astir with excitement. Sure enough, there stood Paul and Silvanus! She greeted each with a warm embrace.

"I know you've probably already told Luke and Elias how you got here, but I want to hear it too. So start at the beginning and tell it all."

She noticed several of the servants standing by the door, trying to hear what happened. "I can see there will be no work done until we all hear this story." She gave orders for all the servants to gather in the portico so they could hear for themselves.

Paul recounted how they had been beaten and taken to jail. "About midnight there was a great earthquake."

His listeners affirmed that they had felt it during the night.

"The prison was shaken to its foundations," Paul went on. "I thought we would choke to death in the dust. All the doors flew open and the chains of every prisoner fell off. Our stocks did as well. It was surely the work of the Lord God!

"The poor jailer was so certain that all the prisoners had escaped, he started to cut his own throat. I yelled at him to stop. Not one man tried to escape. That was a miracle in itself!

"The frightened jailer fell down in front of us as if we were gods. He led us out of the dungeon and into his own living quarters. He asked many questions. We spent the next few hours telling him and his family the good news from the Lord and how Jesus died on the cross that all men might have their sins forgiven. We encouraged him to believe the Lord Jesus and be saved. When they learned of the resurrection of the Lord, a happier household would be hard to find.

"The jailer tended to our backs and put some healing salve on our stripes. At the first sign of daybreak, we baptized them. We returned to his house and his wife prepared us a sumptuous breakfast. You should have seen how they rejoiced!

"We had no sooner finished our meal when two officers came to the jailer's door and told him the judges had ordered that we be set free. I decided it was time those judges learned a lesson. They had publicly beat us without a trial and jailed us. And now they wanted us to leave secretly? Not on your life! I sent the officers back to tell the judges to come themselves and release us. I wanted the people of the town to see that we were innocent."

Luke chuckled. "I would like to have seen their faces when they learned you were Roman citizens!"

"So would I," Paul replied. "Silvanus and I went back to our cell in the dungeon because we did not want to make trouble for the jailer. Before long the judges came and begged us to leave. Not just the jail, mind you, but the city as well. They want us gone!"

"But you aren't going, are you?" Lydia asked.

"Yes, dear Lydia," Paul replied. "I have taught here for many days now. There is no point in my staying here repeating myself when others have never heard the good news. We will be leaving for Thessalonica as soon as young Timothy arrives."

Lydia could see that protests would not change his mind. They must make good use of whatever time was left.

She sent the servants back to their duties. Two runners were dispatched to notify all believers to come to hear Paul one more time before his departure.

CHAPTER 9

Neapolis

Luke left immediately for Neapolis, where he planned to meet Timothy and take him straight to Philippi. If his ship was on schedule, they could leave Philippi in two days' time.

He did not have long to wait. The boat from Samothrace was docking just as he rode into town. By the time he arranged for the care of his horse and hired another for Timothy's use, he spotted his young friend helping a gaunt, half-starved man through customs. Luke looked more closely, Could this shadow of a man be Gaius? It was! If this was Gaius, where was Menalcus? Even as he came near he saw Gaius struggle to follow the officials moving toward a man being carried on a litter by two strong black men.

Luke pushed through the noisy throng of hawkers and onlookers, past people leaving the ship with their bundles and boxes. He waved at Timothy and motioned for him to follow as attention was directed towards the invalid on the stretcher. His blood ran cold when he recognized the man's face.

"Menalcus? Is it you?" Luke struggled to reconcile this thin pretense of a man with the person he remembered.

Menalcus opened his eyes, trying to focus against the bright sun. He moistened parched lips to speak, but no words came.

Luke put his hand on Menalcus's cheek and confirmed that he was burning with fever. He must get him out of this sun without delay. He weighed the possibility of getting him to Philippi and decided against it. Unless he could do something to reduce the fever, Menalcus might never reach Lydia.

He asked the customs officer for the location of the nearest hospital, only to find it was filled to capacity He was directed to a nearby inn where a room was prepared to receive Menalcus. The apothecary was across the street and a local doctor would be there to assist Luke.

By the time all these arrangements were made, Luke had determined that Gaius and Timothy should ride to Philippi and bring Lydia to Neapolis with all possible speed. He prayed that nothing would delay their return.

Luke urged the litter carriers to be as gentle as possible, even though Menalcus was unconscious again. As the group strode down the busy road, Luke made a mental list of the supplies he would need. He was angry with himself for not bringing his own medical bag.

At the inn, the two men transferred Menalcus to the bed as easily as if they were lifting a child. Luke asked them to stay, thinking he might need their strong arms again.

When Menalcus regained consciousness, he was delirious. He accused Luke of all manner of things, spoke of the terrible heat of the desert, relived the journey with all its rigors, and often cried out in pain. Many times he called for Lydia, not understanding why she didn't come when he needed her so.

Luke allowed him to talk. All that day he worked over the emaciated body, fighting to bring his temperature down. He did not like the odor coming from the stump of that leg. He opened the bandages and was dismayed at what he saw. Red streaks were already starting into the upper thigh. The poison could spread through his entire system in no time.

A quick consultation with the innkeeper secured the extra bandages and strips needed for making a tourniquet. A table was brought into the room. When the doctor from the hospital arrived, Luke wasted no time in showing him Menalcus' leg and explaining what he knew of the circumstances, which was very limited indeed.

Both men understood the danger of operating while the patient was running such a high fever, but there seemed to be little choice. Further amputation was necessary, and quick, if there was to be any chance of survival for Menalcus.

A slave brought the necessary instruments from the hospital, and the two men set to work at once, thankful that Menalcus was unconscious.

Luke sat by the patient all night, trying to bring down the fever. He prayed that God would be merciful and help where his own knowledge and skill ended. He prayed for Lydia. He would have to prepare her before she could be allowed to see her husband.

"Go before me, Lord God," he prayed. "Prepare her heart. Give her strength. Give me wisdom. Help me. Help us all."

CHAPTER 10

Philippi

Lydia was sitting in her workroom going over some accounts from the shop when she heard a commotion in the courtyard. She looked up and saw Gaius standing in the doorway. She had been watching for his return for so long that, for a moment, her mind had trouble accepting what her eyes were seeing.

"Oh, Gaius! You're back!" She jumped out of her seat, raced to him, and threw her arms around his thin shoulders. "Oh, I knew if anyone could bring Menalcus home, you would." Still dazed, she looked behind him, expecting to see her husband. "Where is he?"

"Milady..." Tears softened Gaius's eyes. "Menalcus is in Neapolis. He is gravely ill. So much so that he could travel no further. Luke is taking him to the hospital there. He sent me to fetch you."

Lydia felt the blood drain from her face. Menalcus was within a day's ride! She blocked his last words from her mind. His illness could not be serious. She would not let it be.

Her legs suddenly gave way. She would have fallen if Gaius had not caught her.

"I should have found a better way to tell you, but there's no time." Tears streamed down the slave's face.

Myia nearly fainted when she saw Gaius. But since her duty was to her mistress, she immediately ordered a servant to bring some wine for Lydia.

"I'll be all right," Lydia assured her. "Thank God, Menalcus is almost home. We must get him here quickly and make him well. Myia, bring my cloak. Hurry! I will dress myself for riding."

As Myia left to do her bidding, Lydia turned to Gaius and steeled herself to ask the question she'd been trying to push to the back of her mind. "Just how ill is he? Is he simply very weak and tired?" She took a deep breath in a feeble attempt to gain some measure of courage. "You must tell me if he—" She could not finish the sentence.

"I know he will fight to get well when he sees you, milady," Gaius answered.

Lydia gave him a searching look, then started up the stairs to prepare for her journey.

When she flew out her front door, she saw Paul and Elias waiting there with Gaius.

"Traveling in the dark will be extremely hazardous," Paul cautioned her. "Would you consider waiting until dawn to depart? It will do Menalcus no good if some misfortune should overtake you. Besides, Gaius needs rest and food."

Lydia fought the nearly uncontrollable urge to rush past him and jump on her horse and race all the way to Neapolis by herself. She recognized the good sense of Paul's thinking, but she did not want good sense. She wanted Menalcus! After long days of watching and waiting, her husband was within hours of her touch. She would soon be able to hold him in her arms. How could she wait another minute?

However, one look at Gaius settled the matter. He was indeed at the point of collapse. She could tell he had not spared himself or the horse in order to bring her Luke's message. She also knew he would return with her if she but asked.

With many thanks and tears of gratitude, she embraced Gaius. She ordered Myia to see that he was fed and cared for immediately. She did not fail to note how quickly Myia took his hand. Was it really his weakness that caused him to lean on her shoulders as they withdrew?

CHAPTER 11

Neapolis

L uke heard the quick beat of horses' hooves on the street outside the inn. A glance at his patient showed Menalcus still sleeping under the effects of the drug he had administered. Luke hurried out and lifted a weary Lydia from her horse. Gaius gathered up the reins and led the animals away for a good rubdown and some hay.

Lydia's face was radiant. "Where is he?" she asked, tears of joy streaming down her face. "It's been such a long time. Please take me to him right away. I can't wait another minute!"

Luke took her hands in his and led her to a small bench near the doorway. "Lydia, please sit down for a minute. I need to talk to you. Menalcus is asleep. I promise to take you to him as soon as he stirs."

Lydia sat perfectly still on the bench beside him. Even her breathing seemed to stop.

Luke wanted to spare her as much as possible. He knew he could not gloss over the truth, but he was not sure how Lydia would receive what he had to say.

"Lydia, Menalcus is terribly ill. Last night we had to amputate more of his leg in order to keep the poison of the infection from spreading throughout his body. He is consumed with fever. If he does regain consciousness, he might not recognize you." Luke squeezed her trembling hands. "Lydia," he said softly, "we are doing all we can to save him."

"We?" The tiny word came out in barely a whisper.

"Yes. A doctor from the hospital has been helping me. He just left for a few hours of sleep. He will return tonight to keep vigil."

"I want to see my husband," she said, her voice growing stronger. "Don't ask me to wait any longer. I must see him for myself."

"All right. He should be waking soon. But don't be dismayed if he doesn't say anything."

Lydia stepped into the room that was permeated with an unpleasant odor. She had to stop a moment to pull herself together. She was almost afraid to approach the bed.

What a small body lay under the covers—hardly that of her big, strong Menalcus. Had Luke put her in the wrong room? Even as these thoughts surged through her mind, she crept softly toward the still form.

When she saw the thin cheeks under a full growth of beard, sunken eyes still closed, and the pinched nostrils, she dropped to her knees, choking back a sob. "Oh, God," she moaned, "please let him live. Just let him live!"

Lydia placed her hand over the bony fingers that had once caressed her face. She touched his beautiful hair, now heavily streaked with gray and matted with perspiration and grime. She would bathe him herself once she had him at home.

Menalcus seemed to sense her presence. He stirred restlessly, then turned his head toward Lydia. She wanted to kiss his parched lips and those poor, thin cheeks, but she dared not. She would wait until he opened his eyes.

She would not let him die. Her love was strong enough for both of them. She would care for him day and night. She would make him well.

Menalcus stirred again. This time his eyes opened wide and then just as quickly closed. He did not seem to see her at all. Lydia laid her face on his hand. It was so hot! His skin felt like dry parchment.

She kissed his fingers one by one. She tried to say his name, but no sound would come from her throat.

After a time she raised her head. When she did, she found those marvelous brown eyes staring at her in disbelief.

"Menalcus! My darling!" She kissed him again and again.

The lucid moment soon passed. Menalcus lapsed into delirium. Disjointed words, joined with long sighs and groans, were intermingled with calling her name.

When Menalcus lapsed into unconsciousness again, Luke came in. He introduced Lydia to his young friend Timothy. She barely nodded. Her mind was on the restless figure on the bed.

"Give me something to do," she begged Luke. "Isn't there some way to break that fever?"

Luke handed her a cool towel with instructions to continually bathe his forehead. The instant she laid the cloth on his head it absorbed the heat from his skin. Nevertheless, she hoped it provided some comfort to the fevered brow she adored so much.

The other doctor arrived, and the two men checked the results of their surgery. The stump looked clean, they remarked. If only they could bring down the fever, Menalcus might stand a chance.

Timothy offered to relieve Lydia, but she shook her head. Menalcus belonged to her. She wanted to do any task, no matter how small, if there was the slightest chance it would help.

Luke suggested Timothy return to Lydia's house with a report of how things were progressing. Before his departure, Timothy knelt by the bedside and offered a prayer for God's will to be done.

Lydia frowned. "Why didn't you pray for Menalcus to get well? Surely God would hear your prayers. Paul said you have much power in prayer."

Timothy took Lydia's hands. He looked into her face with such compassion and sympathy, she had no choice but to listen to him.

"Lydia, if God wills for Menalcus to get well, we will rejoice greatly. But if Menalcus does not recover, we must rejoice in that also. He will be with our Lord, and that is much better."

When her frown deepened, he continued. "I was at my uncle Nathan Ben Kobath's home when Gaius brought Menalcus there. We talked for long hours, and as I unfolded the Scriptures to him, he became a believer!"

Lydia swallowed hard. Could it be true?

"When Menalcus was a strong man, he believed he could manage his own life. But as a result of this injury, your husband had a long time to think. He knew he had to find strength outside of himself to face his future."

Lydia did not want to think of her husband suffering, no matter what the reason.

"He trusted God," Timothy continued. "You must trust Him too. God, in his infinite wisdom, sees all of our life, not just our present hurting. You would not want Menalcus to live if he would suffer more than either of you could bear."

Lydia longed to argue, to protest. She wanted Menalcus to live, no matter what. She needed him. The children needed him. There was so much she had to tell him.

And if God had any compassion, he would know she could not quietly hand her husband over to that horrible enemy, death. She would not!

"You can trust God, Lydia," Timothy repeated. "He will do right by his children."

She could only nod as Timothy said farewell and departed. Had she tried to speak, she could have given way to hysterics.

Luke made arrangements for Lydia to spend the night at her husband's side. He had the innkeeper bring her a cot. After Luke assured her he would keep watch while she slept, she finally agreed to lie down awhile.

Morning came, bringing a sunny day. Lydia made her toilet, then returned to the room and sent Luke to breakfast.

Shortly after the doctor left, Menalcus opened his eyes. They were clear and bright. "Lydia." His voice sounded strong and steady.

"Menalcus," Lydia shrieked, clutching his hand. "God has heard my prayers. You are going to get well!"

"Yes, Lydia," he said. "I am. I am going to be completely and wholly well."

Menalcus's eyes were shining so brightly Lydia thought he might be delirious again. She laid her hand on his forehead and found it cool. The crisis had passed!

She turned to call Luke, but Menalcus stopped her. "Lydia, I want to talk to you. You must not grieve for me as one having no hope. Timothy was right when he told you to trust God."

He nodded at her look of astonishment. "Yes, I heard his prayer and your words. I could not speak but I heard. Now, you must listen to me carefully because I may not have long to speak with you."

"Dearest one," she said, "save your strength. We will talk when you are better. Please rest. I promise to stay right here."

"We must talk today, Lydia. I had to come home to tell you about Jesus and how much he loves us. I could not leave without knowing you would be with me in heaven. I wanted to tell you again how much I love you. I never told you enough."

"I am a believer too," she cried. "I've been wanting to share that with you!"

His face glowed with relief and joy.

"Now, rest," she said. "We will talk more in a little while. We will go to heaven when we are old and gray and all of our children are grown. If you will save your strength, I will tell you all about the children and everything that's happened since you have been gone."

Menalcus put his fingers over Lydia's mouth. "Only if you take your time and not talk like a frightened pigeon."

Lydia took his levity as a sign that his mood had shifted to a more positive one. She told him about the new baby and the progress of their other children. When he had been completely satisfied with the details of their life, she told him about her visit to the riverbank.

He did not seem surprised to hear of Luke's coming or the visit of Paul and Silvanus. She described how she had come to be a believer and been baptized.

From time to time as she talked, Menalcus would raise one hand and cup her cheek in his fingers before they fell limply to the covers again. Lydia stroked his hand and stopped often to press her lips to his cheeks and lips. She felt as if she were willing her strength to be transmitted to his frail body.

"I hope you don't mind," she said, "but I invited the church to meet at our house until the congregation gets a good start. Of course, now that you are coming home and will need to be quiet, I will tell Paul they must seek another meeting place."

Menalcus again touched his fingers to Lydia's mouth. "You will not need to move the church. I am honored to know that our home can be of some service to our Lord. Now, you must let me speak of my love for you and the children."

Menalcus spoke so quietly, Lydia laid her face next to his. She dared not move lest she miss a word. She was glad he could not see the tears that wet her cheeks and the sheet beside his pillow.

Luke opened the door and rejoiced at seeing Menalcus awake. He tried to get Menalcus to swallow some wine, but after one or two spoonfuls, he could take no more.

"I'm very tired. I'd like to go to sleep now."

"Of course." Luke left the room quietly.

"Good-bye, my dear Lydia," he whispered as he closed his eyes. "Remember, always trust God."

"Good night, dear Menalcus. I'll be right here when you wake up."

Menalcus smiled. soon his breathing became deep and regular.

Lydia took the opportunity to stretch out on the cot. She had not realized how tired she was. The sound of Menalcus's steady breathing soon lulled her to sleep.

She was not sure what roused her, but she awoke to find Menalcus still asleep, even though it was well into morning. He looked so peaceful. His breathing seemed very slow and somewhat louder. She tried to still the alarm that ran along her nerves.

Luke came at her summons and felt Menalcus's pulse. He examined his friend closely before turning to Lydia. "It won't be long now, Lydia. He will not likely wake again."

Lydia's hands flew to her mouth. "No!" she screamed. Surely this was not happening. He was going to get better and they were going home, where he could completely recover. She had prayed and God heard her. Luke was wrong. He had to be!

A look at the tranquility on the dear face of her husband brought her to her senses.

She walked to the window and looked out at the sea. Long, lazy waves rolled in toward the white sand. Far down the beach some fishermen cast their nets. Closer at hand, a family with three children frolicked toward the water, picnic basket in hand.

It has no right to be such a beautiful day, she thought. *Menalcus is dying. The sky should be overcast and stormy. The whole world should be weeping.*

The deep, steady breathing behind her continued, slightly more labored than before. When Luke left the room, she did not turn around.

Gaius entered and stood by her side. Neither spoke. Menalcus's slave had been through so much with his master; he would want to be with his friend to the end.

Lydia leaned her head against the casement. She went over and over in her mind all the things she and her husband had said to each other in this room. More things than most couples say to one another in a lifetime of living together.

Then it dawned on her. Menalcus had known! He had tried to tell her that his time on earth was at an end! That was why he said good-bye instead of good night!

The silence surrounding her shattered her thoughts. There was no sound at all in the room. There was no sound of breathing. She turned, knowing it was over. He would suffer no more. Menalcus was dead!

CHAPTER 12

Philippi

Tell me what happened." Lydia glared at Luke as they sat in the garden after Menalcus's funeral. "I want to hear everything."

"I only know what Timothy told us," he said. "By the time I saw Menalcus, it was too late to save him. Timothy can tell you the rest when you are able to hear it."

"I don't want to hear it from him. I want to hear it from you. You call yourself a doctor and you let him die!" Part of Lydia knew she was being cruel without reason. But another part of her wanted to hurt whomever she could. She wanted someone else to feel the pain that had lodged in her body and soul.

If Luke took offense at her words, he didn't show it. His jaw tightened a little but he spoke as gently as ever. "Timothy was with his Uncle Nathan when Gaius arrived with Menalcus. Your husband was very weak, but not really in danger. He asked Nathan to make arrangements for them to stay at your father's place until he could continue the journey."

"Go on," Lydia demanded.

"Nathan told him about the sale of your father's property and insisted on caring for Menalcus. He sent you a letter telling of your husband's arrival."

"I never received it," she insisted, knowing full well that the courier system was not always reliable.

Luke continued without acknowledging her outburst. "Timothy explained the Scriptures to Menalcus. Gaius, already a God-fearer, had been talking to Menalcus about Jesus as they traveled. They were both ready to become part of God's family."

Lydia was glad, of course, that her husband had come to a belief in Jesus before he died. But at the moment, even that knowledge could not penetrate the layers of grief that gripped her soul.

"When Menalcus heard that Timothy was headed this way to join forces with Paul, he insisted on coming with him, even though he was not well enough to travel on such a journey. Nothing could sway his determination to get home to you.

"By the time they reached Troas, Menalcus was running a fever and in pain from the inflamed leg.

Timothy had a doctor examine him. They did everything they could to persuade him to be admitted to the hospital. Menalcus knew it would mean another entire winter away from home, so he refused. He ordered Gaius proceed with him to the dock.

"The fever was raging by the time the boat docked. That's when I arrived. We did our best to save him. But it wasn't enough. I'm sorry."

Luke turned Lydia toward him. The tender touch of his hands and his gentle, pleading words penetrated her soul. She pounded her fists against his chest. He let her hit him again and again before he finally drew her into his arms, where she wept until there were no more tears.

"At least Menalcus is at home with the Lord," he said softly. "That should bring some consolation."

"But I want him at home with me." Lydia's voice was flat, drained of all emotion. "I need him. The children need him. Does God need him more than we do?"

Luke did not answer. Lydia knew there was no answer to give.

She spent that evening wandering from her bedroom to the children's room to the head of the stairs and back again. Everywhere she went, the air was hot and stifling. She lifted wet tendrils of hair from the nape of her neck, her movements as sluggish as the air that moved fitfully through the bedroom window.

She listlessly tasted a grape, the warm juice flowing thick and sweet over her tongue. She was not the least bit hungry. Still she ate another, and another. When her fingers no longer found the firm, round fruit, she looked at the empty stem in surprise. Surely she had not eaten that entire clump of grapes!

She poured tepid water from the bedside pitcher over her sticky fingers and headed for the stairs. There was much work to do, if she could only settle her mind to the task. The accounts needed to be updated. A caravan had arrived from Thessalonica, and she must make arrangements for a return shipment. Household accounts needed to be discussed with the head steward.

She sat in the workroom and pulled a clean sheet of parchment toward her. She stared at the paper for some moments. Perhaps if she sat very still, the air would not be so hot.

Restless, she took the sheet with her into the garden. Perhaps the water splashing down into the bottom of the fountain would cool her some. She sat on the low wall surrounding the basin, hoping the spray would alleviate some of the oppressive heat.

Myia appeared with a tray of cheese, olives, figs, and sweet wine. Lydia was not hungry. Still she ate Even after she reached the point of feeling stuffed, she ate.

Why am I doing this? Why don't I simply send this food away? Even as she asked herself these questions, she bit into a plump fig.

I'm going to be sick if I eat another bite. The thought crossed her mind as a simple statement of fact. It took a supreme effort of will for her to wave the tray away.

Breathing a deep sigh she leaned against the fountain and let the water play over her hands and wrists. Her longing for Menalcus was a physical pain. Hatred for those miserable, plotting, troublemaking Jews in that desolate end of nowhere called Palestine rose in her like bile. Why did they always have to stir up trouble? The fact that no one made Menalcus's horse fall did not enter into her reasoning. Someone had to be blamed for his death.

She cupped water in her hands and bathed her hot face. Big, salty tears joined the water dripping from her cheeks. At first she cried quietly. Then, as if a locked door had been triggered open from within, great wracking sobs convulsed her.

Myia came, frightened at first, then instinctively withdrew just out of sight. Tears fell from her own eyes. She, too, had loved him.

Lydia regained her composure as she bathed her face in the water again and again. Myia stepped forward and led her unresisting mistress to a shaded couch. She gently dried Lydia's face and hands with a linen towel.

Lydia made room for Myia to sit beside her. The two friends sat without speaking until long shadows touched the top of the garden wall.

Lydia broke the long silence. "It's all my fault. I had no business leaving the worship of the gods I know to listen to Elias and Paul prattle on about an unknown god. Now the gods have taken Menalcus away from me, to show me who really has the power."

Myia stared at Lydia in astonishment and dismay. "How can you say that? You didn't make Menalcus go to Palestine That was his job. You couldn't have stopped him from going. Even if that accident had happened right here in Philippi, you couldn't have prevented it."

"Nevertheless," Lydia continued, "I will make sacrifice to Cybele and Isis tomorrow. I will hear no more of Yahweh. If he is a god of such tender mercy, why didn't he answer my prayers? Why did he let Menalcus die? I believed, and what good did it do me? How am I going to comfort the children, especially this baby Menalcus did not even live to see?"

Myia had no answers It was just as well. Lydia wouldn't have listened.

Lydia talked on and on, forgetting Myia was even there. Perhaps, she reasoned, if she talked enough the pain would go away.

A servant came to inquire about dinner and Lydia waved him away. She would eat no more until she made sacrifice in the morning. She allowed Myia to take her to her room.

The children came in, quiet and subdued. Lydia could scarcely bear the sadness in their eyes. They wanted to talk about their father, to ask questions for which she had no answers. She could not talk about Menalcus tonight. Maybe tomorrow—or the day after that.

Old Elizabeth ushered the children out. "I'll take them to the kitchen," she said. "Cook will find something to give them."

Moments later, Lydia saw the children enter the yard below her window, milk and sweet cakes in hand.

Elias joined them. Krysta climbed onto his lap, Diana sat in the shadows nearby, and Hermanus leaned his head against Elias's knee.

Elias lifted his head to the heavens, his eyes closed. Then he told the children the story of Job. Lydia was familiar with the tale. But something about Elias's soothing voice forced her to listen.

When he came to the part where Job's wife wanted him to curse God and die, Hermanus spoke up. "That's what Mama wants to do."

Lydia stifled a gasp.

"She said she never wanted to hear the name of Yahweh again. I heard her when she was crying in the garden. She thinks it's his fault Daddy died."

Elias stroked the boy's head. "Sometimes, when we are hurting a great deal, the way your mama is right now, and like all of you are, we say and do things we don't really mean. When it hurts so much it seems we can't stand it any longer, we take our hurt and anger out on the people we love. Right now, your mama is angry with Yahweh."

"But won't he be mad and punish Mama?" Diana asked, her eyes open wide.

Elias gave her a small smile. "No, my child. Yahweh understands. That's why he is the great I AM. He knows exactly how your mama is feeling and how you feel. He wants to take the hurt away."

"Then why doesn't he?" Krysta demanded. "Why doesn't he just send Daddy back to us?"

Elias pulled in a long breath. "I cannot answer all of your questions. If I could, I would be a god. But one of our great kings once said, 'To everything there is a season. There is a time to live and a time to die.' "

Unwilling to listen to any more of Elias's platitudes, Lydia left the window and went to the *protas* in the center of the house. She had not been in this room, sacred to religious devotions, since the arrival of Paul and her acceptance of Jesus Christ as the son of the one true God. There had been no celebrations of family rituals since Christ had become the head of this household.

She stood in front of the family altar and gazed at the statue of Hestia, the protector of the hearthstone. No garland graced her brow. No food offering lay in front of her. No oblations had been poured to her spirit. Lydia proceeded to remedy that immediately. She carefully lifted a garland of sweet-smelling jasmine, picked that very morning, and placed it over the head of the goddess. As she placed a smaller wreath over her brow, Lydia involuntarily drew back for a moment when her hand made contact with the cold marble head.

A platter nearby held an offering of fresh figs, grapes, and pomegranates arranged on a bed of myrtle. A fleeting picture of Paul breaking the loaf of unleavened bread, as a reminder of Christ's broken body, passed through her mind, but she immediately pushed it away. Lydia lifted a *hydra* of the best wine and poured an oblation at the bottom of the pedestal.

"This is my blood. Drink all of it, in remembrance of me."

She shook her head to clear the remembrance of Paul's teaching about the shed blood of Christ. Those words rang empty in her heart today.

She knelt to worship, her eyes on a level with those of the statue. She stared in dejection. A feeling of desolation such as she had never known swept over her heart.

"You are only a stone," she said to the statue. "You cannot hear me. You cannot see me. You just sit there and stare. You have no heart to care for me. No one has a heart to care for me."

Lydia fell to the floor. Great tearing sobs wracked her body, then gradually subsided to the kind of weeping that threatened to never end.

While she lay prostrate and disconsolate, feeling lost and abandoned, she suddenly sensed that she was not alone. No visible presence was in the room, but words came to her mind as clearly as if Jesus stood there and spoke them to her.

"I will never leave you nor forsake you. I am the resurrection and the life. He who believes in me, though he were dead, yet shall he live: and whosoever lives and believes in me shall never die. Do you believe this?"

Paul had spoken those words at Menalcus's funeral service. She had been so numb with grief she'd paid little attention.

"I did believe that once," Lydia said aloud. "Menalcus believed it."

She rose from the floor to her knees. She gazed into the unblinking eyes of stone. Once again she heard Menalcus's last words: "Always remember, trust God."

She had not remembered. She had not trusted God. She had wanted—even demanded—God to heal Menalcus according to her wishes. If she really trusted God, she had to believe he knew what was best. Instead she had allowed herself to become so enmeshed in self-pity, she had almost let all she believed slip away.

For the first time since Menalcus's death, the things Paul had said penetrated her mind and heart. *"Menalcus is not dead. Oh, yes, his poor pain-filled body is gone. But his spirit is not dead."*

"Oh, God, I do believe," she said, her words echoing in the small room. "Forgive me, and help my unbelief."

The desire to strike out at the world disappeared with her tears. She was at peace. Tears of a different sort trembled on her lashes. How good to know God was alive! No statue of stone, he could see and he could hear and he cared about her. And Menalcus was with him! His Holy Spirit had sent those images of the bread and the wine to her mind and heart to remind her that she was a person worth dying for, not a thing to be manipulated by a distant god who did not participate in the affairs of men.

A lovely light of gladness dispelled the dark, haunting shadow that had enveloped Lydia since Menalcus's death. She was released from the despair and flooded with the reality of her salvation. She would see Menalcus again! God had promised, and He could never lie.

She would remove the idol with her own hands. Fresh flowers would be placed on this altar—not to honor a stone god, but to commemorate the day God had become her *Abba* Father. It would be her private place of worship and prayer for the rest of her life—until the day she joined her beloved husband in heaven's eternal embrace.

Myia took an extra-long time dressing Lydia's hair. She fussed unnecessarily over her toilet. She dogged Lydia's footsteps all morning until finally Lydia turned in exasperation. "Why are you hovering over me?"

"I'm not hovering, milady."

"Yes, you are. You haven't been two cubits away from me all day. What is the matter?"

Myia licked her lips several times, then mumbled, "Gaius and I wish to be married."

For the first time in many weeks, Lydia really looked at Myia. She was still a crippled slave, but there was no longer a look of defiance in her face that dared anyone to feel sorry for her. Her eyes danced with joy and her lips curved in a lovely smile. How much of this was from her newfound esteem as one of God's beloved children? How much was from loving and being loved by Gaius?

Whatever the cause, Myia was a grown woman with grown-up needs. Lydia felt ashamed that she had paid so little attention to Myia. She had been so caught up in her own feelings and thoughts, the whole world could have changed and she would not have noticed.

Lydia took so long to answer Myia began to tremble. Tears began to well up in her eyes.

Gaius appeared at Myia's side. "It is the custom among my people for the man to ask permission to marry." He took Myia's hand. "I now ask for the right to marry Myia."

Lydia gazed at the tall slave. He had regained the weight he had lost while bringing Menalcus home, but the fulfilling of that task had left its mark. There was a maturity and serenity in his expression that was found in few men, rare indeed among the pleasure-loving Greeks of Philippi.

Lydia dropped her eyes, lost in thoughts of her own anticipated marriage years before. Finally she rose, smiled, and embraced them both. "Menalcus would be pleased."

Tears stood in her eyes as she saw the look of happiness and love that passed between them. Her heart grieved that she would never know that happiness and love again. But she was pleased that these two had discovered what she had once known.

Timothy and the other men talked most of the night before Paul's departure. Paul had expressed a sense of deep frustration. The need to press on to Thessalonica urged him to depart from this place. He knew from experience the believers would retain more and grow faster in the faith if they accepted the work for themselves. On the other hand, he did not want to leave before a solid foundation for the new church had been established.

"I have resolved the situation by leaving Timothy behind," Paul announced. "Although young in age, this man has a vast background of Scripture from which to give instruction and guidance."

Timothy felt a deep sense of humility as the mantle of authority was passed on to him. But he also sensed an excitement for the task that lay ahead of him.

After Paul and Silvanus left, many of the remaining believers complained. "Paul was so sure of his beliefs," one said.

"And so good at making the Scriptures clear to us," another commented.

One or two people did not return for the nightly meetings after the two leaders of the faith left their midst.

But those who remained continued to meet together in the evenings and to worship at the river every Sabbath Day. A large group of people gathered there each week, divided into two distinct groups. The Jewish believers sat on one side of the speaker, and the new Gentile believers congregated on the other side, with a noticeable expanse between them.

On one Sabbath day, after the singing of a hymn and the reading of the Torah, a visitor from Jerusalem, who had been standing between the two groups, asked to speak. As was the rule in their meetings, he was allowed to address the gathering.

After many ingratiating remarks, he faced the Jewish believers and quoted the laws given to Moses. He then turned his back on that group and addressed those who had accepted Paul's message. Timothy and Lydia sat near the front of the small group.

"Holy brethren," he began in a solemn voice, "we who are the descendants of Abraham, Isaac, and Jacob—we who have followed the teachings of our fathers and the prophets—are we not the true followers of Yahweh? Some of more eloquent speech would have us forsake these laws and the traditions of our forefathers. They would have us forget that we—" He stopped to smite upon his breast and raise his voice for emphasis—"*we* are the children of the covenant."

He turned again toward the Jews who had accepted Christ. "Now, does it not stand to reason that if those of other nations wish to become part of that covenant, they should also accept the standards of that covenant? We must decide if we are the people of Yahweh or not. If we are, let us stand for the laws of Moses and the traditions of the elders!"

There was much murmuring among the Jewish people. Some cast black looks in the direction of the new believers.

Timothy stepped forward and asked permission to speak. The leader of the congregation hesitated. It was the right of every male to speak at these meetings, as long as what he said pertained to the Scriptures. But if these Judaizers were offended by what Timothy said, they would report the leader to the Sanhedrin, who could cause no end of trouble for the burgeoning group.

Timothy knew he had put the leader in a difficult dilemma. But he had to speak. At the man's tentative nod of affirmation, Timothy stood to address the full congregation.

"Brethren, our purpose as the chosen people of God is to lead others to know him, not to put restrictions upon them that they cannot keep, thereby making their worship impossible."

The murmuring increased until it became a mighty roar. Timothy tried to reason with them, but their shouting only grew more intense.

"Very well," he finally hollered, loud enough to still the crowd. "We will withdraw from your congregation and meet henceforth at the home of Lydia, who has graciously opened her home to us."

The dissention abated as everyone in attendance waited to hear what Timothy would say next.

Filled with conviction, Timothy stated, "Since our Lord rose on the third day after his burial, which was the day following the Sabbath, we will meet for worship at sunrise tomorrow."

The visitor from Jerusalem shook a fist in the air. "This is one more example of the departure from the law of Moses," he shouted. "Did not our Lord God say, 'Remember the Sabbath Day to keep it holy'? Do you need further proof?"

Amidst the shouts of the crowd, Timothy led the little band of Gentile believers away from the riverbank. A few of the Jewish people started to leave with them, but after a few steps, they seemed to realize they were breaking with the traditions and rituals of their heritage. They turned back and were welcomed with many gestures and much talk.

It was a small group indeed who gathered in the atrium at Lydia's house the next morning. But Timothy gave them encouragement and lifted their spirits. After a meal together they had a time of prayer and sang a hymn before going to their various homes. They agreed to meet again at sunrise the following morning after the Sabbath, to have the first regular services of the church in Philippi.

As time passed, the change in their lifestyle, their outlook, and the joy and excitement of their new purpose in life became catching. The Philippian jailer and his family continually brought those who were released from prison and their families.

The slaves of nearby households came as often as their duties allowed. Their changed attitudes caused some inquiry on the part of their masters, and as a result some entire households accepted Christ and asked to be baptized.

Timothy saw the need to set some of the older women over the children and young women. Lydia agreed to teach several of the young slaves and the children of other believers. She told them the stories Elias had taught her children, then showed the lessons they needed to learn from those stories. In so doing, he could see her own faith being strengthened.

He knew she could not shut out the pain of missing Menalcus. But she seemed quite pleased to share her house with the church. With people in and out of the house so often, she would not have to be alone, and she would have less time to dwell on thoughts of her loss.

Timothy received news of Clement, a longtime friend of his family, who was not only eloquent in preaching but was gifted in starting new work and getting it well established. He sent for him. As soon as Clement arrived, Timothy placed him in charge of the work.

A short time later, a letter from Luke to Lydia convinced Timothy that he needed to rejoin Paul.

Greetings to Lydia and all in her household.

Much has happened since our visit with you, and I wanted to keep you abreast of our work and to thank you on behalf of all of us for your wonderful hospitality

Our arrival in Thessalonica was in one sense a repeat of our stay in Philippi, although our lodging did not compare with our quarters in your gracious home.

Thessalonica is an exciting city and a busy one. Situated as it is across the Via Egnatia, the main street links the east and west. Trade pours in from both directions. Paul is aware of the importance of planting the gospel in this strategic place. If God's grace is accepted here, it is bound to spread east to Asia and west to Rome itself.

It is too bad Alexander, the great conqueror who wanted to unite the world, could not have lived to meet Paul. We have talked much of him and compared Paul's vision of a whole world for Christ with Alexander's desire to make the world a universal place.

Paul preached three Sabbaths in the local synagogue. The Holy Spirit gave him mighty power, and many people became believers and were baptized.

Many Greeks forsook their idols and accepted the good news of Christ's death, burial, and resurrection.

Our old "friends" from Philippi were not long in dogging our footsteps. They stirred up all kinds of trouble, exaggerating Paul's arrest in Philippi but not bothering to tell the end of the story. They said Paul is deluded, that he preaches for what he can get in the way of money and flattery. They have even misconstrued his kiss of peace to say he is after women! You know Paul well enough to see the humor and irony of that.

However, they were successful again. We had to leave town in a hurry. I am now with Paul in Athens. The good news is that Timothy returned to Thessalonica to find the church is growing by *leaps and bounds. The people are faithful to their commitment. Praise the Lord!*

I want to share with you one message Paul preached. It concerns Christians who die in the Lord. When we were with you, the death of your beloved Menalcus was too recent for you to listen to sermons. I am sorry we had to leave without doing more for you.

I shall forever praise God, our Father, for Timothy's faithful witness to Menalcus while he was yet strong enough to hear and comprehend it. How precious to you must be the knowledge that Menalcus died in the Lord. You must make that a cornerstone of your thinking, even while you grieve.

Though all of us look for the coming of our Lord very soon, there has been concern about those who die before his return. Paul urges you not to sorrow as one having no hope. Not even death can break the relationship between Christ and the person who loves him.

Who can describe what will happen when Jesus returns? Paul speaks, he says, from the authority of the Lord himself, of the Lord descending from heaven in the clouds, even as he ascended into heaven. He will come with a shout of command. The voice of an archangel and the trumpet of God will call forth the dead, and they will be taken together in the clouds to meet our Lord in the air. Then we will be with him throughout all time.

What a wonderful time to anticipate! And so, dear Lydia, you do not need to accept Menalcus's death with bleak hopelessness nor despair. Your tears must be for yourself and the loss of the physical presence of Menalcus, but never for him, because his spirit is even now with the Lord. If I understand Paul's message correctly, when Christ returns, a perfect body will clothe the spirit, and we will see Menalcus again!

I do not tell you not to weep. I only urge you to trust God.

Paul is trying to arrange a return visit to Macedonia. We so look forward to seeing you again. Greet all of your household, especially the children and Elias. May the grace of our Lord Jesus Christ be with you all.

Luke

With Timothy's assistance, Lydia composed a reply.

Greetings to Luke and all the Christians with you.

It is hard to believe that two years have passed since you were here. It seems like forever, but we have been so busy I scarcely know where the time has gone.

It is dusk—and I miss Menalcus so much. His absence is a knife that turns and twists. I try to fasten my mind on our Lord at these times, but it is difficult. Am I even worthy of the name of Christ? Some of our widow women appear so content in the Lord and have such joy and peace in their lives. I try to emulate their example, but I end up having to fight feelings of resentment toward them, as well as my distress and loneliness. I am convinced that if one more person says, "This, too, shall pass," I will lose control and do something shameful!

Enough about me. I will survive. Most of the time I find the sustaining grace of our Lord to be sufficient. There are times, however, when a memory comes rushing in from nowhere and floods my thinking,.

I had a wonderful experience last week. One of the mule drivers with a load of goods from Thessalonica was talking with Elias about the Lord. You were right in your prediction that the gospel would spread if it was planted in that busy crossroads. It seems Paul's preaching has borne much fruit in that country.

This man told of bitter opposition and stirring up of trouble by some of the same people who were here. But the marvelous news is the growing number of people who are believing in the Lord Jesus for the forgiveness of sin. It seems the more those troublemakers try to suppress the gospel, the stronger it becomes.

The thing that made the gospel believable was the way all of you worked day and night at your trade to support yourselves. I appealed to Paul to let me help more, but he insisted that people must see him practice what he preaches. He is very strong in his declaration that a man who will not work does not deserve to eat.

346 · Acts Chapter 16

I hear a certain doctor has not been slack in putting his skills to good use, especially among the poor. May God bless you, dearest Luke.

We yearn to see you again. May God grant your quick return to us. We keep you in our prayers. Elias, the children, Myia, Gaius, and our entire household send greetings to all of you.

Lydia

Then, together, they wrote a letter to Paul.

Greetings to you and to all who are with you, especially Luke, Silvanus, and Timothy.

The church is moving along slowly. We have people coming but not much commitment. People seem to have other things to do. The women are the mainstay, although several men are faithful. Pray for us that our men will be the dedicated leaders we need.

The church continues to meet in our home. Sometimes I yearn for a little peace and quiet without so much coming and going, but most of the time I am glad my days are filled. I miss Menalcus so much. Some say time will heal the hurting, but I find time moves very slowly. It is an uphill fight but the Lord is good.

Clement has a lot of preaching opportunities. Every day he is in the marketplace, answering questions and expounding on the Scriptures to any who will listen.

I understand the men from Jerusalem who stirred up so much trouble here have followed you, not only to Thessalonica, but to Corinth as well. They surely will have much to answer for in that day when our Lord comes again.

The children are well. Hermanus is always at the gymnasium or the barracks. I worry that he will pick up the bad habits of the soldiers, but he remains thoughtful and kind. I find myself much in prayer on his behalf, as he is easily persuaded. I pray the things he has learned from Elias and from you, dear Christian brothers, will bear much fruit. I am sorry Timothy can stay no longer with us, but I know you have need of him.

We are so excited to know you may soon be coming to visit us again. There have been many times when we have needed your good advice. But we will discuss all of that when you come.

In the meantime, I am enclosing a little contribution to your needs. God is blessing my business, and I can think of no greater way to show my gratitude than to share with you in the ministry.

We count the days until you come again.
Lydia

Lydia continued to fill her days with work. Business at the shop was progressing. The quick availability of materials from the dye yards made it possible for her to prepare large shipments to Thessalonica and beyond to the west, to Troas and Turkey to the east, as well as a greater variety for the local people. Orders were coming from Corinth, Ephesus, and Athens to the south.

The work of the shop was left mainly to Elias. Lydia closely supervised the dye workers and the artisans who wove designs into the cloth after it was dyed. Some designs were stamped on, but borders and simple designs were woven into or embroidered on the material.

She preferred this work because it left her tired at the end of the day. If she became tired enough, she would sleep. The trick was to sleep without dreaming.

Lydia hated going to bed. She did not want to think about the absence of her husband. They had not lived like most of their countrymen, where the husband slept in one section of the house and paid a visit to his wife as often as his physical needs required, then returned to his own bed.

Menalcus had always shared Lydia's bed. She could not put into words how much she missed reaching over in the middle of the night to touch his warm body. She had often bent her leg so the sole of her foot contacted his leg, just to have that communion with him. Early morning had been the best. She would wake to find him curled against her back, his strong, muscular arm holding her close. Even when he was away on his courier duties, she could smile in anticipation of his return and the joy of their reunion.

Now there were no smiles. She woke to silence every day. No matter how much she hugged the pillow to pretend he was there, the bed was empty. Menalcus would never lay his head there again. His soft, gentle breathing had ceased forever. She was alone.

Sometimes Lydia doubted her own commitment as a Christian. She felt like such a failure! If all she believed were true, why was it so difficult to throw off the despair she often felt? She had made progress. She had managed to struggle out of the abyss of grief. She believed she was ready to face the future with courage and intelligence, if not elation. Then a word, a turn in the conversation, a certain feel at dusk would bring it all crashing back. Would God never deliver her from the shadow of this sorrow?

To fill the long night hours, Lydia worked on invoices and household lists. Correspondence concerning the many facets of the buying and selling of merchandise, and writing letters to her friends, filled much of her time at home. Many nights Myia had to remind her that tomorrow was another day.

For the first time in almost two years of cramming every waking moment with activity, Lydia came face to face with the honest admission that busyness was not enough. The truth was, she needed and wanted to love and be loved again. But how could any kind of love be possible for her? Could she put her love for Menalcus aside to love another?

Dear God, she prayed, *if I am to finish out this life alone, please give me peace. If there is another for me, help me to know him. I give myself to you in commitment. You have given me wealth, family, and loyal friends. Am I selfish in asking for love again?*

You know all my thoughts and my ways, so I will not pretend to be other than I am. Please give me your peace and I will be content.

One way she attempted to alleviate her loneliness was by taking on the problems of others. When she visited the homes of the dye workers, she was appalled at the way they lived. Most had but a single room for their family. Those who had a sleeping loft where a little breeze could be felt were lucky.

On a visit to the home of a worker whose wife was ill, Lydia decided she must do more. The family of five lived in one room. The oldest looked to be about six. The wife, obviously pregnant, was trying to fix a thin gruel for their supper when Lydia arrived. It was all the mother could do to stand, let alone cook. Lydia remembered how sick she became each time she was with child. And she had servants to do her bidding, plus a large, airy room to rest in.

She left food from her basket and promised to send more. Inquiry revealed that most of the men who worked for her business lived a very frugal life. Often not as well as the slaves in her house. Many drank away their small salary before coming home.

She left the village determined to change the situation, at least for the women and children. In the meantime, she sent slaves to each family with enough fruits and vegetables to feed them.

Employment at the dye works offered better jobs than most of her workers had ever had. Lydia could have used slave labor, as did many of the employers around her. She believed Elias when he argued that free men, who had a hope of making a living for themselves and their families, would make better workers and need less supervision. She came to see that putting some spirit and encouragement into these men was pleasing to the Lord.

With the help of Elias and Gaius, plans were developed, and a man from the carpenter's guild built living quarters near the dye works. A small garden plot and room for a chicken coop comprised the back garden of each small house. A trellis for grape vines ran the length of the block of homes. While the women and children tended the garden, they could also enjoy shade from the hot sun.

Together with Elias, Lydia sought means for a fair wage for her workers, one that would enable them to do more than simply exist. They developed a list of incentives whereby good work would be rewarded.

It was within reason that a worker might eventually earn enough to buy his own living quarters.

Such innovations did not go without notice in the city. Other employers did not hesitate to voice their disapproval. They had no intention of taking money out of their profits to better the lives of their workers. Those who made use of slaves did not even consider improving their lot. Had not the gods given special privilege to some and ordained others to maintain that privilege?

Though the upper class looked upon Lydia and her workers with suspicion and veiled threats, her workers adored her.

Lydia constantly heard pleas from other men for a place in her employ. Her endeavors provided increased production and the best quality of work known in the empire.

The church also benefited. More and more of the workers began to slip into the services. The women and children seldom missed a chance to listen. Whole families came to accept the Lord and were baptized.

Nothing had aroused such a warmth in Lydia since the shock of Menalcus's death. She wanted to hold on to it, to feel the hope and joy she had once known. She liked experiencing the satisfaction and challenge of competing in business. Most of all, she was glad to realize her worship was more than cold ritual, more than mere duty.

The church continued to meet in Lydia's house. Each Sunday found the small band of worshipers steadfast in their commitment to this new way of life. They gathered for prayer and mutual encouragement on one or two nights during the week. Their number increased slowly.

Clement carefully examined each new candidate for baptism. He spent many hours instructing and teaching the truths Jesus left for his followers.

Some problems arose. There were those who simply wanted to tack Christianity onto their present religion, as if Jesus were just another god to add to the phalanx of gods they already worshiped. When it was made clear there was only one true and living God, some departed. Those who remained needed constant reminding that the goal of the Christian life was to grow in the likeness of Christ and to act like him in the world.

Two women, Euodias and Syntyche, kept things in an uproar much of the time. Each one was afraid she was not getting the proper attention. Their jealousy threatened to work dissension in the little band. Lydia exercised all of her abilities as a peacemaker to keep things on an even keel. She tactfully reminded them that Christ rules from righteousness and hatred of evil, not from self-interest. In a world where the

Christians were a definite minority, they needed the wholehearted response of every person.

Satan was ever ready to prey upon their natural fear of death. So far, their group had not experienced persecution, other than the sneers and snubs of former friends and business acquaintances. But every time news of the horrible things that were happening to Christians since Nero became emperor reached their ears, the members grew wary.

When Lydia learned that Paul, Luke, and Timothy were planning another visit to their part of the country, she decided to send another letter.

Greetings, dear friends.

We are so excited at the news of your coming! Five years is a long time and much has happened to all of us. There will be so much to talk about, I doubt there will be time for sleep. There will be time to eat, however, as the church is planning a feast in celebration of your arrival.

Be prepared to answer many questions. Each time we find something we are not clear about, someone says, "Wait until Paul comes. He will tell us."

Hermanus can scarcely contain himself. You will be here in time for the games. He is participating in the races and wants me to invite you to attend. It will be a real holiday since almost the entire city will be there. Perhaps you will indulge us and take a day to relax from your work also.

Elias stays busy at the shop. He always finds some way to get a bit of the gospel across to our customers. If all were as zealous for the Lord as this dear friend, our little church would soon be too large for my small house.

I have much to discuss with you when you come. As you may recall, I gave Gaius and Myia their freedom when they married. They have remained with me, more loyal than ever, and are a tremendous asset to the church.

Now, however, Gaius is getting anxious to tell his own people the gospel. How I dread their leaving! Myia may have some difficulty adjusting to the colder climate in the north, but she is so in love, I am sure she will endure. Perhaps you will assist Clement in ordaining Gaius before they depart. He will need the help and encouragement of the church as he takes on this new work.

We are hoping you will be able to stay with us through the winter, and even longer if God wills. We send greetings to all until such time as we can greet you in person.

Lydia

The three leaders of their faith arrived a few days before the annual games. Hermanus was pleased beyond measure when their guests accepted his invitation to visit the gymnasium.

He proudly escorted the men to the shady grove encircled by a promenade under great arching branches of oak trees hundreds of years in age.

With head held high, he introduced Paul, Luke, and Timothy to his training master and secured permission to conduct a tour of the facility.

There was much light-hearted conversation as they walked past porticoes reserved for those older men who no longer participated in the exercises but still liked to observe. Everywhere possible, there was an altar dedicated to the gods, ornamented with statuary and garlands of flowers.

This large gymnasium included areas for all the sports: wrestling, casting the discus, hurling the javelin, and racing. The group paused at each one for a few moments, but stayed the longest at the area set aside for racing. It was here Hermanus waxed the most eloquent, for racing was where he excelled. No matter what other sport one might choose to practice in, everyone must run.

The bottom of the extended race course consisted of loose, dry sand. The purpose was to impede the runner by making his footing uncertain. As his proficiency increased, the runner might be weighted with armor—sometimes completely outfitted; sometimes with only a shield and helmet. Hermanus and his guests watched several contestants bounding through the deep sand, their naked young bodies straining to reach the goal.

The next area was for the practice of leaping, either for distance or for height. Those practicing this skill were allowed no artificial aids, not even a pole. The muscular force of the arms was added to the power of the legs for the sudden exertion of strength required of the leap. If the natural spring of their muscles could not make the leap, they must keep trying or go to some other sport.

The throwing of the javelin and discus held the interest of the visitors for a while. Time passed more quickly than anticipated.

When Hermanus brought his visitors home they found the evening meal ready to be served. They had scarcely finished their last bite of melon before the believers gathered to hear Paul speak.

Hermanus was delighted when Paul told of their afternoon together and used the rules of the games as illustrations of how Christians were to live. Paul spoke of wrestling against the powers of Satan and the unseen rulers of the spirit world. He warned against shadow-boxing or just playing around, insisting one must run the race to win. This might call for denying oneself many things that would keep one from doing his best. The Christian, he explained, seeks more than a laurel wreath of flowers; he seeks a heavenly reward that will never fade or disappear.

"Dear brothers," Paul said, "I am still not all I should be, but I am bringing all of my energies to bear on this one thing: forgetting the past and looking forward to what lies ahead, I strain to reach the end of the race and receive the prize for which God is calling us up to heaven, because of what Christ Jesus did for us."

Lydia noted the impression Paul's words made on Hermanus. She was grateful her son had been able to spend the entire afternoon with these men. She had been dreading the upcoming games when all the youth of the city would compete. Most boys would have fathers and grandfathers in the stands cheering for them, even if they did not win. There would be no one for Hermanus, except Elias and maybe Clement and herself. What better person to place a garland around Hermanus's neck than Paul, his spiritual father? Or Luke, his grown-up friend?

When Paul finished speaking he answered questions for a while. With the promise to speak again the following day, after the games, he ushered the believers to the door. For the first time in many months, Lydia ascended the stairs with a light tread.

The morning of the games began with a brilliant sunrise over the distant mountains that touched the edges of the few clouds with pink and gold.

The entire household was astir with excitement. Today was holiday! Only caretakers of the infirm and infants would remain at home. Businesses were closed. Some prisoners were released. And for once, women were welcome to participate.

The men accompanied Hermanus to the gymnasium. They would see first hand the final preparations of the young athletes for the upcoming competition.

By the time Lydia and the women started for the arena, the road was crowded with a happy throng of families and women from outlying farms who shed their plain, dark, everyday garb for their festival dress. Full skirts and tight bodices embroidered in beautiful designs were covered with black aprons embroidered with bright flowers ending above a decorative border around the bottom of the skirt. Gold braid at the waist and around the neck accented the heavy gold jewelry worn so proudly. Black veils fastened on one shoulder and trimmed with gold completed their outfits.

Venders selling their wares lined the roadside. Wine sellers wore skins strapped to their backs, and each carried a cup in one hand. Sellers of fresh, warm bread shouted their wares, the round, eight-sectioned loaves carried on racks above their heads.

Horse dealers, sellers of amulets, jugglers, mimes, and acrobats performed under the shade of the large oaks lining the stone streets. Artists, showmen, and charlatans came to the games. It was a unique time of excitement, competition, and the exhibition of skill.

Occasionally a slave cleared the way for his master's sedan chair by running ahead and announcing the name in a loud voice. Some, who sought recognition, had their slaves walk in front of them, calling their names, indicating that a path should be opened for such an important personage.

Flower girls, laden with garlands for the neck and head, smiled prettily as they presented their wares. Poets recited their verses, singers sang their songs, jesters called out their doggerel.

Soon Lydia and the women arrived at the city gates. The processional began. A band of flute players led the column, followed by soldiers from the garrison. The officers rode on horseback, the rest of the men marching in formation.

Athletes of past years, fresh myrtle wreaths on their brows, made up the next division. Many tales of past glory were exchanged as they strode along. The priests from several temples came next, carrying offerings of fruit and wine to present at the various shrines as they passed by. The old men of the city came next, ranked according to the prominence of their office or their family.

Women made up the last group. Slaves were free to attend but could not be part of the procession unless their assistance was required by their owners. The procession arrived at the arena just as a drum roll announced the opening ceremonies.

A troop of Roman soldiers marched to the center of the arena, in perfect formation behind their commander, each step matching the cadence of the drum. A flag topped by the Roman eagle was raised. The spectators stood to their feet and smote their breasts. A cry of "Hail, Caesar!" resounded from the packed stadium.

Many present, especially the older men, were veterans of the Roman wars. There was a swell to their chests and a lift to their heads as they paid homage to their emperor. Rome had treated them well. The bitterness and rebellion found in many Roman colonies was not present in Philippi.

The contestants entered the arena by twos. The leader of the athletes carried a torch much like the front runner of the great games of Olympus, of which these games were but a slight imitation. The contenders walked around the arena, their chests arched, their limbs straight, their carriage erect.

Their naked bodies, bronzed by exposure to the sun and air, already glistened with perspiration. A light coating of oil had been carefully massaged into their muscles back in the gymnasium. Their features glowed with anticipation that reflected on the beholders like sunlight. The skillful and persistent exercises that produced such wonderfully elastic bodies were soon to be put to the test of competition.

The crowd roared and cheered through successive events of wrestling, discus throwing, and tossing of the javelin. Each winner was led before the judges to receive a laurel crown and garland of flowers amid the ovations and applause of the spectators. Winners received amphorae of olive oil, shields and cloaks, and other items of value.

At last it was time for the races. Lydia tensed with anticipation. How would Hermanus perform? What if he did not do well and disgraced himself and his instructors?

"Don't worry," Luke chided her. "There are no losers in the race. Everyone does his best. That's what the judges require, even though only one will get the prize."

Of all the gymnastic sports, the race was everyone's favorite. Hermanus's event came near the end. The runners maintained a marvelous speed. Some were swifter than horses, with endurance that seemed undiminished even at the end of a long race. They stood in front of the judges, where the waiting prize was displayed, with arms uplifted and eyes flashing. It was a stirring sight for the spectators.

At last Hermanus stood in the starting line with six other young men of his age. What magnificent specimens of physical manhood! Muscles, which would lend power to the legs and provide momentum to the arms, rippled and gleamed in the sunlight.

Once their feet were firmly planted, the signal was given and they bounded forward like splendid young animals, straining for the goal.

The runners would take the course around the arena twice. By the end of the first circuit, the crowd was standing, cheering not only for a winner, but out of sheer exuberance for the display of energy being witnessed.

Lydia was on her feet with the rest. In the upper sections of the stands where the slave population stood, Gaius and Myia and the other members of her household cheered for Hermanus.

Two of the runners appeared to be at the point of dropping. One more fell to the ground and grabbed his leg, obviously suffering from cramps. The three remaining men sped on like sleek creatures of the field running from a hunter. Arms flung wide, eyes reflecting the joy of giving their all, the runners flashed past the winning marker and stopped in front of the judges.

Hermanus came in second! Lydia was so proud.

As the judges intoned the names of the three young men and placed the laurel wreath on the elated winner, the commander of the garrison stepped forward and placed the garland for second place around Hermanus's neck. The officer untied a leather corslet from his arm and presented it to

Hermanus as well. Lydia recognized this as the special body armor Menalcus had worn while carrying out his duties as courier to the Roman army.

A sudden chill shot through the joy and pride she felt for her son. She deliberately pushed it aside and gave full attention to the ovation the runners were receiving from the throng of onlookers. For a fleeting second her eyes met those of her firstborn son over the heads of the crowd. His eyes shone with pride. Lydia threw kisses with both hands. Her smile belied the sting of tears that threatened to escape and run down her cheeks.

Luke took her hand and raised it with his in salute to the young man. Paul and the other men likewise demonstrated to Hermanus their approval of his effort.

The slaves left immediately after the games. The evening meal must be in readiness when their masters returned home. There would be many banquets this night. Songs would be sung and verses composed to honor the winners of the day's events. The winners would be welcome to go from house to house, where praises would be heaped upon them again and again. Shrines and temples must be visited on the way home and homage paid to the gods and goddesses for victories won.

Lydia and her party would not be stopping at any of the shrines or temples. They no longer needed to make sacrifices to gods of stone. They strolled leisurely along, reliving the day. A rosy glow hung in the evening sky.

Hermanus beamed and sparkled as he acknowledged the accolades Paul, Silvanus, and Timothy attributed to his honor. He tousled Darius's hair and accepted the hugs of his sisters. Elias clasped Hermanus in a tight embrace. This man, who had so often been a refuge for him as a child, now held him at arm's length. The look that passed between the two said far more than words.

Lydia told Hermanus how proud she was of him. She want to tell him how much she loved him, but she would not behave like a possessive mother in front of these men.

Luke seemed to understand her feelings. "Being a mother is a difficult task. You see what your years of training have produced and you can say to the world, 'Here is my finest. He has more to offer than you can ever receive. Treat him well.' On the other hand, when you know the dangers that lie ahead, you want to hold him close and say to the world, 'Not yet! I still have need of him. You'll have him soon enough. Wait your turn!' A most difficult task, but one you will handle wisely, God being your helper."

Lydia nodded in affirmation of Luke's words. Only God knew how difficult it was to wish

Hermanus God's speed as he ran ahead to join the celebrants. She knew without looking that his steps would turn toward the barracks before he returned home.

There would be no formal ceremony that marked his rite of passage into that mysterious place called manhood, but both Lydia and Hermanus knew the journey had begun.

Hermanus had barely disappeared into the crowd when he came running back. "Fire! Fire!" he cried. "Mama, the works are on fire!"

Lydia thought surely she must have misunderstood her son's cry of alarm. But a look toward the dye works showed a red glow nearer and brighter than the sunset. Even as she looked, flames shot into the air like a geyser. The people around them shouted as they realized what was happening.

Running as fast as she could, Lydia and those with her came within sight of the place where the dye works had been. Most of the yards lay in smoldering ruins. Heaps and piles of material burned. Fumes from the dyes filled the air. Lydia gasped as she saw the angry flames racing down the row of workers' homes, devouring the wooden structures like a hungry giant.

Children cried. Mothers gathered their families with frantic screams. Men vainly tried to rescue household goods from their burning homes.

Fortunately for the city, the homes had been built near a vacant lot. The surrounding houses were of stone, and the owners were able to stamp out any sparks the wind carried in their direction. A bucket brigade was formed. But the best that could be done was to contain the fire.

Lydia gave Hermanus the responsibility of seeing that Darius and his sisters were safely returned home. She and Elias walked among the workers, making sure all were accounted for. Paul and the other men joined her in comforting the weeping mothers and dejected fathers. Homes, possessions, and jobs were gone.

Lydia directed everyone to her house. The bedraggled, soot-streaked crowd slowly headed in that direction. She stayed behind with the charred remains of all that she had accomplished. Tears made little paths down through the dirt on her cheeks.

So much destruction. What could have been the cause of such a catastrophe? Perhaps a worker failed to extinguish the fire under one of the dye pots. A spark on dry wood could have done it. With everyone at the games, no one would have been there to safeguard against such a disaster.

Some of the businessmen, who had been hostile to Lydia's treatment of her workers and had openly criticized her methods, came to express sympathy.

Lydia accepted their words with a nod, unsure of how sincere such condolences were.

She picked her way past charred beams, all that remained of the drying sheds. A growing number of people gathered near where the main building had stood. She approached the group and looked at what was drawing their attention, only to pull back with a gasp of horror. There among the smoking embers lay the body of a man. His clothes were burned from his body as was much of his flesh. His skull had been crushed by a falling timber.

Lydia recognized the man's eyes, which were still open to the sky. They seemed to reflect the same evil that had marked them in life. The bully who had lost Janis, and her ability to make money for him, had finally wreaked his vengeance.

Lydia raised her head to meet the baleful look of his companion, who turned abruptly on his heel and stomped past the cluster of businessmen who were covertly watching Lydia. They could not meet her gaze. It did not take much deduction on her part to know who had paid for this day's work. The bully had not received the wages he expected, but he had received what he earned.

Lydia returned to her house, she soon found that Paul had organized the families into groups to be fed. What had been intended as a victory dinner for Hermanus turned out to be an assembly line for feeding the children and wives of the workers. The men ate in the yard.

Lydia's announcement that the fire had been intentionally set evoked angry growls and expressions of desire for revenge.

News of the fire quickly swept through the city. Members of the congregation appeared at Lydia's door with offers to shelter the families. Lydia was moved by their compassion and concern. Some of them had barely enough for their own needs and yet they were reaching out to bear the burdens of those in trouble. She thanked God for their dedication and concern. They truly were growing in the grace and knowledge of the Lord!

Paul gathered the men into the atrium, where prayers were made, thanking God no one was injured. He also prayed for those responsible for this misfortune. He praised God for the response of those Christian friends who stepped forward to offer help to these distraught workers and their families.

Lydia assured the men that work would begin as soon as possible on rebuilding their homes and then the yards. But she knew it would take a few days to get things in order.

"Miss Lydia," one of the dyers asked, "why can't we help with the rebuilding? We have nothing to do until we can go to work again. We can at least clear the debris from the land so the work can begin."

This idea was greeted with enthusiasm by the rest of the workers. They were not forgetful of where they had been and where Lydia had enabled them to be. Now they had a chance to show their gratitude.

The church in Lydia's house soon realized that being a Christian did not make one immune from trouble. Travelers and tradesmen carried news of fresh waves of persecution against the Christians in many parts of the empire. Christians were often sent to prison or worse, condemned to the mines. Others hid in the wild rather than be put in prison for debts they could not repay. Sometimes Christians were held as hostages by robbers and brigands.

So far nothing of this sort had taken place in Macedonia, but there was no guarantee persecution would not come. To be known as a Christian was to be fair game for the rest of the Roman world.

Nero had little patience with anything that upset his personal lifestyle or interfered with his pleasures. He knew little of the faraway provinces of Rome and did not care to be informed. Let them pay their taxes like good citizens and be quiet about it. How they fared was their concern.

The church in Philippi wept when they heard of the straits of the Christians in Jerusalem. Many had lost their jobs because of their confession of Jesus as Messiah. Some had their property confiscated. A famine in the land added to their suffering. Unless relief came soon, many would die.

Lydia reflected over her own life. She had left home and father to come to a strange land and take up a new life. She had been terribly homesick for a short while. Then the children came, and her love for Menalcus grew. Now she had lost her husband and a large portion of her business. But she had never known hunger or deprivation of any kind. She did not know what it was like to be homeless.

I wonder how I would handle a situation like some believers are facing? she pondered.

At the next gathering of the church in Lydia's house, Paul again brought up the subject of the Christians in Jerusalem and their suffering. He reminded them of their abundance. The bracelet on Lydia's arm seemed to grow heavier and heavier. Strange, she had worn it all these years and most of the time did not even realize it was there.

There was one stone left, but she had plans for that. A large portion of the money would be used to rebuild the dye works and the houses of the workers. Several of the large dye vats had cracked from the intense heat of the fire and would have to be replaced. Beyond that, she and Elias had often talked of the money they could save if they owned their own ship. Word had come of one for sale that was in port in Neapolis right now.

It was also time for this growing church to seek a building for worship. Lydia looked around the atrium. The room was filled to capacity. People were standing in the doorways, sitting on the stairs, and standing in the portico. She planned to contribute a substantial amount toward building a church or buying a place for one in the near future.

"You are the most generous people I have ever known," Paul praised them. "I ask nothing for myself. But for our brothers and sisters who ask only enough to sustain life, I ask that you become the answers to your own prayers for them, so they will not fall by the wayside."

The congregation was dismissed with prayer. They would bring their offerings for the relief of the saints in Jerusalem at their next gathering. Paul planned to depart for Jerusalem as soon as possible and would be personally responsible for distributing the money.

Lydia retired to her room after the other believers had gone home. She needed time to think.

She rehearsed again the way she planned to spend the last of her inheritance from her father. It was a good plan. The more profit she could turn from selling the purple, the more money she would have to share. Then she could freely send an offering to Jerusalem or wherever there was need. Hadn't she helped Paul before? The more money she could put in the offering, the quicker the church in Philippi could be built. Even Paul had commented about that need.

Her father had taught her sound business practices. He would be pleased to know she was putting them to use.

Slowly she removed the bracelet from her forearm. It had grown shiny from the long years of wear. She slipped the catch and gazed at the last of the precious diamonds. Was this one really more beautiful than the other two, or did it only appear so because it was the last?

She held the stone in her hands as her mind traveled back to that long-ago day when her father had given her the bracelet. She could hear his voice as if it were yesterday. *As long as you keep this bracelet, you will never go hungry or be in want, nor will any member of your family.*

Lydia gazed at the stone, seeing the fire reflected back to her as she turned it from side to side. *You will never go hungry or be in want, nor will any member of your family.*

How could Loukas have known she would become part of a much larger family, the very household of God? Could she truly enjoy buying a ship, knowing that part of her family was hungry and in want?

She knelt by the window. She did not bow her head but lifted her face to the cool breeze. Overhead she could see the first stars of evening. A full moon bathed the city in soft light.

Heavenly Father, I come to speak to you only because of your love and mercy. I am so selfish. I am not worthy to mention your name. You have given so much, even your own dear Son. I have given so little; only the extras, only the fringes that cost me nothing. Forgive my selfish heart.

Lydia removed the stone from the bracelet. She placed it in the box with her wedding necklace. The memory of that day and the happiness that marriage had brought flooded over her. She glowed with the certainty that Menalcus would be pleased with her decision.

The next morning Lydia returned from the agora with her gift for the relief fund.

"Use this as you see fit," she told Paul. "But I have one request. You are not to reveal the amount of this gift to anyone. Some might think I am giving it for show. Others may feel they have so little in comparison, they would give nothing at all. I kept enough to rebuild the dye works and the homes for the workers. The men can go back to work, and their families will no longer be a burden to our brothers and sisters in the Lord."

Paul was so overwhelmed when he saw the amount of Lydia's gift, he wept.

The saints in Jerusalem rejoiced greatly over the generous gift Paul delivered. While this provided the means for immediate relief and enabled many to endure, it did not stop persecution by Rome or by those religious leaders who insisted the Jewish laws and customs must be observed.

Paul languished in a Caesarean jail for two years for charges brought against him by the same troublemakers who followed him everywhere he preached. Only his Roman citizenship kept him from being killed.

He wrote to the church in Philippi, encouraging them to continue in the faith and urging them to use the gifts God had given them to work in building up the church.

A letter from Luke brought the disheartening news that Paul was still in jail, this time in Rome. He was allowed to live in a house, rather than the dungeon, but was constantly under guard. However, he could receive visitors, and he used every opportunity to preach and teach.

Lydia, along with the other believers in Philippi, wondered if God would perform another miracle and release Paul as he had in Philippi. But Clement reminded them to anchor their faith in Christ alone, not in man—not even in such a man as Paul. Paul had been their spiritual father, who spoke on behalf of God, but Christ was God. Regardless of what happened to Paul, God would be the same yesterday, today, and forever.

An offering was received to send to their beloved friend. They could not free Paul, but perhaps they could make his incarceration a little easier.

After much prayer on Paul's behalf, Clement dismissed the congregation, then remained behind to talk with Lydia and Elias. They discussed what might be the best way to send the money to Rome. Ships did not ply the open sea during the winter months because of the peril of sudden storms. Perhaps they could send a special messenger with a caravan going overland from Thessalonica.

Elias sat for a long time, lost in thought.

"You seem quiet tonight," Lydia observed. "Are you still worried about Paul, or is something else bothering you?"

"I was just thinking," Elias replied. "The work in the shop will not be heavy during the winter months. You could handle it alone. I have not had a holiday in many years. What would you say if I were to take the money to Paul myself?"

Lydia looked at Clement and saw the same surprise on his face that she felt in her heart at this unexpected idea. But the more they discussed the plan, the better it sounded. Elias could find out first hand what Paul needed. As a Jew he could help Paul in ways his Greek friends could not.

Preparations were made for him to leave early on the second morning. He was laden with messages and good wishes and many gifts for Paul. Lydia did not forget to include something for Luke and Timothy. Sylvanus was somewhere else, preaching in Paul's stead.

Daily prayers were offered for Elias's safety. Hazards on the overland route could prove as dangerous as the uncertain storms at sea.

Lydia was surprised at how much she missed Elias. He had given stability to her family in the years since Menalcus's death. Suppose something happened and he did not come back?

Much happened in the two years Elias was gone. Hermanus joined the Roman legionnaires, as Lydia had expected. She prayed he would hold on to the things he had been taught and perhaps teach them to others he would meet.

Diana seemed content to stay in the house. She enjoyed planning meals, arranging rooms to accommodate guests, supervising the marketing, and doing the many things required of the mistress of a household. In fact, she enjoyed the very things about housekeeping that Lydia found odious. Lydia strongly suspected Diana was thinking ahead to the time when she would be mistress of her own home. The glances of one or two of the young men in the congregation in the direction of her daughter had not gone unnoticed.

Krysta was enrolled in a newly opened school for young ladies. Lydia was not sure what she was learning about being a lady, but she was definitely learning a lot about business. She pestered Lydia endlessly about facts and figures of the dye works and the shop. Lydia had never liked the task of balancing accounts and struggling with interest rates and freight costs. After watching the ease with which Krysta grasped the intricacies of handling the accounts, Lydia gladly turned the work over to her.

Darius continued to follow Lydia around at the dye works. More and more he reminded Lydia of her father. His suggestions created several labor-saving devices that made the work easier and faster. He continually worked at designs for the material and was elated beyond measure the first time he saw a lady wearing a peplos with his design around the hem of her garment.

Loukas would have been proud of his grandchildren. And Menalcus? Would he think she had done a good job? Lydia recalled all the decisions she had been required to make alone, the discipline she'd had to administer, and the instructions she had managed in spite of the need for a man to share these times with the children. Yes, she had done a good job. With God as her helper and Elias as her right hand, these children had grown into fine young people, ready to take their places in the world.

Where would they be as a family without the hope and strength that came from their belief in God? Where would she be? She remembered the emptiness of her sacrifices to Cybele and Isis. The searching of her heart had been an actual pain. The cry of her heart for acceptance and peace had become a part of everything she did and everywhere she went, even weaving in and out of her dreams. The search had ended when Paul introduced her to Jesus.

Her attempts to worship at the feet of Cybele and other gods brought none of the warmth of heart that came when she offered a sacrifice of praise and prayer to the living God. There was none of the uplifted spirit and encouragement of hope she knew now as a child of God. And the peace that came from knowing sin was forgiven and she was accepted was indescribable. Even that feared enemy, death, would only reunite her with her loved ones and put her in the very presence of God himself.

Her thoughts were interrupted by the porter bringing a letter from Paul. Much of it was directed to the church, with praise and thanksgiving for their generosity. He implored them to work together with one mind, one heart, and one purpose: that of convincing everyone they met of the reality of sin and the forgiveness offered through the death of Christ on the cross.

He closed with a few words for Lydia.

If the Lord is willing, I will soon send Timothy to see you. He can bring me news of all that is happening in Macedonia. He has been very concerned about all of you.

Meanwhile I think it best to send Elias back to you. He has been closer than a brother and helped me in spreading the gospel as no one else. How can I thank you for sending him? Welcome him home. I only wish I could be making the journey with him.

Greet all the friends for me. The brothers here send their greetings.

Springtime brought a lift to everyone's spirit. Lydia had just returned from lowering the shutters on the shop for the night when she heard horses arrive at the rear of the villa. To her astonishment, Elias and Luke walked through the door.

Runners were sent to summon the believers while the two men ate a hearty supper and then refreshed themselves with a bath and clean clothes. Lydia refrained from asking questions until everyone arrived. She was impatient to hear the travelers' report but recognized how weary they were. It would be enough for them to recount their adventures one time tonight.

The church listened intently as Elias and Luke related, with tears and many expressions of grief, the things they had experienced in Rome. The believers listened with horror as the men told of a great fire that burned a large portion of the city, destroying the homes of the poor. Memories of the fire that destroyed many of their homes were renewed in their minds. They shuddered as Elias said the blame was placed on the Christians, despite common knowledge that Nero had hired thugs to set the fires. The congregation could hardly bear the account of the subsequent torturing and killing of those people who claimed the name of Christ.

When Luke told them that Paul had died, many believers cried aloud. Lydia would have sunk into absolute despair had Luke not reminded them of Paul's desire that they remember whose children they were and of the things Paul had taught while in Philippi.

"Paul's last words to Timothy were, 'I have fought a good fight. I have finished my course. I have kept the faith.' " Luke looked at each one long and earnestly. "May we be able to say the same when our time comes to depart this world."

For the next few hours the church reminisced about Paul's teachings. As they recalled his words and his many exhortations to them, they came to realize Paul was not dead. He was with the Lord he loved and had served with all the zeal and strength at his command.

They sang a hymn and encouraged one another before departing for their homes as dawn broke in the east. They had talked all night!

CHAPTER 13

Good-bye

Lydia knew she was dying. She had talked with each of her children during those long days when she could tell her end was near. Hermanus received permission from his army commander to come home. He arrived in time to spend precious hours with his mother. Elias had knelt by her bed for a long time as they said their farewells.

The children sat or stood in the room most of the day. Lydia felt so weak, it was difficult to speak. But she had one more request. She wanted to see Luke one final time. Hermanus left to summon him and then ushered his brother and sisters out of the room for a while.

When Luke came to her bedside, she managed to smile weakly and lift her hand to this friend who had seen her through so many trials. "Dearest Luke. It's time to say good-bye once again."

He pressed her hand to his cheek. She could feel his tears.

"You must not weep for me, dear friend."

"I weep for myself. What shall I do without you?"

"You will continue your writing, of course."

Luke bent close to hear Lydia's words.

"I want my children and my grandchildren to know about you and about Paul and the others. But most certainly about our Lord." Lydia's voice faded and she resumed with an effort. "I want them to learn the facts from one who was not a Jew so they will understand that our Lord died, not for one group of people, but for all of us."

"I promise. I have been honored to have met and talked with so many who knew Jesus in person. I've written down much of what they told me as first-hand information."

Realizing that Lydia needed to conserve her strength, he continued. "My most cherished memory is of speaking with Mary, the mother of our Lord. She was quite old when I met her, but she was able to tell me all the details of the visitation of God and the wonderful news that she had been chosen to bear his Son. She shared the time of his birth and the events that followed. I think it did her heart good to remember how honored she was in being chosen as the mother of the Messiah. It helped in some ways to ease the pain of seeing him crucified. She, more than any other, affirmed the fact of his resurrection and his Sonship. The apostle John cared for her in the last years of her life."

As Luke started to place her hand back on the cover, Lydia gripped his hand with a slight pressure. "Have you ever regretted coming to Philippi to live?" she whispered.

"Would I regret living in peace, in the midst of people who are constantly trying to help others, surrounded by friends who have become my family, and most of all, near to one who has been my own true friend? No, Lydia, I have no regrets."

A gentle smile graced Lydia's face.

Luke kissed the back of her hand. "You have given me a friendship that few people on earth are privileged to enjoy. There has never been a time when I could not come to you and receive encouragement, insight, and—" He smiled—"sometimes correction."

"We have had our moments!" Lydia closed her eyes. When she opened them again, she smiled at Luke. "I want you to know how much having you in my life has meant to me. You were the rock I could lean on. No matter what came along, if I needed you, I only had to call."

Lydia felt her strength waning. "Please tell the children to come in, and dear Elias."

Luke turned to do her bidding.

"Luke."

He leaned close to catch her words.

"White robes are beautiful—but do you think our Lord would allow mine to be the faintest of purple?"

At Luke's bidding, the children entered the room and came to stand by Lydia's bedside. Hermanus knelt to kiss her cheek.

"I was with your father when he died," Lydia's voice was weak but very clear. "He left me with some precious words: 'Trust God!' You must not forget them. I can think of no better words to leave with you."

She closed her eyes for a long moment. When she opened them again, she looked at her family: four beautiful grown children, making lives of their own. And Elias, faithful partner and friend, with his great kindness and wisdom. And Luke with his gentle strength and compassion. She had truly been blessed!

"Remember," she whispered, "trust God. Nothing will make you a greater or better person."

Lydia closed her eyes and slept.

To order additional copies of

Heart Cry of a Dreamer

Have your credit card ready and call:

1-877-421-READ (7323)

or please visit our web site at
www.pleasantword.com

Also available at:
www.amazon.com
and
www.barnesandnoble.com

CPSIA information can be obtained at www.ICGtesting.com
Printed in the USA
BVOW070109120113

310331BV00001B/2/A